THE RISE OF

RENEGADE X

CHELSEA M. CAMPBELL

2nd edition published by Golden City Publishing, 2013

Originally published by Egmont USA, 2010

Cover art by Raul Allen.

ISBN: 0-9898807-3-7

ISBN-13: 978-0-9898807-3-2

Books by Chelsea M. Campbell

Renegade X
The Rise of Renegade X
The Trials of Renegade X

Harper Madigan: Junior High Private Eye

DEDICATION

FOR SÄNNY MCSÄNPANTS, MY SECRET NOVEL TWIN,
WHO READ THIS BOOK TO ME IN HIS ATTIC AND HAS
BEEN ITS BIGGEST FAN EVER SINCE.

THE RISE OF RENEGADE X

CHAPTER 1

Golden City isn't your average tourist trap. Sure, it's got its tall buildings, and the one street everyone knows the crazies hang out on—the teens with green hair and lip piercings that tourists think are an attraction somehow. Like they don't have them at home. Traveling to see ordinary stuff like that is the same as going to a restaurant and ordering a peanut butter and jelly sandwich. It's a waste of time and money, and that's *not* why people come to Golden City. Tourists aren't here to throw pennies in old fountains or catch a play—they're here in the hopes of spying some idiot in tights soaring past the skyscrapers. They want to visit superhero-themed diners and order Justice Burgers and Liberty Fries, served to them by an unhappy wage slave in a polyester cape. They want to visit the Heroes Walk in Golden City Park and see all the shining white statues of the superhero do-gooders who made the history books.

But they don't come just to see the heroes. You don't

want to know how many tourists harbor the secret hope of getting accosted on the street by a supervillain with a raygun. As if we have time to go around mugging pointless, ordinary citizens. The *Golden City Daily News* did a report on it last year. Almost 70 percent of all tourists come here hoping for some danger, some excitement, and the chance to see a real-life bad guy. They figure with heroes making up a whole 21 percent of the city's population, and villains only 14 percent—giving us the highest concentration of heroes and villains in the U.S.—a hero is bound to come along and stop the villain before things get out of hand.

They also come for nights like tonight. I'm Damien Locke, only son of the supervillain known as the Mistress of Mayhem, and what's about to happen to me is something every tourist in Golden City is dying to see, and it's invitation only. And let me tell you, most superheroes, despite their supposed generosity, don't invite strangers to their sixteenth birthday parties. It's a huge rite of passage, and they don't want to share the big night with nobodies. Neither do I, but let me put it this way: at midnight tonight, my right thumbprint is going to rearrange itself to form a *V*. It only happens once, and at ten bucks a head— twenty for the whole family—I'm going to make a killing off it.

Seriously, there are over two hundred tourists at my birthday party, and more are pouring in. It's amazing what out-of-towners will pay to watch a random villain's thumb make the big change. Their admission charges will more than pay for the price of the party, which of course isn't at our house. I rented a hall downtown, big enough to hold five hundred people before we become a fire hazard, and all I had to do to get this kind of turnout was post fliers downtown that said, *Supervillain birthday: danger, excitement, and cheap drinks guaranteed!*

Strobe lights and a disco ball reflect off the multicolored tiles on the floor, and music blasts from speakers as tall as I am set up in front of the stage. There's a bar, too, but the owners get the money from that, not me. I've got a camera set up so when the big event happens, people will be able to watch on the giant flat screens plastered along the walls.

I'm mingling and signing the occasional autograph—for a five-dollar fee, of course—and trying not to get bumped too hard by the crowd when someone pinches me on the ass, a privilege that was *not* included in the cover charge. But when I turn around, it's just my friend Kat. Her costume's bright purple with black sleeves and writing over her boobs that proclaims her "The Shapeshifter." She has short black hair, and tonight it has purple streaks in it. Kat can change her shape and form at will. She might not really be wearing that costume. She could, in fact, be completely naked and no one would ever know. Kat's had her power for a little over a year now, but I'm still waiting for mine to come in, even though it seems like all my friends have had theirs for forever. But I bet when I do get mine, it'll be really cool. I'll probably get laser eyes, like my mom, or be able to control lightning, like my grandpa.

"Hey, birthday boy," Kat says. She's holding a cup of punch, which my mom "made." And by "made," I mean she poured three containers of leftover juice from the fridge into a big bowl and added a packet of Kool-Aid. And homemade booze, of course. If you're ever at a party with my mom, don't drink the punch unless you want to wake up naked in a horse pasture with your underwear on your head and a hobo licking a banana split off your stomach. I warned Grandpa last Christmas, but he didn't listen. You'd think he'd know better, being her father and all.

The punch isn't for the tourists, just the real guests, and Kat must not have tasted hers yet because she sips it and makes a face. "Wow. Your mom drop one of her chemistry beakers in this stuff?"

Probably. "You look hot. In both senses of the word." Did I mention my friend Kat is actually my *ex-girlfriend* Kat? I'd be seriously regretting breaking up with her right now if she hadn't cheated on me last year. We might have grown pretty close lately, but there were a couple months when I wouldn't even talk to her, and I have to keep reminding myself of that. "Thanks," Kat says. She looks over the black spandex supervillain costume I've got on, ignoring the cool interlocked *M*s on the front and staring at the goggles I'm wearing. They're round and make me look kind of like a bug. Kat raises one eyebrow and grins, and I can't tell if she's serious or teasing me when she says, "You look like a total loser in those."

"All part of the act."

"What? That you got hit by the ugly mad scientist stick?"

"Why, Kat," I gasp, pretending to be offended, "that's

an insult to my mother." My mom's a mad scientist. It's a lot like being a regular scientist, except without worrying about legal or moral limitations, and it's a common profession for the scientifically inclined supervillain. You can even major in it at Vilmore, the local supervillain university. Kat and I have both applied for next fall. Ordinary citizens might not go to college until they're eighteen, but that's how your enemies get ahead. Villains have to work a lot harder than that and start as soon as we get our *V*s. Especially since heroes have their own school, Heroesworth Academy, and start at about the same time, though I'm sure their coursework isn't as rigorous.

Kat takes another sip of her punch and coughs. "It *is* hot in here," she says. Then she freezes up, her eyes on the crowd. "Oh no, Pete's here. He thinks it was worth ten bucks to come here and torment you? Crap, he's already seen me."

"Don't be so hard on our dear pal Pete. He didn't pay anything, not yet—I invited him." When she says Pete's here to torment me, she means his presence torments *her*. Which is a step up from my last birthday, when I caught her making out with him at my party. In my room. On my bed. And they couldn't blame it on the punch because Mom was buried too deep in her work—an experiment in splicing goldfish genes with a shark's—to go to the store for the Kool-Aid. Though Kat's shapeshifting power coming in a couple weeks before that might have had something to do with it. I liked her how she was, and I *thought* she liked me. I guess she just didn't think she could do any better, because as soon as she could turn herself into a supermodel, I was out of the picture.

I lean over and whisper in Kat's ear, "Don't shake hands with him."

If Pete were smart, he would have burned his invitation. Instead he comes straight over to us. Ah, Pete, as thick as ever. Just like old times. Pete's a year older than me and Kat, and he's been going to Vilmore since last fall. His superpower is that he can broadcast signals, like to a radio or a TV. He doesn't need a phone to call someone—it's kind of creepy. He locks me in a quick embrace, clapping his hand against my shoulder. "Good to see you, man." It's not good to see him. He moves to Kat, but she's too busy downing her punch in one gulp to notice.

"Happy birthday," Pete says, shuffling his feet. He's not sure if he should meet my eyes or not. Pete has dark skin, glasses, and a well-muscled torso, if you're into that sort of thing. "When I got the invitation, I ... I'm glad there's no hard feelings."

And I'm glad he's been living at school the past six months and hasn't been around. It's made it easier not to accidentally run into him. Of course, it's also made it harder to get revenge.

"Damien," Kat says, her voice rough from the punch, "I'll catch up with you later." She looks at Pete, like she owes him some kind of explanation. "Big, um, bathroom emergency."

Pete stares longingly after Kat. In a room with over two hundred people in it, I think the last thing he expected was to end up alone with me. "Listen, Damien, about last year—"

Mom dances over. She bumps her butt against Pete's, startling him and possibly scarring him for life. "Whoo," she says, tugging on her collar. Strands of wavy red hair cling to her neck, stuck with sweat. She was in the papers at least once a week before I was born. Now her supervillainy is more low-key, limited mostly to tinkering in her lab, making punch the FDA wouldn't approve of, and extorting money from the government to make ends meet. "I hope midnight gets here soon—we're running out of punch. Oh, look, sweetie, I knew you'd take my suggestion." She smiles at the two silver *Ms* on my costume. "Master of Mayhem."

"Midnight Marvel." Not that Mom's supervillain name isn't cool, but naming myself after my mommy? Yeah, that would make me the lamest villain on the planet. "It's a stage name, just for tonight." I haven't decided what my *real* villain name is going to be, but I figure I have two years at Vilmore to figure it out.

"Pete!" Mom says, as if she just noticed him—I guess she didn't care whose butt she was bumping. "I haven't seen you in ages!"

"Pete's been busy," I say, saving Pete from stupidly gaping at her for five minutes, struggling to come up with an excuse for why he never got invited back to our house.

"Very busy," he repeats, sticking his hands in his pockets and avoiding Mom's gaze. You can't blame Pete for that one. Mom can shoot lasers out of her eyes.

"Oh, there's Taylor!" Mom spots her boyfriend in the crowd. I don't really like that she's dating or that she brought him to my party without a cover charge, but he *is* the dean of Vilmore, so I suppose I can let it slide until the admissions process is over. "You boys have fun," Mom says, getting ready to bounce her way across the dance floor again. "And don't forget, honey, you've only got about twenty minutes before midnight."

"I didn't know if I was going to come," Pete says after Mom leaves. "I only got your invitation today." He takes his hands out of his pockets and relaxes his shoulders. "But we used to have a lot of good times, and I wanted to apologize."

"You had a whole year to do that, Pete."

He stiffens. "I was afraid you'd be mad."

"Getting mad's a waste of time."

"Oh, good, I'm glad you feel that way, because there was never anything between me and Kat. Not *really*. We were just friends, and now I'm seeing this new girl, Vanessa, and she's great. Not that Kat isn't, you know, great, 'cause she is. It's too bad you and me, all three of us, couldn't still be friends, you know?"

"Yes, it is." I take out a long, thin piece of paper, the kind you might put a grocery list on, that I'd rolled up into a little tube and stuffed under the band of my goggles. I unroll it and hold it out to him. "You know what this is?"

He squints at it. It's hard to read in the dark party hall, and the disco ball only makes it worse.

"This is my list, Pete." My list of people who need "dealing with," to put it lightly. Nobody messes with me and gets away with it. Well, except maybe Kat. Not talking to her for months was getting off easy. I was going to put

8

her name on my list, I really was, but at first I was too depressed to bother. Then I kept putting it off, and then we were talking again, and then … we were friends, and I didn't have the heart. It just worked out that way. It's not like I'm a sucker for her or anything.

I point to the name at the top of the list, where it says *Pete Heath*. "And here's you."

Pete knows all about my list, and his eyes go wide behind his glasses. "Damien, I told you, I'm sorry."

"It's too late."

"It's never too late—"

"No, really, it is." I sigh. "I laced your invitation with a little something Mom concocted."

"What, moonshine?"

"No." I roll up the list and stuff it back under the band of my goggles. "I hope you washed your hands after you touched it. I hope you didn't, say, go to the bathroom or anything. Or eat. That would be just awful."

"What?!" Pete bites his nails, a nervous habit, then pulls his hands away from his mouth like they're diseased.

I take my cell phone out of my pocket—I hate keeping anything in my pockets in this skintight supervillain costume; it's revealing enough as it is without any extra bulges—and check the time. Fifteen minutes till midnight. "Let's see, you probably picked up your mail about noon … and you knew it was my birthday, and you knew the invitation was from me. So … quarter after twelve? That accounts for enough time for you to stew over what happened last year before deciding to open it." I tap my fingers against the side of the phone. "I'd say you've got half an hour to get home before the ugliest, itchiest rash you'll ever have bursts to life on your skin." I wiggle my fingers at him for emphasis. "Lots of pustules. It should last about two weeks." I grin as pure terror spreads across his face. "Oh, and Pete? I'd bind my hands if I were you. To keep from scratching, especially *down there*." I nod toward his crotch. "You wouldn't want to scar or get infected."

Pete gapes again. He looks at his arms like he's got bugs crawling all over him. I see him scratch, but it's only because I've creeped him out. I know it doesn't itch yet. Mom's good at what she does. If her concoctions are known for anything, it's for being consistent and precise: same results every time.

Pete swears at me, tells me to do something with my mother that I most certainly will *not* be doing, then storms off, flailing and cursing. "Bye," I call after him, giving him a little wave. "So glad you could make it."

I check the time on my phone again before stuffing it in my pocket. I look down at the embarrassing bulge it leaves on my hip, like I have a weird growth or something. I need to get one of those gadget belts, so I can put my high-tech supervillain gizmos in it. You know, like my cell phone.

Kat creeps back after Pete leaves. "What'd you say to him?"

"Nothing."

She bites her lip. "Damien, I'm *so* sorry ... about last year and ... everything." She leans in close. She looks up at me, and there's a moment where we gaze at each other, like in the movies. I'm considering kissing her for the first time in a year, even though I know it's a bad idea, when she pokes at my eye through the goggles and says, "What the hell's wrong with you? You look like an insect."

"All the cool kids are wearing them." I back away, so I'm not standing within lip-touching range. "I guess you're not cool."

I hold out my wrist and check the watch I'm not wearing and head for the stage. "Time for the Midnight Marvel."

Kat grabs my arm. She pulls me back to her. "Damien, wait ... I—"

I push up the goggles, so we're actually looking in each other's eyes this time.

Her forehead wrinkles, and her bottom lip trembles, and she looks like she wants to say something serious. Then she sighs and says, "I wanted to wish you happy birthday."

Before I can respond, sparkling lights shimmer to life onstage. Mist pours out across it, and the loudest version of "Happy Birthday" I've ever heard blares through the room. I shove my goggles back into place. I take my cell phone out and give it to Kat to hold. No embarrassing bulges for the camera. These people have paid to see a show, but not enough for *that* kind of show. I stand up straight and salute her before heading backstage.

X·X·X

To get on the stage, you have to go up a set of stairs.

There are only about ten steps, but it's enough to send my stomach lurching and my heart pounding. I might not know what my superpower is yet, but I certainly have my weakness down. I hate heights, and anything that takes me off solid ground.

I tell myself it's only a couple of steps, it's not worth freaking out over, and especially not when I'm expected onstage to live out one of the most important moments in my entire *life*. I sweat on my way up, but my internal pep talk works, and before I know it I'm safe on the back side of the stage and my heart rate returns to normal. Thankfully there are curtains separating me from the audience, so no one but me had to witness my struggle.

The crowd cheers when I make my appearance on the stage, my face over three feet tall on the big screens. I raise my arms up, and they cheer even louder. I grab the microphone. My voice echoes through the giant hall. "Hey, Golden City!" That one gets me some whistles. These people are all from out of town, from cities all across the U.S., and maybe even other continents—I think I saw a Japanese tourist or two when I was making my rounds—but they like to feel like they're part of the *real* Golden City and not just the museums and guided walking tours. "For those of you who've never been to one of these, you're about to witness the most spectacular transformation in your life. At the stroke of midnight, my body will fulfill the role laid out for it by the wonders of genetics, sealing my fate as the Midnight Marvel."

Except it's science, not destiny, despite what my cheering audience would like to believe. When the whorls on my thumb rearrange themselves tonight to form a *V*, it's because way back when, some scientist did experiments on the differences between supervillains and superheroes. It turns out we're similar in a lot of ways—like, you know, we're both *super* and everything—but there are also distinct differences in our DNA. Enough so this scientist guy could make a virus that affected only villains. In an effort to "bell the cat," so to speak, he worked out this genetic alteration for supervillains and spread it amongst the populace, outing anyone with supervillain ancestry.

Big surprise, some villain scientists got together and retaliated, making a second strain that affects heroes, giving them an *H*. They also started Vilmore way back in the day, to support the education of the best and brightest villains, so we could always fight back against crap like that. Mom says we're related to one of them, and that's why she became a scientist, but I have yet to ask my grandparents to confirm this.

There's one other letter possibility, if the two virus strains mix, but heroes and villains don't exactly hook up a lot, so it's only happened a couple times. *If* those stories about kids getting "the third letter" are even true and not urban legends. It's always supposedly happened to someone's cousin's friend or whatever. Not to anybody anyone actually *knows*.

And then, of course, there are also plenty of ordinary citizens in Golden City, and they get squat for their sixteenth birthdays and can only hope to get invited to a really cool party like this one.

But as I said, my thumbprint changing into a *V* tonight isn't destiny, it's the result of Marianna Locke losing her cool for some guy sixteen years and nine months ago. It's not even a marker of how great a villain I'll be, or that I'll be able to make a career out of it. I'm going to have to work hard to do well at Vilmore and turn myself into a successful, front-page-worthy villain.

"Can I hear a 'happy birthday'?" I ask the crowd.

They scream it back at me in a wide range of accents. A clock appears on the big screens. 11:59. *Tick, tick, tick*, it counts down the seconds. This beats New Year's any day. My heart pounds. My whole body's going to explode. The cameras zoom in on my thumb.

The clock changes to 12:00. I feel a wave of relief—this is it—and watch as my thumbprint changes ... *not* into a *V*. I blink, hoping my eyes aren't working right under the stage lights. But no. My stomach churns with horror. There's a letter on my thumb all right, but it's not a *V*. It's not an *H*, either—it's something even worse. I quickly hide my thumb in my fist. My nerves tingle. *This can't be happening. This doesn't happen to real people.* The lights pouring down on me suddenly feel really hot. I sweat underneath my costume, and it starts to itch.

The audience is still waiting for their moment, the people in the front rows looking at me, everyone else staring up at the screens, wondering why I'm not giving them the show they paid for. A murmur runs through the crowd as I pretend to be sick, stumbling off backstage behind the curtains. It's not hard to fake. Maybe my eyes were playing tricks on me, since I was so nervous. I double over in case anyone's watching and try to work up the courage to examine my hand.

Kat's the first one to run after me. She skids to a stop, misjudging the distance between us, and practically falls over on top of me. "Damien, what happened? You okay?"

"No," I say, clutching my stomach. "I shouldn't have eaten the shrimp." I fake gag to prove my point. My stomach really is a mess, though, and if I pretend much more, it's going to turn into the real thing.

Kat steps back.

If I'm right about what I saw, I can't go back out there. I promised these people a show, and they're going to get pretty pissed if they paid ten bucks for nothing. My mind races, wondering what the hell I'm going to do, when I remember Kat's a shapeshifter.

"You have to be me," I croak.

She nods and works her magic. That's one of the great things about Kat—she doesn't ask questions when I'm in trouble, she just helps out and gets things done. There's a shimmer, and then it's *me* nodding. Well, almost me.

"Your ... nose is ..." I fake another heave. "Crooked."

But she doesn't listen. She straightens her new insect goggles and hurries back onstage. I hear the crowd liven up, and by the extra loud applause and cheering, I take it Kat's given them the show they wanted. She can change her looks at will, so no one has to know her thumb transformed four months ago—she could make a living off of stupid tourists with that trick.

I relax as much as I can in this situation. My hands tremble. I feel dizzy, like I'm looking out the window from a ten-story building. I hold my thumb out, willing it to have changed into a *V*. It hasn't. On my thumb is an *X*. A big fat stupid *X*! I feel the vomit rising in my throat as that sinks in. I'm shaking all over and I think my heart is going to stop. And that's when I know I'm tainted. The third letter isn't just an urban legend. I have *both* strains of the virus, and there's only one way that could have happened.

Mom, who has a lot of explaining to do, tromps backstage, out of breath. "Damien!" she wheezes. Her high-heeled boots make loud clomping noises on the floor. She puts a hand on my back. "Sweetie, what happened?"

"I don't know," I say, glaring at her with my thumb in her face. "You tell me."

CHAPTER 2

"**M**_other,_" I call out, knocking a couple times as I open her lab door, "do you have a moment?" It's been three days since the party. I have to admit to spending more of that time than I'd like wallowing in self-pity. But now I have a plan.

Mom is bent over a microscope, in the middle of rolling up the sleeves of her white lab coat. She clenches her teeth when I come in. "Damien, not now. I'm busy."

For the first day or so, she tried to comfort me about my lack of a _V_. She said at least an _X_ was better than an _H_, and it wasn't the end of the world. Conveniently leaving out the part where she could have told me this was going to happen or, you know, _why_ a perfectly respectable villain like her stooped to doing it with a superhero.

I ignore Mom's half-hearted attempt to get me to leave and make my way across the lab. The scent of sulfur and cleaning chemicals wafts through the room, along with a slight odor of sweat. One whole wall is shelves filled with everything from harmless stuff like table salt and dried rose petals to more dangerous ingredients like gunpowder and various acids. There's also half a bowl of SpaghettiOs Mom left on the shelf last week and forgot to clean up. Nothing is in order, and it takes her forever to find something she needs. I told her she should get someone to alphabetize it for her—I even offered to do it myself, at a discounted rate, but she declined. She said that much organization would cramp her style.

One row of shelving used to be taken up by lab rats, but I freed them a couple years ago when I found out Mom was planning on testing a particularly lethal potion of hers on them. If she didn't want me doing that, she shouldn't have encouraged me to play with them and give them names. Looking back, I think that was her way of getting me to feed them and clean their cages for free. And maybe I could have overlooked her testing lethal concoctions on faceless lab rats, but on Mr. Whiskersmith and Twitcherella? That was going too far. So I rescued them by sort of letting them go *in the house*, and they got into the cupboards and chewed through the walls in the kitchen and the bathroom. They also chewed through the cord of the microwave, and we had to cook our TV dinners in the oven until we got it fixed. Did you know they take, like, an hour? And you have to preheat. It took forever to make our house rat-free, and when we did, Mom vowed never to keep vermin again, even in cages. Not until I move out anyway.

At the moment, the lab is rat-free, but there *is* a man

chained to the wall above my head. He mouths, *Help me*, and I reach over and untie his shoes, because I can. I like pulling the shoelace and watching the bow go *pop*, and then there's just a pile of string. Something that holds everything together, so easily defeated with a simple tug in the right place.

"Wow, is this the mayor?" I ask, pointing with my clipboard at the guy on the wall. He struggles to kick off his shoe at me, and I hop out of the way.

"Flattery will get you nowhere." Mom doesn't look up from her microscope, but I still see her glare at me. "You know perfectly well that's the same intern I captured last fall. Seems the mayor's office invited him back, even after I twisted all that information out of him. But you've seen him before—don't be rude." She finishes with her microscope and sighs. "Did you read that article I gave you?"

I groan. "I might have glanced at it." Yesterday, Mom got tired of me moping and looked through all her books until she found an article documenting a case study about kids like me, who got *X*s for their sixteenth birthdays. Except there haven't been a whole lot of them, what with my particular brand of "mixed parentage" being so rare, and the ones the article talked about were all separated by at least five to ten years. Yeah, heroes and villains hooking up isn't exactly popular.

Mom looks up at the whiteboard next to her lab table, which right now reads *Hypno Formula for use with Dr. Kink's Device* across the top, followed by a bunch of boring math scribbles, and mutters some equations to herself. She adds some more numbers to the board, then pauses her work long enough to smile at me. "If you read the article, then you know your situation isn't the end of the world, right, Damien? We can fix this."

The article said the one thing all the kids had in common was that their *X*s eventually matured into an *H* or a *V*. The kids' actions and choices shaped which letter they got, but the time frame for the change varied from a year to more like five. That doesn't work for me. I only have six months before Vilmore starts up, and my prospects aren't looking good. I mean, will they even take me with an *X*? Especially since it means I'm half *hero*?

"At least it's not an *H*," Mom says, like I should be grateful for what I have, instead of getting mad that my life as a villain is essentially over. And maybe an *X isn't* better. At least if I had an *H*, I'd have a *real* letter, not this "in the middle" crap. With a real letter, you know where you belong, and all you have to do is show the right people your thumb to find acceptance. What's a stupid *X* going to do for me? If I show it to people, are they going to laugh and treat me like a joke? Freak out because I'm an urban legend come true? I'll be shunned for life by *everybody*—heroes, villains, and even ordinary citizens off the street are going to know there's something wrong with me. It would have been better if my thumbprint hadn't changed at all. I'd be a nobody, but at least I'd have other nobodies to hang out with. There are barely enough known cases of *X*s to write an article about, let alone to form a support group.

I ignore Mom's misguided optimism and step over a

puddle of green liquid sliding across the floor. I'm careful not to bump the glass beakers on her lab table as I pick my way over to her. Some of the beakers are full of dangerous chemicals, and some are empty, but she's in the sort of mood where she won't care—she'll get pissed no matter which ones I knock over. On accident, of course.

"Damien, don't get too close!" Mom throws out a hand, warding me off from the beaker closest to her, like she's trying to keep a little kid from touching a hot stove. "This is a *very* important project Taylor and I are working on."

Lately, all Mom's projects seem to involve her boyfriend, Taylor, and they're all *very important.*

"And if I get it right," she adds, "this concoction could be very dangerous—I don't want you breathing it in."

"You're breathing it in." I set my clipboard down on the edge of the lab table and pick up a palm-sized plastic rectangle. It looks kind of like one of those mini tape recorders, except it doesn't have anywhere for a tape to go. One half is covered in blue cellophane, the other half in red, like someone made it out of recycled 3D glasses, and there's a band of duct tape around the middle. It looks more like a crappily made theater prop than something that belongs in Mom's lab.

"Well ... it's not harmful to supervillains. Only regular people and ..." She can't bring herself to say "heroes." Or "half heroes." Mom scratches the side of her head with a pair of tweezers, her voice constricted with guilt. "I don't know how it will affect you, that's all. And *please* don't play with that—it's the only one of its kind."

I ignore her and press the on and off switch on the side

over and over. If she didn't want me messing with her stuff, she shouldn't have hidden the truth from me for sixteen years and let me find out in front of hundreds of people. "Where did you get this, a garage sale? I hope you didn't pay more than a quarter—I think you got ripped off."

"It's actually quite innovative." Mom brightens, thinking I'm somehow interested in this piece of junk. Especially when I have more important things to worry about, like how bleak my future looks through *X*-colored glasses. "It's a hypnotic device. It alters the mental state and makes the brain susceptible to suggestion. Most use visuals to get the job done, like swirling circles or a swinging pendulum, but what makes Dr. Kink's invention here so special is that it uses audio signals."

Blah, blah, blah. "Sure, Mom. Whatever you say."

"It is a tiny bit flawed, in that it's not strong enough on its own, but that's where this comes in." She gestures at the beaker I'm supposed to stay away from. "I believe all I need to do is make the brain more open to the effects of the device, and then my victims won't know what hit them. Literally."

There's a square plaque on the wall behind her. About twenty keys, all different colors and sizes, dangle from the hooks. The keys are the only thing in here that Mom keeps carefully labeled and organized—when you have that many keys, you don't want to mix them up, especially when one of your man-eating plant experiments goes wrong and the only thing keeping you from the extra-strength herbicide is a locked cabinet—except the key to this lab, which she keeps on her person at all times. I guess she doesn't want anyone to get in uninvited, not even a certain beloved son of hers. Luckily, that's not the one I'm after.

I set the garage-sale reject hypno-thingy back on the table and tap my pencil on the clipboard. "I have a few questions for you." I prefer pen, but pencil puts people at ease, because they think they can change their answers, like doing another take on camera.

"Damien." She glares at me, lasers charging in her pupils. Mom's not always good about keeping her temper, or controlling her power. "If this is about ... about ... *that man* again—"

She can't even say the word *father*. "It's not."

The lasers in her eyes dim. She glances back and forth between me and the clipboard, then swallows and reaches up to pull a strand of hair out of her face. "We've been over this, Damien. You never showed any signs of caring who he was before. I don't see why that should change."

Before now, there wasn't an *X* on my freaking thumb. She's right, though. I could have cared less who he was. The way she refers to "the incident" that spawned me, I always knew she was ashamed of him. Anytime someone even mentions Father's Day, she scrunches up her eyebrows, flares her nostrils like she's training to compete in some sort of Olympic nose gymnastics, and puts her hand to her chest as if she's going to have a panic attack. Then she changes the subject.

The only thing I could guess about my father is that he has dark hair, like me, since Mom and my grandparents are all redheads, and that he must really have sucked as a villain for Mom to be so ashamed of him. I had to make up the rest. I always pictured a shabby little man with a drippy nose who still lived with his mother, despite being in his late thirties. I pictured him carrying a sagging briefcase in and out of the house every day to and from work. Probably someone who couldn't cut it as a villain and became an accountant or an insurance salesman. Someone we're better off not mentioning, because if Mom had told me I was related to someone like that—that I was probably going to grow up to *be* someone like that—I wouldn't have been able to sleep at night. My secret fear was that he had a really crappy power, like being able to command slugs or having a sixth sense about not stepping in gum or dog poop. Something useless that kept him from having an edge as a villain, and that I might inherit it.

But it turns out, all that was wishful thinking, because in reality, the situation's even worse than I ever imagined: now I know my father is a superhero.

"Damn it!" Mom mutters, abandoning the microscope and scratching out some equations on her whiteboard. "Oh, Kat called about a million times, by the way. She has your phone." A mischievous smile twists up Mom's mouth. "If I didn't know better, Damien, I'd think you were avoiding her." Mom would love it if Kat and I got back together. She doesn't know about the cheating, though.

"She has my phone—how am I supposed to call her?" I raise my eyebrows at Mom like she's not fit to wear that lab coat with such faulty logic. And of course I'm avoiding Kat—she's a supervillain, and I'm not. I can never see Kat or any of my other friends again. At least, not until I get a nice pair of gloves, since I can't afford a fake thumbprint. And okay, maybe that article is right and I can turn this *X* into a *V* if I commit enough villainous acts, so possibly I can see Kat again in only a few years instead of never. I press the pencil to the clipboard. "Would you say you're quick to anger?"

Mom glares at me.

"I'll mark that as 'yes.'" I scribble on the paper, making a big deal out of writing down one check mark. "Would you call yourself a go-getter? What about team player? Do you find yourself attracted to people who are similar to you, or your opposite?"

Mom squeezes a drop of purple liquid into a beaker full of something red. The chemicals sizzle as they make contact. "I thought this wasn't about … *him.*"

"It's not. It's about you. Would you say you're prone to one-night stands? What if the guy has a really great sense of humor?"

"You'd better be starting a dating service."

"Then I'll need a more flattering picture of you than any I have." I give her the once-over, like I'm deciding if there's anything I can do with her. "Though I suppose some guys might find the lab coat a turn-on. I'm just worried about the bags under your eyes. Let's rethink this and change your first answer to 'no.' You don't want to scare anyone away with a bad temper."

She scowls at me. "I'm taken, thank you, and go call your girlfriend."

"I told you, she has my phone."

"Use mine. So, she *is* your girlfriend, then?"

"No, we only meet to have sex. She's probably calling because she has a ..." I cup my hand ⌐o my mouth and glance over my shoulder to make sure the intern's not listening. "... a you-know-what." I balloon my hands out over my stomach, gesturing the shape of a pregnant woman. "It's a product of passion, unlike me, whom God planted in your womb in a fit of divine and spermless inspiration."

"Damien!" Mom's laser eyes flash. She shuts them, clenches her fists, and counts to ten.

While she's not looking, I reach into my jeans pocket and pull out a tiny key. I accidentally bump her precious hypno device with my elbow, sending it clattering to the floor. Mom must hear because she speeds up her countdown. I hurry and slip the key's look-alike off the rack on the wall behind me and make the switch. I shove the real key back into my pocket right as Mom finishes her count and opens her eyes.

"For a slightly higher fee," I inform her, "you can get a video interview that other people can watch. We've had a lot of success with those."

Lasers shoot out of Mom's eyes and zoom across the room. They plow through every beaker on the table and singe the knees off of the intern's pants. He cries out in pain or fear or maybe a little of both. "Damien," Mom says, her face bright red as she points to the door, *"get out!"*

I have a very unpleasant task ahead of me. One whose results will probably haunt me for the rest of my life. I'm going to find out who my father is.

I sigh as I step into Mom's closet and slide the door shut. It's dark, but I know where the buttons are. I press the down arrow, and a light dings on the opposite wall. A new set of doors opens up, and I step into the elevator. Once inside, I press the button marked *V*. Not *V* for *villain*, but *V* for *vault*. Talk about a walk-in closet.

Once the elevator stops, I get off and use the key I stole from Mom to open the door. The inside of the vault looks like Mom's been beating up five-year-old girls and stealing their stuff. The carpet is pink. An old rocking horse sags in one corner, with fading red bows tied around its ears. It's almost buried by a pile of stuffed animals. A stack of old diaries dominates the center of the room. And when I say stack, I mean a three-foot-by-three-foot cube. Mom still writes in her diary every night, and she's kept every single volume she's had since she was seven.

My chest tightens as I approach the stack. I'm not worried about Mom catching me so much as I am reading about her exploits. The truth is in this pile of R-rated literature. Great. Time to get to work. I put on a pair of latex gloves. Hopefully Mom won't notice someone's disturbed her diaries, but if she does, this way she won't be able to prove it was me. Without the gloves, my *X* would be a dead giveaway, even if she didn't have my prints on file.

The diaries are arranged by date. My stomach twists as I slip the one from seventeen years ago out of the pile. It's green and smells like lighter fluid. I smile—maybe Mom considered burning it. A promising sign.

Luckily Mom likes to keep her diary nice and readable and doesn't write on the backs of the pages, making my job here a little easier. I flip through the book, trying to only catch the dates and not the content. Yikes. My eyes spot the words *leather*, *cape*, and … *vibrator*. I think I'm going to be sick. Heat rushes to my face, even though there's no way Mom knows I'm reading this. Life would be so much easier if mothers stuck to making cookies and moonshine and didn't have sex. Not that Mom ever makes cookies.

I find a section dated during the month of my conception.

Dear Dairy,

She spelled *diary* wrong, and the writing leans heavily and is hard to read, like somebody wrote it in a hurry or in a panic.

The Mistress of Mayhem has struck again. What have I done? I need more men in my life. Or at least one good one. If I had, I wouldn't have acted out of desperation. One kiss wouldn't have turned into a hundred, with his hands sliding down my back and me tearing my suit off. And his. So much for secret identities.

I scrunch my eyes closed. My ears are so hot, I wonder

if my superpower has come in and I've somehow inherited laser ears. I take a deep breath. I can do this.

It happened so fast. One minute we were fighting our way through the subway tunnel, locked in a high-speed chase, and the next thing I knew we were in the subway bathroom, locked in a fast embrace.

Do you think Mom will notice if someone pukes on her diaries? Do you think she'll have to analyze the puke in the lab, or do you think she'll instinctively know it was me?

I lost my shoe in the toilet, and my hairpin fell to the floor and bounced under another stall from all the commotion. We didn't say anything the whole time— that would have ruined it—and I closed my eyes to keep my lasers at bay.

Now that it's over, I wish I'd controlled myself. I can't believe I did it in a dirty bathroom stall with the enemy, with

That's the end of the page. I look to the next one, my face burning and my palms sweating inside the latex gloves. This is it. My father is—

a foil pan and a turkey baster. Can you believe that? I tell Mother that I'm going to cook Thanksgiving this year, and she brings over all the supplies, even though it's not for six months! She thinks I can't cook, that I can't take care of myself! I'm twenty-two years old, and I'm doing just fine on my own. She's always treated me like a baby, even after I got my V, like it didn't mean anything.

There are obviously a couple pages missing between Mom's subway scandal and her Thanksgiving plans—I can tell by the torn edges—but I'm desperate enough to keep reading, just in case. I scan through the part about Grandma oppressing Mom with baking equipment and a lack of trust in her Thanksgiving skills. Believe me, Grandma's the one in the right here. I've experienced Mom's cooking. It's a lot like her punch, only without the alcohol, so you don't even have the benefit of blacking out halfway through.

But as far as my father goes, no luck. I close the diary and slip it back in its place in the stack.

I lock up and take the elevator to Mom's closet. I peer into her bedroom before emerging, making sure the coast is clear. As I'm hurrying past her bed, I notice her current diary on the nightstand. I walk over to it, drawn despite my will, and flip to the entry from a couple days ago. My birthday.

My worst fears have been realized. I was hoping the stories weren't true, that he'd get his V anyway. I never had the heart to tell him the truth. My poor little Damien! And now he knows, he knows that his father must be … one of them.

My parents are going to disown me. They always

suspected his father "wasn't of the right sort." I hope they don't take it out on Damien. He's going to have it rough as it is, and there's no way he'll make it to Vilmore—

I'm sure that sentence ended in something slightly upbeat, like that I won't make it to Vilmore *this fall,* or that I won't make it for visiting day later this spring. But I don't find out because I hear the bedroom door opening and slam the book shut. I drop it on the nightstand and dive under the bed as Mom bursts into the room. She flings the door open so hard, it bangs against the wall. I peer out from under the dust ruffle. Her boots thump against the carpet, kicking up dust. She has the hypno device in one hand. It might have looked like a busted-up piece of junk before, but now there are even more wires hanging out of it, and it rattles a little as she moves. Oops. I guess knocking it off the table wasn't such a good idea, but it's not my fault she buys such crappy equipment. Mom mutters something under her breath about me not being allowed in the lab anymore. She scowls and slides open the closet door.

I wait until she's safely in the elevator before getting the hell out of there.

CHAPTER 3

The Gallant Gentleman, a superhero in one of those red fox-hunting outfits British people wear, twirls his riding crop and scowls at me. He's not actually British, since I know he was born in Golden City—I did my homework—but he talks with an accent. He's got a pack of hunting dogs with him, because that's his power: talking to dogs. I guess if you're really serious about it, you can make a career out of any superpower, even a really dumb one. Of course, he's not exactly fighting crime anymore. I cornered him in the park, where he gives lessons in obedience training every afternoon. He's kind of washed up, relying on the name he made for himself years ago to keep his obedience school going. He's only got two students today, and they're both busy practicing guiding the dogs between the statues in the Heroes Walk. The Walk is a brick path that wanders through Golden City Park, surrounded by blindingly white statues of superheroes who have supposedly done something really awesome for society, like kill off supervillains. I know the woman who defeated Kat's grandfather has one of these statues, but I haven't actually seen it.

The Gallant Gentleman takes one look at me, in my hooded sweatshirt and baggy jeans, and I can see his lip twitching in disgust. God, I hope he's not my father. It didn't take long to narrow down my suspects. An hour at the library pouring over old newspapers on microfiche— after stopping to pick up a pair of gloves first; they're black and fashionable enough that no one will question me wearing them until the weather warms up—and I had it down to three. Judging from the description in Mom's diary, my father wasn't just any superhero, but someone she was specifically at arms with at the time. And you can bet their adventures made the headlines in this town. That left only four potential people, and one of them is a girl, and I don't think she did any siring.

My three suspects are the Gallant Gentleman, the Forensic Avenger, and the Crimson Flash, all three some of Golden City's most moral superheroes. None of them sounds like a good candidate for doing it in a filthy subway bathroom with my mom, so that makes it hard to narrow down my choices without DNA samples. Hence the visit.

The Gallant Gentleman smells like mothballs and Altoids. "Excuse me," he says in his nasally voice and fake accent, "do you have *business* here, young sir?"

He says "young sir" like it's polite, but the tone of his voice is the exact opposite. I can tell he doesn't like kids, or at least teenagers. I smile at him, though I'm cringing on the inside. What if he's my dad and I inherit his power? What if it's already come in and I didn't notice because I'm never around dogs? I picture myself and this guy wearing matching dog whistles and bonding over playing fetch. Though I guess if we have some sort of psychic connection to the dogs, we probably wouldn't need the whistles.

Ugh. I try not to shudder at the thought and concentrate on getting back to business. It's not like it matters anyway, because I'm not going to bond with him even if he is my dad. That's not what I'm here for—I just want to *know*. If I know who my dad is, I can determine how bad this *X* situation is.

I raise my eyebrows at him and point at some dog poop on the ground. "What are you going to do about *that*?" I ask in my snottiest voice. As I do, one of the dogs from his pack gets excited and slurps my hand. I don't feel it until the slobber soaks through my glove, and then it's extra gross. G.G. gives it a *look*, and I imagine I can see the psychic beams radiating from his brain to the dog's. Probably not, but the dog whimpers and sits down.

"Good boy, Jack. We don't touch ... *strangers*."

I clear my throat. "Dog leavings count as litter, you know. It's people like you who make the park unpleasant and ruin everyone's experience. So, I hope you were planning on cleaning that up."

He stands even straighter, as if the stick up his butt still had a few kinks in it and he just fixed them. "What are we coming to, when our young people don't trust their local heroes? Do you know who I am?"

I do, and I'm not impressed. He'd better not be my

father. Not that I can picture Mom losing her cool for this guy, even in a moment of misguided passion, but I could say that for any superhero, so it's kind of a moot point.

"I know you think you're better than everyone else in the park. Otherwise, you'd clean up that mess!" I point at the poop again, waving wildly and raising my voice. He humors me by turning to look, and as soon as he does, I reach over and snag a loose hair from his coat. I hope it's his and not one of the dogs', but it's gray like his and looks longer than any of their fur.

I'm not quick enough, and the Gallant Gentleman catches me in the act. He whirls around, sucking in a deep, horrified breath, and grips his riding crop in shock that I actually touched him. Or that I stole a DNA sample, which is kind of serious business in a town with so many villains looking to do in their "local heroes." Of course, at this point in his career, he'd be *lucky* if a supervillain took him seriously enough to want to mess with him.

I hold on to the hair sample for dear life, not caring that I've been caught. He looks at me holding the hair between two gloved fingers. Then he scowls and looks to the dogs, who are now growling at me. I don't need any superpowers to know what's coming next, so I turn and run.

$$X \cdot X \cdot X$$

One rip in my pant leg—these were new jeans, too—and a lot of strenuous exercise later, and I'm on to contestant number two. The Forensic Avenger is hosting a Junior

Forensic Team meeting at the Golden City Public Library. I'm a little old for it, since the other kids here are all under twelve, but I'm so enthusiastic about forensics that none of the parents or librarians have the heart to tell me I shouldn't be here.

Today is a stressful day, let me tell you. Investigating the Gallant Gentleman—a.k.a. Mr. Snobby Pants—and getting chased across the park by his pack of dogs, who are probably specially trained to sniff out supervillains, really wore me out. And now I'm here, sitting cross-legged with a bunch of children on the scratchy library carpet, pretending to *loooove* detective work, all so I can find out which one of these guys did it with my mom and ruined my life.

The Forensic Avenger is dressed like Sherlock Holmes, with the hat and everything. He holds up a magnifying glass. "Who can tell me what this is?"

My hand shoots up in the air. "Oh, *me*! I know! Pick me!"

He smiles—a genuinely nice smile—but goes with someone younger. I guess as a first-time participant in the group, I can't expect special treatment.

I hate myself for thinking this, but I really hope it's this guy. He has to be better than the Gallant Gentleman, who hated me the second he saw me. And I haven't met the Crimson Flash yet, but I know he's a loser because I've seen him on TV. He has his own show where he teaches kids how to safely cross the street and stuff. I watch it sometimes at Kat's house. We think it's hilarious. So out of the three, the Forensic Avenger is looking the least crappy.

And as for his power, you know how investigators shine black lights onto stuff, to look for body fluids? Yeah, well, he can see that without the black light. Which makes him perfect for forensic work. I don't think I want his ability, but at least he doesn't wear a fox-hunting outfit or sic dogs on me.

"Suzy?" the Forensic Avenger says, pointing at a little girl in the front row.

She's really quiet, suddenly not sure she wants to say anything, and in a very tiny voice manages to mumble, "Magnifying glass."

"Very good!" He claps his hands for her, and the rest of the group joins in. I almost forget to fake my enthusiasm and have to kick my clapping up a notch or else risk looking like I don't value little Suzy's cleverness.

"Forensics is all about finding clues that might normally go unseen," the Forensic Avenger says while a librarian passes out magnifying glasses to everyone. "So let's take a minute to see what we can discover right here in this room."

I bet with his power, he knows all sorts of stuff about this room. Like how many kids have wet themselves.

I accept my magnifying glass with a smile, though even my fake enthusiasm is waning. I just want to get this over with and go home. I hate to call it quits with only two samples, but I'll catch the Crimson Flash tomorrow morning, when he's out filming his show.

"What's this?" I say as I pluck a hair from the brim of the Forensic Avenger's Sherlock Holmes hat.

He doesn't seem worried that I have his DNA. Maybe

because I'm sixteen and joining a kids' group, seemingly without noticing I don't belong. Maybe he thinks I'm a little slow or genuinely that interested.

The Forensic Avenger laughs. "You're really crazy about this stuff, huh?"

My mind blanks, since I hadn't expected him to speak to me. "Uh, yeah. I'm especially interested in fingerprinting."

He scratches the back of his ear. "You know, I have a class at the community college that might be more suited for you. How old are you?"

"I just turned sixteen." I wait for that to ring any bells, like maybe he'll go, "Huh, that's funny, sixteen years and nine months ago, I did it with some woman in the subway bathroom. Boy was *that* place disgusting."

"You might be old enough, if your school supports taking college classes in high school."

High school. Right. I've heard of that, and it doesn't sound pleasant. "I'm homeschooled. But, um, thanks anyway."

"This group is really for the kids." He looks sort of guilty when he says, "You're not going to get anything out of it." He pauses, then digs through his bag of props and pulls out a brochure about going into detective work. "Here. I'll trade you." He offers me the brochure while holding out his free hand for the magnifying glass.

I make the trade, not caring that he's oh-so-subtly kicking me out of the group. I got my sample, and that means my detective work is over for the day.

X·X·X

I intended to go home, but then I remembered Mom's pissed at me for "breaking" her stupid whatsit device. I say "breaking" because I don't buy that it worked in the first place. But instead of getting chewed out, I opt for a detour to Kat's house.

Kat lives in a two-story, three-bedroom house with a white picket fence. Walking by, you'd have no idea the people who live here and keep their lawn trimmed and their roses pruned and their music quiet after dark are actually supervillains. Kat's dad has some kind of superpower that lets him commune with machines, or at least know when and how they need fixing. He could have used his ability to repair tractors or something, but instead he used it to start a tech business. He's the CEO of Wilson Enterprises, a computer company with good stock options and about a hundred million slaves— I mean, factory workers—under its thumb. Her mom is his secretary. They started the business together a little while after Kat was born, and it's only in recent years that it's really taken off. Their products are pretty good, if you don't mind your CPU sending out mind-control signals, telling you to buy more Wilson Enterprises merchandise. As a bonus, it waits until the computer is in energy-saving mode, so it doesn't use up all your processing power while you're playing games. Or, you know, working.

"Did you get your hair trimmed?" I ask Kat's mom as she shows me in. "It looks very ... modern. And high-tech."

She fluffs the bottom of her shoulder-length 'do, her whole face lighting up. "Why, thank you, Damien. I didn't expect anyone to notice."

I make my way up the staircase to Kat's room, keeping close to the wall and not looking down. I'm always torn between keeping to the inside of the stairs, where there's less chance of falling over the edge—but where you have nothing to hold on to if you slip—and gripping the railing for dear life and taking the risk. So far, I've always chosen the wall. Even if I'm terrified of slipping, railing can break at any moment; you can't trust it.

"Damien!" Kat shouts from the top of the stairs. She sounds excited to see me. "Come on, get up here! Show some hustle!"

I pretend to be distracted by the painting on the wall of Kat's notorious grandfather, Bart the Blacksmith, as if *that's* the reason I'm slow getting up the stairs, even though I know I'm not fooling anyone. Kat's known about my phobia for over a year and a half. "I think you should move your room to the first floor. The guest room's a lot bigger than yours. You're sixteen now—you deserve some respect."

She tromps down the five steps I have left and grabs my arm. "It's only stairs, Damien. Lots of people have them. And you know what? They go up and down them every day, and *nothing happens.*"

I jerk my arm back, like I'm offended she tried to help me. Really I don't want her getting careless and making us both fall.

"Keep your door open, honey!" Mrs. Wilson calls from

downstairs. "You know what your father said!"

"Yes, Mom!" Kat rolls her eyes. She slides her octopus statue as close to the edge of the doorframe as possible, so that the door's open just a crack, obeying only as much as she has to. Kat had a real octopus for a while, and when it died she got this foot-tall stone replica in its honor.

I'm still wearing my new gloves, by the way. If she saw my *X*, she'd know about my dad. I haven't even figured out who he is yet, let alone how I'm going to tell Kat—*if* I tell Kat instead of finding a hole to crawl in and die so I'll never have to see anyone again. It's a tough decision.

Kat has pink streaks in her hair today. She bounces down on her bed, a frilly purple canopy. She doesn't even pretend it's leftover from when she was a kid. They couldn't have afforded one then, plus I was with her when she picked it out at the store last year.

"Here's your phone, before I forget." She grabs it from the nightstand and tosses it to me.

"Thanks." I lie down on the floor and stretch out, resting my arms behind my head. Her ceiling is covered in thick spackle. She has a poster of Falling Super Pants, the all-supervillain emo boy band. All five of them have their shirts off and seem to have walked into a fountain without realizing it. They're standing around in the middle of it, getting sprayed by the water and shrugging and laughing. And holding sci-fi-looking rayguns. Their expressions say: *Wow, how'd we get here? I don't know, but let's splash each other some more!* They are all, how you say ... more "finely toned" than me. Some might even use the term "rippling." I shake my head. "Falling Super Pants?"

Kat glances up at the ceiling and gasps, like she forgot that was up there. Her face turns pink. *"So?* You've only heard the one song they play on the radio all the time, 'Poisoned Lipstick in My Heart.' The rest of the album's way different."

I sit up. "You have their whole *album*? Next you're going to tell me you downloaded all the bonus tracks, too."

"Whatever." She throws one of her pillows at my face. "Like you can talk. I know about your Superstar collection."

Superstar is one of those stupid pop bands made of, like, eight teens who won some contest for a record deal. The ones in the band aren't actually super, but they dress up like heroes and villains in their videos. I'm ashamed to say I own both their albums and their six singles and listen to them on a regular basis. To my credit, I resisted buying concert tickets when they played last month. Of course, I was completely broke at the time, but I guess I could have borrowed the money from Mom. And maybe the real reason I didn't go wasn't the money, but because I'd have wanted to take Kat with me, and taking her to a concert would be kind of like a date. And asking Kat out on a date would be kind of like getting back together. Which we're not, even if we spend all our time together and are closer than we ever were when we were actually going out.

Here's how I see it. I might secretly still have a thing for Kat, but as long as we're not technically together, she can't cheat on me. If she takes up with someone else, it's not like we're dating, so it's not like she can break my heart or make me feel like crap. At least in theory. But if we go out? Then I couldn't help but take it personally if she chose someone else over me again.

"I hoped you'd stop by," Kat says. The bedsprings squeak as she leans over one side of it and rummages around underneath, her knees digging into the mattress. I hear paper crinkling, and then she sets something on my stomach.

"I would have given it to you on your birthday, but I didn't want to risk it getting broken at the party."

I lift my head to see what it is. It's a birthday present, wrapped in leftover silver Christmas paper. Wherever it said *Merry Christmas*, Kat crossed out the Christmas part and wrote in *Birthday!* with a black Sharpie.

"Merry birthday," she says.

The present is tall and thin and oddly shaped. It must have been hell to wrap.

Footsteps pound up the stairs. "Kat, honey, I thought I heard something," her mom calls. She pushes the door all the way open, quickly surveying the situation, her eyes flicking from me on the floor to Kat on the bed. "I told you to leave this open." She drags the octopus over to hold the door open as wide as possible. "Were you two ...?" She struggles to come up with the right way to phrase it. "... *sitting* on the bed just now? I thought I heard squeaking."

Kat folds her arms and sticks out her chin. "Were you going to oil the springs for us, Mom? That's so kind of you."

Mrs. Wilson's mouth hangs open. I set Kat's present down on the floor. I hold up a finger, signaling for Kat to wait a minute, then I take her Mom's arm and lead her into the hall. I pat her hand. "I feel your pain, Mrs. Wilson."

She stands too close to the stairs and I draw her over to the wall. She has a quizzical look on her face, not sure what the hell I'm talking about.

I cup a hand around my mouth and whisper, "Did you know your daughter has a poster of *half-naked men* on her ceiling?"

"Oh, dear." Mrs. Wilson touches a hand to her chin and glances into Kat's room, where Kat's still frumped on the bed, glaring at her.

"Don't look!" I grab her sleeve and pull her farther into the hall. "It's such a rare trait these days for a parent to care as much about their kid as you do."

Mrs. Wilson squeezes my hand. "Oh, Damien, you know your mother loves you."

"I know, I know." I sigh. I shift my weight, shuffling my feet. I scratch my ear and look away. "Mrs. Wilson," I whisper, "can I ask you a favor?"

She nods, her face pale, her eyes hooked on my every move.

I open my mouth and take a deep breath, then turn away. "No, I can't, it's … it's too much."

"*Damien.*" Mrs. Wilson puts a stern hand on my shoulder. "Now, you know if you have a problem, or you need something, you have to ask someone. Keeping quiet isn't going to get anything solved."

"You're right. But, please, don't tell Kat. I don't want her to get mad at me."

"Go on. Your secret's safe."

"I'm …" I cover my eyes with my hands. "I'm offended by Kat's taste in décor. The naked men—"

"I thought you said they were only half-naked!" Mrs. Wilson whips around, her eyes darting to Kat's room.

"Half-naked. Same difference." I point to my face. "These eyes can't take the vulgarity."

"Now, Damien, it's … it's nothing you haven't seen before. It's not that"—she twitches on the word —"*unacceptable* in present-day society."

"I know. I guess I'm too old-fashioned. But, if you could … if you could talk to her for me, about the posters and the … the *magazines*."

"The what?!"

I wave my hand, dismissing it. "Never mind, Mrs. Wilson. I think I'm going to have to face the facts. Kat and I are too different to be friends. If I can't tell her to her face that her … her obvious carelessness when it comes to these matters disturbs my soul, how can we maintain a relationship?" I shake my head. "What's the man she marries going to think when he finds out that she *looked at posters*?"

Mrs. Wilson's brows knit together in concern, though whether she's concerned about Kat or me, it's hard to tell. "Damien, it's … it's no problem. I'll talk to her. Kat needs more influences like you in her life."

I hide my eyes under my hand again. "Is it … is it okay if we shut the door, just this once? I don't want anyone to hear me crying—"

"It's fine, fine!" Mrs. Wilson wraps her arms around me,

pulling me into a hug. I press my face against her shoulder, and she pats my back like she's comforting a little kid. "Don't worry about it. You know, Damien, you need to relax more."

"Thank you, Mrs. Wilson." I sniff and drag my sleeve across my nose. When she's gone, I stride into Kat's room, grinning. "You can shut the door now."

Kat storms over, pulls the octopus out of the way, and slams the door as hard as she can. The sound seems to set off my birthday present, which starts twitching on the floor.

I raise my eyebrows. "What the hell is that?"

Kat grabs the present and sets it in my hands. "Don't talk that way about Mr. Wiggles."

"Mr. Wiggles?"

"Have you been crying?"

"Just faking it." I rip open the wrapping paper. It falls away, revealing a plastic sunflower in a flowerpot, wearing sunglasses and holding a guitar. It's one of those dancing flowers that wiggles around when you play the radio for it. "This is Wiggles?"

"Mr. Wiggles." Kat jabs a finger into my stomach. "He was my favorite toy when I was a kid, so you'd better take good care of him."

"You should have sent him to grad school. Then he'd have his PhD and be Dr. Wiggles." I sit down on the bed. "If he's your favorite toy, why are you giving him to me?"

"Because. It's your sixteenth birthday, and I wanted you to have something really special."

I stare hard at Mr. Wiggles. I still have a teddy bear

from when I was two. His name is Damien II, and he's so faded, you can't tell what shade of brown he started out as, and one of the ears is worn through. I can't imagine giving him away. But Kat's giving her favorite old toy *to me*. As a special present.

I feel like a jerk for not taking her to that concert. For avoiding even getting tickets because of her. Not that she'd want to go—she hates Superstar. But if she'd give me her most prized possession from her childhood, something that can't ever be replaced, maybe she'd go see a band she hates with me.

Kat picks up her remote from her nightstand and clicks on the TV. A grin tugs on one side of her mouth. "I've got a whole week's worth of episodes recorded. Two and a half hours of *The Crimson Flash and the Safety Kids*. I *know* you want to watch it."

"You know me too well." I set Mr. Wiggles down on the floor and join Kat on the bed. As the theme song plays —"The Crimson Flash is here, and everything's okay; trust his word and not the herd and have a neato day!"—I decide he's got to be the worst of the three candidates. The Gallant Gentleman might be a fake British snob who sicced dogs on me, but at least he doesn't wear a bright red cape and tights. He doesn't make it his mission in life to save kids from burning orphanages or to help old ladies with their groceries. And best of all? The Gallant Gentleman can't *fly*.

I wince as the Crimson Flash zooms through midair across the screen. If the Crimson Flash turns out to be my dad, that might mean *I'll* be able to fly someday. I shudder at the thought, and not just because I have a fear of heights. Some superpowers are unique to villains, and some to heroes. Just as no self-respecting superhero would have laser eyes like my mom, no self-respecting villain would be able to fly. And if they could, they'd never be taken seriously as a villain. Don't get me wrong, there are a lot of villainous things you could do with flying, like swooping down on your enemies and dropping Mom's concoctions on them, but that's what jet packs are for. Of course, most villains don't have to worry about getting flying powers and becoming the laughingstock of the universe, since superpowers are genetic and inherited from people in your family. I'm just lucky that way, I guess.

"This episode's all about taking your pets to the vet," Kat says. "I've seen it before. You want to skip to the next one? Oh, I know, I've got the one where he wears a swimsuit and teaches everyone about beach safety. A *swimsuit*, Damien. With stripes."

I'm staring too intently at the screen to respond. Is the Crimson Flash's hair the same color as mine? It doesn't matter. I know my mother well enough to say it definitely wasn't *this* guy. My mom and *him*? He stands for everything good and lawful in the world. Mom's exact opposite, and the guy in her diary entry was clearly ready and willing to do it with her. I bet the Crimson Flash doesn't have sex. Like, ever.

"Damien? Are you okay?" Kat's giving me a worried look.

"It's fine," I tell her. "Let's watch this one."

"You seem really nervous." She twists a string from her purple-flower comforter around her finger.

I run a hand through my hair, almost simultaneously with the idiot on the screen. That doesn't mean anything. So we have a few of the same traits—complete coincidence.

Kat holds up the remote and presses the pause button. The Crimson Flash freezes in mid-motion, right before he gives the intro and tells us what today's show is going to be about. He looks like he's staring directly at me. Great.

Kat doesn't say anything right away. I notice how close we're sitting. She smells like her watermelon shampoo and the laundry soap her mom uses to wash their clothes. I guess they're real and she's not secretly naked. Our shoulders are touching, and if I wasn't busy gripping the bedspread in outrage that the Crimson Flash has the same hair as me, my hand would probably be lying really close to hers. Like, resting against it. Which doesn't sound like a big deal, except when you consider how far we've come in the past year, going from me not talking to her to getting all cozy on her bed and making fun of stupid TV shows. Also, there's the fact that I *want* to touch her hand—and other, less public, places—but it's never going to happen. I'm not going to let it.

"We need to talk," Kat finally says. Her voice is quiet. "About us."

"There is no us, Kat."

"I think I freaked you out, at your party. When I almost ..." She let's out a deep breath all at once. "I almost kissed you, okay? Now you're acting weird."

No, *I* almost kissed *her*. And any freaking-out on my part is due to the fact that my dad is a superhero, possibly the one staring at me from the screen. It's got nothing to do with Kat, but I can see how she might get that from my behavior right now, not knowing about my *X*.

"I wanted to," she adds, her eyes darting toward mine, then down at the bed. She sets the remote on her nightstand and hugs one of her frilly pillows. "We're practically back together as it is, so—"

"Whoa." I hold my hands up in a "stop" gesture. "We are *not* back together." I laugh. I actually laugh, even though I've had the same thought myself. "I don't know where you're getting that."

She chews her lower lip. "Oh, so you're over at my house all the time, hanging out and snuggling up with me for no reason?"

"There's no snuggling." To be honest, there has been a fair amount of what I would call snuggling in the past couple weeks, but I'm not going to admit to it. I scoot a little farther from her to make my point. My heart is racing because I think she's on to me, and I'm not ready to get caught. I'm only okay liking her in secret—it's not all right if she knows and wants to do something about it. "I'm … I'm so over you, Kat." It sounds like a lie, even to me. Hot guilt spreads through my chest, and I can't look at her.

But every time I think about how great it would be to kiss her again or put my arms around her or tell people she's my girlfriend, I have flashbacks of walking in on her kissing Pete. She was shapeshifted, so she didn't look like

50

her. Long blond hair, tight muscles, and extra curves in all the right places, with her hands all over my best friend. She shifted back to her usual self as soon as she saw me, with a horrified look that must have rivaled my own. If she hadn't—if she'd had her power longer and had more control over it—I might never have found out.

"Damien," Kat whispers, "don't be like this. I know that you—"

"We can't get back together, Kat. You told me you liked me last time, too, and look how that turned out. If you really liked me, you wouldn't have made out with Pete. Why did you have to ruin everything?"

Tears spring up in her eyes. "I'm sorry," she says. Her voice is tight and squeaky and the tears spill down her cheeks. "I made a mistake. I just … I didn't know what I had with you. I didn't know how much it meant, and then I got this power, and I could be anyone I wanted. I thought I wanted to be somebody else."

"On my birthday, Kat? In my room? On my *bed*?!"

"I didn't mean for it to be like that! I wanted to get away from the party, and Pete came to see what was wrong. He was comforting me."

"I'll bet he did. So you stuck your tongue down his throat. Nice."

Another sob tears through her, so she can't talk right away. I can tell this is hard for her, but after a year of only guessing at why she broke my heart, I deserve some answers.

Kat clutches her pillow even tighter. "We started out just talking. Pete was telling me how cool it was that I could look like anyone I wanted. And then …"

"And then you miraculously turned into someone even hotter than you already are and made out with him."

"Something like that. I was so sick of being me, and there were a lot of girls at your party, Damien. You flirt with everybody. I didn't know you as well then; I thought that meant you liked some of them. I didn't think I could ever be as cool as they were. I couldn't compete."

"I was with you, Kat. I wouldn't have done that."

"You think I don't know that now?!" Her face is puffy from crying and her eyes are red. "I liked you so much, and I couldn't see why you would ever like me, not with a dozen other girls to choose from. Pete came to see what was up. One thing led to another, and I let myself think it wasn't a big deal, that you were stringing me along anyway, until I saw you standing in the doorway. You looked so devastated. You weren't the only one who got hurt, you know."

"Yeah, sure." I believe she was hurt by us breaking up. I wouldn't have believed it then, but I do now. It's just not enough. "That doesn't change the fact that you ruined things, and now I'm over you."

She covers her eyes with her hands and sobs again.

Part of me wants to put my arms around her and comfort her and tell her I'm sorry, I didn't mean any of that, and it's going to be okay. I could have her back, and maybe it really would turn out all right this time.

But the other part of me feels like she's getting what she deserved. She hurt me, and I didn't see her crying about it then.

Eventually I slide my arms around her, because I can't stand being so mean to her, but I don't tell her it's going to be okay. "You're my best friend, Kat. You mean a lot to me. But we're never going to be more than that. We could have been, but we're not. Okay?"

Her shoulders heave harder and snot slides down from her nose and onto her lip. She nods into my shoulder, too upset to talk.

There's a long, awkward pause. The Crimson Flash is still staring at me from the TV, only now it feels like he's angry at me for lying to Kat. But if I told Kat the truth, that I'm actually crazy about her, and if we got back together and things didn't work out again? I don't know that we could stay friends. How many rounds of not talking to someone can you take before it's really over?

"Kat, I—" *I like you. I really,* really *like you, and we should spend all our time together and make fun of superheroes and listen to dumb pop bands and go to Vilmore and be some kind of supervillain duo.*

I'll bet Kat and I would make great partners in crime. But ... my throat constricts when I try to tell her that, and instead I get up from the bed. In other words, I chicken out. "I should go."

"Wait." Kat jumps up and catches me before I get to the door. Her face is red and blotchy and covered in tears. She picks up Mr. Wiggles from the floor and shoves him into my arms. "Don't forget your birthday present."

I nod. I hug her before I go—as if I hadn't played with her feelings enough—and she clings to me, her fingers gripping my sweatshirt. There's a wet spot on my chest when she finally steps back. "Bye, Damien," she says. She says it like it might be the last time she'll ever see me.

"Bye, Kat," I tell her, feeling like I'm losing her all over again. Then Mr. Wiggles and I are out of there.

CHAPTER 4

The next morning, I'm on the trail of the Crimson Flash. It was a little more difficult to track him down than the others, since he's out wandering the streets of Golden City with his camera crew at half past the crack of dawn—did I mention I hate getting up early?—but I sweet-talked the secretary at the TV station into telling me what neighborhood he's visiting this morning.

The Crimson Flash is a right, upstanding citizen, and I *so* don't want him to be my father. Not only can he fly and not only does he do good deeds all the time, but he has to go blasting it all over television. If one of the others was my dad, I could forget about it and not have to have the shame rubbed in my face all the time.

I catch up to the Crimson Flash on the street. He's with his film crew, getting exciting footage of rescuing a kitten from a tree in someone's yard. Square jaw, neatly combed hair that does *not* look anything like mine—even if it is the same shade of black—and a billowing cape. When he's not out raising money to save orphanages and helping people down from flaming apartment buildings, he's on TV, helping lost kittens out of trees.

I cross the street, ignoring the sounds of the man in the next yard arguing on his cell phone and kicking his lawn mower, which apparently doesn't work. I approach the film crew and act like I'm a curious bystander, edging my way closer. Then I pretend I don't notice what's going on and walk over to the Crimson Flash. The camera guy's assistant sticks his arm out to block me. He doesn't say anything, just jerks his head in the other direction, indicating I shouldn't get too close.

Damn. This is going to be more annoying than I thought.

"Don't worry, kids," the Crimson Flash says, pointing straight up at the mewling kitten, "the Crimson Flash is on the job."

"Excuse me, sir!" I say, before he can fly six feet in the air and pull the fluffball to safety.

Everyone turns and looks at me, like they think I'm nuts if I don't realize they're filming.

I run up to the Crimson Flash, beaming at him. "You're all about helping people, right?"

Genuine concern wrinkles his brow. "What can I do for you, son?"

Son. Great word choice. "I need a hair sample, if you don't mind. It's for school. For a project." I've never been to school. That makes it harder to lie about it, but saying you're doing a project seems to make people listen.

The Crimson Flash frowns. A breeze tugs on his cape.

The kitten mewls nonstop in the tree, and the camera crew mutters angrily about how they're not going to get out of here on time.

"A hair sample," he says, eyeing my gloved hands with suspicion. He knows that a single hair could prove fatal for him if an enemy got ahold of it.

"Please, mister Flash, I only need one more. Everyone else in my class already has theirs."

His mouth slips open as he ponders my request. He's about to give in, and then he shakes his head. "I'm sorry, son, but I can't do that."

The camera crew breathes a collective sigh of relief now that they can get rid of me and get back to work.

"I'll make a bet with you," I say as the Crimson Flash readies himself to save the kitten. I nod at the tree. "If I can safely get that cat out of there without moving from this spot, will you give me the sample?"

He looks up at how high the branch is, then raises his eyebrows at me.

One of the crew mutters, "I gotta see this."

The Crimson Flash thinks it over. Then he folds his arms, a superior smile on his face. "All right," he says. He doesn't think I'll win; he's probably a man of his word, he'll probably give me the hair sample when I do, but I'm not taking chances. "And what if you lose?" he asks.

"I won't." I bend down and pick up a pebble. I squint at a branch in the tree, pinching the pebble between my forefinger and thumb, getting ready to shoot it. I take my left glove off and lick my forefinger, then hold it up to test the wind. Everyone is mesmerized. Nobody makes a sound except the cat in the tree and the neighbor in the next yard, too afraid of interrupting my calculations. Carefully, I position my hand, lining up the stone with the tree and muttering to myself about angles and carrying the one.

Then I shoot. The pebble sails through a pair of branches and over the white picket fence, beaning the neighbor on the head.

"Ow!" he shouts. "Who threw that?" He forgets about his lawn mower and glares at me.

I hold out my hand. "I need to borrow your phone. It's an emergency!" I left mine at home. Plus, bothering this guy is more fun.

He eyes the film crew suspiciously. He doesn't seem to notice the man in full superhero garb standing next to me. Maybe he doesn't realize it's a TV show about the real thing. Finally, he says, "I'll call you back," and hangs up, then grudgingly tosses the phone to me.

I catch it in both hands and dial a couple of numbers before going, "Oh, oops, that's not how you work this thing. ..." I bare my teeth at it and keep pressing buttons. I hear everyone around me groan, except the Crimson Flash, who stands patiently beside me. Finally I finish dialing. Before the phone stops ringing, I hold it up to my ear and start talking into it, as if there was another person on the line. "I've got an emergency here. You're going to need to send a truck out right away."

Mom answers the phone. "Hello?"

"Er, hold on ..."

"Damien? Is that you?"

I cover the receiver end with my hand and turn to the

Crimson Flash. "What's the address here?"

He scrunches his eyebrows together in distrust. "Who are you calling?"

"Just the fire department. Do you know the address or not?"

"The fire department?! Kid, you can't—" He takes a deep breath, all flustered, and grabs the phone from me.

"Hello?" he says. "This is the Crimson Flash. I'm afraid there's been a mistake. We don't need any—" All the blood suddenly drains from his face. He swallows.

Damn. I shut my eyes, hoping this isn't happening, but when I open them again, he still has the same reaction, which is more revealing than a DNA test. He stares at me, his expression completely blank. His hand goes limp and the phone slips and lands in the grass. I can hear my mother's voice.

"That boy! I can't believe he told you. I don't know how he knew. I wasn't going to say anything. I didn't put him up to it, believe me—"

I reach down and hang up, then toss the phone back to the neighbor across the fence. The Crimson Flash probably would have kept his word about giving me the DNA sample, but I don't want promises, I want results.

"You okay, boss?" the cameraman asks.

"Let's take a break," the Crimson Flash says. The camera crew shuffles off, groaning, but he paces in front of the fence, his head in his hands.

When no one's watching, I take out a portable laser from the pocket of my hooded sweatshirt. It's not the kind of laser jerks use to point at the screen with in the movie

59

theater. It's the kind of laser you carry around so you can make jokes like, "I have my mother's eyes." Well, if you're me. (And then people glare at you like it's not even a little bit hilarious.) I point it at the tree and tap the button. There's a quick *joop* sound as the laser slices through the branch, then a yowl as kitten and branch hurtle through the air. I reach out and grab the kitten before it can hit the ground.

I turn and grin at the Crimson Flash. "Don't worry," I tell him. "You can keep the hair sample."

X·X·X

This is a nightmare. The Crimson Flash, superhero extraordinaire, *is at my house*. Who does he think he is, coming here to confront my mom like this? And saying things like, "He's half superhero—it's not fair for him to only be around villains!"

Like I'd want to be around anyone else. Plus, who cares if I'm half hero? Once my *X* changes into a *V*—which it will, someday—we can put all this "half superhero" business behind us and never mention it again. And no cape-wearing loser is going to tell me otherwise, even if he is my father. *Shudder.*

The Crimson Flash stands all straight and tall and can't quite look my mom in the eyes.

Mom is furious. She charges her lasers in my direction, then gets hold of herself. It's like witnessing a bullfight. She's about to kill someone, and he's got the red cape. If only she had a nose ring.

"What gives you the right to come in here and demand that *my* son—"

"I'll remind you, Marianna, he's half *mine*. As is evident by that mark on his thumb."

Mom cringes. "Like hell he is. You didn't raise him! You didn't spend sixteen years putting up with—"

"He's half superhero! He doesn't know anything other than villainy, but that's not his fault—"

"If you interrupt me one more time!" Mom clenches her fists. She stomps around the living room in a big circle, shaking her finger at the Crimson Flash. "What we did was a big *mistake*. You don't have any right to come here."

"No right?" The Crimson Flash gestures to himself with both hands, outraged. "He's my kid!"

I slump down in an armchair with a bag of potato chips. I pick out the folded ones and crunch on them as loud as I can.

"Maybe I didn't tell you about him for a reason!" Mom jabs her finger into the end of the Crimson Flash's nose.

"Aw, you don't have to fight, guys," I say. "There's enough of me to go around."

They ignore me.

"He's only a villain because you raised him that way," the Crimson Flash says with conviction. "He could be a real hero, deep down."

She laughs. "Gordon, have you *met* him?"

"I resent that," I say with a mouthful of chips. "I'm quite charming."

Mom tugs on her hair, practically ripping it out. "You can't take him. You can't take my little boy."

The Crimson Flash—"Gordon"—rubs the side of his face. His determined expression falters. "It's the right thing to do," he says, looking like he's about to cry, like he'd rather do anything in the world than take me home with him, and I know he's not going to get his way. You have to have a stronger attitude than that if you want to win a fight with my mom. "He's going to need someone to train him."

"He's got me," Mom says, jerking her thumb to her chest. Her thumb with a *V* on it. "He's a villain, and I'm doing fine training him on my own, thank you very much."

"He's got a choice, Marianna." The Crimson Flash shakes his head and bites his lip, like Mom is making a grave mistake in wanting to keep her only son instead of giving him away to a stranger. "He needs to see that. And the way he runs around doing whatever he wants, it's clear he needs a father."

"Whoa." I sit up in the chair, the bag of chips spilling onto the floor. "You want to say that to my face, Mr. Subway Bathroom?"

"DAMIEN!" Mom stomps over—sometimes I think she wears heavy platformed boots so she can stomp extra loud —and grabs me by the ear. She fakes a smile and growls through clenched teeth. "Can I have a word with you, sweetums? *Alone?*"

She drags me into the bathroom and locks the door. It's a cramped space: just me and Mom and her lasers.

"Maybe I should let him take you, after all the crap you've pulled today! It'd serve you right!"

"I didn't think he was going to come over here," I mutter. "I only wanted to mess with him."

"That's sweet, dear, but now you know why I was right. Why I didn't want you getting involved."

No, I'm pretty sure that was because she was ashamed of her little subway plunge into the enemy's pants. "Hey, Mom, how much do you trust this guy? Because he's out there, unattended, in our house. Our house chockfull of supervillainy."

Mom shoves me out of the way and presses her ear to the door.

"He might find some kind of damning evidence against you, something that'll make the courts think you're unfit to be my guardian. Maybe you shouldn't be so careless with my future."

"Damien, shut up." She waits a minute at the door, then, satisfied, glares at me again. "I hope you're happy. Things were just fine, and now look what you've done!"

"I'm pretty sure he can hear you when you shout. This place isn't soundproof, you know." I thunk down on the edge of the bathtub.

"You read my diary, you little—"

"Do you want to read mine?" I perk up. I've been waiting for a good opportunity to leave it lying around for Mom to find. "I can assure you, it's full of lots of incriminating anecdotes about my exploits."

Mom sighs. "Is any of it *real*?"

"I think you'll have to be the judge of that."

"So, in other words, no?"

I let my foot swing hard into the side of the tub and

rest my chin in my hands, pouting. I came off too eager. I was saving that fake diary for a special occasion. There was even a tiny camera in it so I could watch her read it. Now it's all ruined. "Mom, I don't want to live with that guy."

"I know, sweetie." She puts her arm around me.

"I bet he flosses his teeth twice a day. I bet he lives in a tidy little bachelor pad on Borington Lane and wears an apron while he cooks Top Ramen for dinner every night."

"On second thought, Damien, where *is* this diary of yours? Maybe I'll show it to him."

"Maybe you'd better not. It might make him think I need saving even more." I tap one of my temples. "Those superhero types, they can't stand not saving people."

The look Mom gives me turns my stomach. She tilts her head, her lips twitching into a half smile. Of *pity*. I partly expect her to ask, *Do you know that firsthand, Damien? Is everything all right? Have you been having superhero...* urges?

Mom pats me on the back. "Don't worry. The last thing I'm going to do is let him take my little boy away from me." She grins and rubs her hands together. "And the Mistress of Mayhem has a few tricks up her sleeve for people who refuse to cooperate."

More like a few tricks up her skirt. "Thanks, Mom."

She kisses my forehead, then throws the bathroom door open, already screaming in a shrill voice at the top of her lungs, "That boy is mine and you shouldn't even be here!"

The Crimson Flash shouts back at her. "You think everything belongs to you! It's just like old times!"

I think about Kat and how right now would be a great time to escape to her house. If, you know, I hadn't told her I was over her and made her cry.

I hide in the bathroom, and when the shouting is finally over, Mom bursts in, grinning. I start to smile, anticipating the good news that she got rid of the Subway Scrambler once and for all.

Instead, she folds her hands together and says, "Get your things together, Damien. You're going to be spending some time with him." She doesn't say "my father," just *him*. I'm supposed to know who she's talking about.

"What?!" I can't believe this. My blood runs cold and I'm considering whether I heard wrong, or if I can never trust my mother again. Talk about betrayal. "You said you wouldn't let him take me!"

"I changed my mind," Mom says. "It's only for a little while, and I think it'll be good for both of us. I've got a big project I'm working on, and I could use the time alone."

By "alone," I think we both know she means "with Taylor."

"And"—she nods at my gloved hands—"you have to turn that *X* into a *V*, and think of all the opportunities you'll have to do that while living with superheroes. Know your enemy. That's what your grandpa always says."

Great advice. Too bad Mom took it too literally. The corners of my mouth droop into the opposite of a smile. My shoulders sag and I still can't believe this. "Gee, Mom, with that much opportunity, I'll be enrolling at Vilmore in no time."

"That's the spirit, honey." She gives me a quick kiss on

the cheek. "Now hurry and get packed. Don't keep your fa
—*that man* waiting. I don't want to have to put up with
him any longer than I have to."

CHAPTER 5

Mom sold me out. She didn't just promise Gordon Tines, better known as the Crimson Flash, that I'd stay at his house for a while and then come home. No. They made a deal. He's got six weeks to turn me into a wannabe superhero, proving I take after his side of the family, or else I get to go back and live with Mom. We're not talking changing my *X* into an *H* or anything—that would take a lot longer than six weeks—just which letter I should be rooting for. Gordon thinks he can prove I have more hero potential than villain, and if I don't stay true to my supervillain genes and survive all of his "teach me to be a hero" nonsense, I'll have to live in this suburban hellhole for the rest of my life. Or until I turn eighteen, whichever comes first. Or, dear God, until they send me to hero school. The only thing worse than not starting at Vilmore this fall would be starting up at Heroesworth.

Which is the last thing I'm going to do *ever*. Plus, I'm pretty sure I could get out of it. I'm half villain, and I'll bet everyone at that school is a big antivillain snob. They wouldn't want me there any more than I'd want to go. And even better than that? It's not going to matter, because in order for Gordon to send me there, he'd have to convince me I'm supposed to grow up as a hero first. Mom says this is a great opportunity to know my enemy, but I've been making fun of his show for years—I *know* what I'm up against, and it's ridiculous. The leader of the Safety Kids is going to convince *me* I want to stay with him forever and learn to be a hero? He might be my dad, but at least I didn't inherit his delusions.

But, for now, I'm staying at his house with him. *With his family*. He's got the perfect setup—superhero wife and three 100 percent superhero kids. And now me. I wake up in the morning in an eight-year-old boy's room that smells like cheese, with dirty socks covering my face, and I didn't even drink any of Mom's punch. I cringe as I fling the filthy socks away. All I have with me is a backpack full of my clothes and Mr. Wiggles. I can see why he and Kat were such great friends when she was a kid. I'm already appreciating his company immensely, as he's the only familiar face in the house.

Alex, my eight-year-old half brother, stomps on my arm as he jumps out of bed. His room is so cramped and small and overstuffed with junk that the only way I can fit on the floor is if I keep my legs folded. They ache, and my neck is cramping from only having a thin couch pillow to support it with all night. I guess this is the kind of five-star service a half villain like me can expect in a house full of heroes.

"Ha ha!" Alex shouts. "I survived a night with a supervillain!" He does a little dance that involves not noticing he's stepping on my ankles until I lift my foot up and trip him. He slips and, luckily for him, lands in a three-foot-tall pile of laundry that I believe to be the source of the cheese smell.

"One down," I mutter, but he just laughs.

I drag myself out of bed—which consists of nothing but a blanket and a hardwood floor—rumpled and still wearing my clothes from last night. I yawn and follow Alex into the kitchen, though not as sprightly as him, bringing Mr. Wiggles with me. Mr. Wiggles and I, we have to stick together.

A slightly pudgy teenage girl with blond eyebrows and dyed black hair sits at the dining table, glaring at us. "You're late," she says. This is Amelia. Amelia is fifteen. She has one of those countdown clocks in her room, like the kind they sell for New Year's, counting down the days until she turns sixteen. She made a point of bringing it down and showing it to me last night. She's got 236 days left. I told her maybe she shouldn't be so impatient, because she might turn sixteen and find out she has latent supervillain genes, and then won't she long for the carefree days of her carefree youth?

"Couldn't you have gotten dressed first?" Amelia asks in disgust. I can't tell if she means me, looking like I've slept in my clothes all night but being otherwise fully dressed, or Alex, who's running around in pajamas with his shirt half unbuttoned.

I sit down at the table directly across from Amelia and

position Mr. Wiggles next to me.

Amelia makes a face. She's wearing mauve eye shadow, which I hope isn't to impress little old *moi*, as I am her half brother, her mortal enemy, and altogether not interested.

"What is *that*?" she says, scowling at Mr. Wiggles.

"This is Dr. Wiggles, formerly Mr. Wiggles. He recently got his PhD in early-twentieth-century literature." Even if he didn't have his degree, I'd still venture to say he's smarter than Amelia.

"Freak," Amelia mutters under her breath, as if her saying it like that makes it okay, even though I can obviously hear her. "Aren't you a little old to be playing with kids' toys?"

"Dr. Wiggles is a highly sophisticated piece of technology. Plus, 'kids' toys' don't go on to get their doctorates." I have her there.

She gapes at me, then says, "Whatever," and rolls her eyes.

Helen, my father's wife and the mother of my three half siblings, limps out of the master bedroom with Jessica, my two-year-old half sister, glomped to her leg. Helen's a superhero, too, but I didn't catch what her power is.

So far, I like Jessica the best because she talks the least, refers to me only as "boy," and has started her own garden in the yard. She has a couple of rows of dirt marked with signs she made herself that have scribbles of what the vegetables are supposed to look like on them. I think one of them might have been a tomato, the others some kind of mutant carrot-cauliflower hybrid. There may or may not be any actual seeds planted there.

"Boy!" Jessica says, hiding behind her mother's legs and pointing a grubby finger at me.

"Yes, Jess," Helen mutters. *"It's a boy!"* She says that last part sarcastically, mimicking the balloons and greeting cards people get when they have a baby. Helen has shoulder-length blond hair and owns an antique shop downtown. She always walks with a slight limp, I noticed, even when Jessica isn't trying to climb her leg.

Jessica takes a risk, leaving the safety of hiding behind Helen, and runs over to the dining table, where she stares at me with wide blue eyes.

"Jess," Amelia says, patting the seat next to her. "Sit here, Jess."

Jessica ignores her and continues to stare at me.

Amelia keeps calling her like a cat until Jessica turns around and says, "No," very sternly. Another reason why I like her.

Amelia makes a noise of frustration that sounds like a train colliding with a herd of mooing cows. "Nobody in this house ever listens to me!"

I rest my chin in my hands, my elbows propped on the table, and stare at her. *"I'm* listening, Amelia. Tell me your problems."

That infuriates her even more, though for a second she thought I was serious. When I won't stop staring at her—not even blinking, I might add—she shouts, "Mom! The mutant freak Dad brought home is *looking* at me!"

Helen steps out of the kitchen, stirring a bowl of pancake batter.

"I can't help it if I'm entranced by her beauty," I say, managing to do it without gagging, which I think should earn me some kind of award.

Amelia looks like she's going to be sick.

Helen scowls at her. "Amelia, *be nice*."

"But, *Mooooom!*"

"Amelia!" Helen forgets she has a spoon in her hand and accidentally flings batter across the floor when she points it at her daughter. Helen jerks her chin toward me in an effort to be discreet, like I won't notice they're talking about me. In a tight voice, her teeth clenched, she says, "We already discussed this."

Helen seems to be under the impression that I was "rescued" from my awful life of living in a filthy den of savage and immoral supervillains. She was not as forgiving of Gordon, however, who had to sleep on the couch, even though they weren't together yet when he sired me. (Almost, though. I've only got an eight-month lead on Amelia.) Helen thinks I'm some sort of deprived refugee and is careful not to hurt my feelings or make me feel unwelcome. Which she would probably not be doing if she knew the truth, that I'm a supervillain at heart and thoroughly despise everything hero related.

"Are you going to learn to fly?" Alex asks, leaping onto the seat next to me.

"No!" Amelia and I both shout at the same time. I squint at her.

"Alex, don't stand on the furniture!" Amelia glares at him, then at me.

Alex doesn't listen to her. "You *are* going to," he says.

"Dad told me last night."

I laugh. Just a little chuckle to myself. "Sorry to disappoint you, Alex, but that's not going to happen."

He doesn't look at all convinced. "How do *you* know?"

Because I'm going to spend all of my time praying I get laser eyes or pretty much anything but Gordon's awful ability. "I'm going to be a supervillain," I explain, "and no self-respecting supervillain *flies*." Unless it's in a cool jet or rocket pack, but even so, that's not going to be me. I'm not leaving the ground anytime soon.

"Who cares if he doesn't want to fly?" Amelia asks Alex. "Flying powers are for superheroes only, and he's clearly not one of us, no matter what Dad says. I'm still going to be the first." She sounds pretty proud of that and twirls a lock of her hair around her finger.

The idea of leaving the ground makes me sick. My chest constricts and my stomach flops. I push my bare feet against the floor to remind myself I'm on solid ground. "It's getting kind of late—I'm already sixteen."

Amelia scowls like I said it to rub it in.

"All my friends got their powers months ago. Maybe I'm a dud. I've got this stupid *X*, and mixing both viruses could mean I'm not going to get a power." I could live with that if it meant getting out of flying. "Or maybe I won't get one until I turn this into a *V*."

"Or an *H*," Alex chimes in. So helpful.

"Either way, flying isn't my ability. I'm sure of it."

"You don't know that," Amelia says, sounding sympathetic for once.

But one thing I do know? I'm *not* flying. *Ever.*

X·X·X

"Dude." Some guy grabs my arm as I go to sit down, apparently thinking he's doing me a favor. "You don't want to sit there. That's Kink." He points to the girl sitting in the desk next to the one I was heading for. "She's a freak."

I look around the classroom. There's a group of four kids off to the side wearing black spandex with black jeans over it, chains around their waists like belts, and gloves. Their gloves look a lot like the ones I'm wearing, except that I've got both of mine on, and they only wear one on their right hand. Like they've got something to hide—kind of like me—only I'm pretty sure they don't, because according to Amelia, she's the only superhero at this school. A fact she didn't sound too upset about.

Unlike everybody else, the black-spandex kids sit on top of their desks. Then there's the teacher, Mrs. Log, who's wearing a plain, flower-print dress and scribbling some equations on the whiteboard. Most of the other kids plowing into the room sit in the middle rows of desks and don't make eye contact with the spandex kids. But nobody sits anywhere near "Kink," the girl in the back.

Kink has crimped, sandy-blond hair, with a hair band pulled over the top of it. It does nothing to stop it from looking wild and poofy and unkempt. A long braided strand of hair runs down the side of her face, with a couple of silver beads woven in that go with the choker made of tinfoil gleaming around her neck. She doesn't seem to notice that nobody wants to sit by her, her nose shoved in a paperback about the world's most notorious jailbreaks. By the looks of it, it's a real page-turner.

Hmm. Supposed freak, or the boring rest of the class? I shrug off the guy who thinks he's doing me a favor and sit down next to Kink. She doesn't look up at me or acknowledge my presence in any way.

It was Gordon and Helen's idea for me to go to high school. When I told Helen I'd never been before, she almost cried. Then I explained that I'd been homeschooled, but that didn't help. She must have been picturing cavemen-like supervillains in capes grunting and showing me how to rub two sticks together to make "the pretty fire stuff."

There are high schools specifically for heroes, but thankfully Gordon doesn't believe in sending his kids there. He thinks going to a school full of boring old regular kids brings you closer to the people you'll be saving later. I asked him why, with that line of thinking, he didn't send us to an old-people home so we could get closer to the people we're going to help cross the street. His face kind of twitched, like he wanted to get mad at me, but instead he smiled and said I could volunteer at the senior center after school if I was concerned. Fat chance. But even if I won't be saving anyone, I'm glad he didn't try to send me to hero school. Regular school is going to be bad enough, and so is living with a bunch of superheroes —I don't need to be surrounded by hundreds of them every day. Ugh.

Gordon and Helen made Amelia walk with me on the

way here, but once we set foot inside the building, she gave me instructions not to talk to her, called me a freak for good measure, and walked off. I will be, as they say, paying her a visit at lunch today. I look forward to it.

"Class," Mrs. Log says once "school" has started, "today we have a new student." She beckons me toward the front of the room. People turn their heads as I pass by, making pointed looks at my gloves, and coughing the word "Poser" into their hands. Maybe word hasn't gotten around that Amelia and I are related, and they think I'm pretending to be a hero. Or a villain. Or this school isn't as hero-friendly as Gordon thought, and they're pissed because I'm not ordinary enough to go here.

Mrs. Log introduces me. "Kids, this is Damien Locke."

I take a bow, which earns me some snickering from the black-spandex kids, who are now sitting behind their desks like everybody else.

"He's, uh, coming to us from another school. Is that right, Damien?" Mrs. Log's brow furrows as she checks over a piece of paper that must have my information on it.

The Mistress of Mayhem's Institution for Underprivileged Boys. "Eastwood," I say, because that's the school Amelia keeps telling me I *should* be going to. Eastwood is apparently where they send kids who can't handle normal society. You know, delinquents, the insane, and pregnant girls.

Saying I came from Eastwood gets me the reaction I wanted. Half the class looks away from me in a mixture of fear and revulsion. The spandexes laugh derisively and whisper amongst themselves. Kink still has her nose buried in her book.

Mrs. Log tries to very casually take a step away from me. Then another. "Eastwood, is that right? Oh, my, that's ..." She wrings her hands together, her attention swiveling to the whiteboard behind her, like she's just remembered she has some very important math to teach. "Well, class, shall we get started?"

That's my cue to sit down. I take my place next to Kink, but she continues to read her book, unfazed by my confession of being either insane or a delinquent, or else unaware of it, too busy learning about breaking out of prison and not paying any attention to the math Mrs. Log is trying to teach us. I don't blame Kink for not listening, because it's boring anyway. We're learning advanced algebra, but I covered this with Mom three years ago.

I learn at roll call that Kink's first name is Sarah, and that Kink is actually her last name and not something people made up. Her hand shoots up when Mrs. Log calls her name, but she doesn't say "Here!" like everybody else, and she doesn't look away from her book.

Mrs. Log doesn't try to call on Sarah or on me, I notice. She gives the black-spandex kids all the really easy questions and even then has to walk them along, feeding them hints about the answers. Everyone else in the class gets normal treatment.

I tap my fingers on the desk. I catch myself playing "Poisoned Lipstick in My Heart," and that puts a stop to that. I'm beginning to think my investment in Sarah was misguided, since she hasn't done anything but read her book, when she suddenly slams it down, looks over at me, and gasps. Her glasses make her brown eyes look huge, and her mouth slips open as she continues to stare.

She stares at me for the rest of class. At some point she takes out a notebook and scribbles in it. She chews the end of her pen. She laughs quietly and shakes her head while she writes, and she doesn't seem to care when I stare right back at her. I try staring at her boobs, which are buried under several layers of clothing, including a wool sweater and a denim jacket. I know she notices, because I hear her mutter, "Drawn to female characteristics of the species," as she writes, but that's the only reaction I get out of her.

She doesn't say anything to me until the bell rings and class ends. While Mrs. Log is reminding everyone to do their homework tonight, Sarah quickly stands up, nods at me, and says, "You look just like him." Then she hurries off, the first one out of the room.

I have to push my way past everyone to catch up to her, the rest of the class now clogging up the doorway. I run after her in the hall and grab her arm.

"What did you mean, I look just like him?"

"Like the Crimson Flash." She points at me with her pen. "You have his jaw and his ears. And you *didn't* go to Eastwood." She laughs, as if she's sharing an in-joke with some invisible person. "They never transfer them in the middle of the semester." Then she takes off.

"Wait!" I grab her arm again. "I do *not* look like him."

Sarah glances over her shoulder, her eyes darting back and forth, like she expects something bad to happen. "I really have to go," she says, pulling herself free from my grasp. "But you do, you look just like him."

"What are you, in his fan club?"

"No, but I used to watch his show. And now I really, *really*—"

Somebody shoves me hard from behind. I stumble and fall forward, landing in a heap on the dirty hallway floor.

"Kink's got herself a boyfriend." It's one of the spandex kids, a tall boy who seems to be their ringleader. He slams his hand into a nearby locker, pinning Sarah between him and it.

Three other kids stand by and jeer.

"What's the matter, Kink? I'm not good enough for ya?" He makes kissing noises at her.

Sarah tries to dart past him, but he blocks her with his other arm.

In the middle of hauling myself to my feet, someone else stomps on my back and knocks me down. They laugh. They sound like hyperventilating chickens.

The girl of the group jerks Sarah's notebook out of her hands, the one she was writing about me in.

"Don't!" Sarah shouts, reaching out to stop her.

The girl holds it away from Sarah and flips through it, but I guess she can't understand enough of it to make fun of it, because she just goes, "Blah, blah, blah. Don't you ever do anything *interesting*, Kink?"

"Give it back, Jill!"

"Leave her alone," I say as I get to my feet.

"God, you're weird," Jill says, ripping off Sarah's tinfoil choker.

"I said leave her alone!" I glare at them, my fists

clenched. I don't have any lasers or poisoned invitations or anything, only sheer force of will. My heart beats wild in my chest and adrenaline surges through my veins. "Let her go."

The hallway's empty by now, though nobody tried to stop them even when it was full. It's just me and Sarah and the four spandex kids.

"Uh-oh, Marty," one of the other ones says, addressing the ringleader, who still has Sarah pinned to the locker. "Scrawny poser boy's mad at you."

"You're *so* scared," Jill says sarcastically to Marty. She says it to him, but she waves her hands around, making "Ooooh" noises like a ghost, at me. Like I'm the one who *should* be scared. Then she nods toward my gloved hands, her face twitching in disgust. "Both gloves? That's lame."

I don't know what she's talking about. Maybe if I'd only worn one glove, like them, they'd think I was cool, but somehow I doubt it.

Marty suddenly slams his hands against the lockers, making a loud *bang!* and getting a start out of Sarah. He grins, says, "Your boyfriend's next, Kink," and lets her go.

Jill flings Sarah's notebook and sends it sliding down the hall, the pages crumpled against the floor.

Jill and Marty move to leave, along with the other two, but I block their way. Jill raises her eyebrows at me.

"You just made my list," I tell them. My list of people who need dealing with. "You're going right to the top." Too bad I'm new here, or they might be more intimidated by that.

Marty shoves me up against the lockers as he walks

past. I slump down to the floor and watch as they disappear, laughing, down the hall.

"Don't worry, wearing gloves doesn't make them supervillains," Sarah says. "They're only pretending. They're not any different than you and me, but you still shouldn't have done that." She shakes her head in frustration, then looks me over, one side of her mouth twitching in doubt. "I hope you have backup."

I hold out my hand. "Can I borrow your pen?"

She hands it to me, then runs down the hall to get her notebook. She dusts it off and straightens out the pages. "Losers."

I take my list out of my pocket and write Jill's and Marty's names down in ink.

X·X·X

I slide into a chair next to Amelia at lunch. I slip my hand into hers before she notices it's me. Her eyes get wide and her muscles go tense, but when she turns and sees me, her look changes from shock to pure disgust. "Get out of here!"

Her friends gape at me, fries and sandwiches held frozen, partway in their mouths. They've all got on mauve eye shadow like Amelia. They mostly wear black, except for one girl who's wearing pink, like she didn't get the dress code memo today. She looks really out of place.

I don't know if I'm as freakish as Amelia says I am, or if the idea of a boy coming up to the table is just too out of the ordinary, but all six girls seem broken, like clockwork toys whose gears all simultaneously fell apart. They look to Amelia for some kind of explanation.

Amelia makes a scoffing sound, like she's offended not only by my presence but by the fact that she has to introduce me. She mumbles into her peanut butter and jelly sandwich with the crusts cut off, red goo oozing out the sides. "This is Damien."

I can tell from their expressions that she hasn't told them about me.

"I'm her brother," I inform them, reaching across the table and grabbing a fry off one of their plates. "We're very close." I put my arm around Amelia and squeeze.

"Eww! Get off me, you creep!" She pushes me away.

The girls eye me with interest now. "This is your brother?" the pink girl asks.

"*Half*," Amelia corrects her. "He's not sitting with us. Not if he knows what's good for him. And you look like such a poser with those gloves on."

She could have told me this morning. Not that it would have changed anything. Apparently the deal with the spandex kids is they wear a glove on their right hands to pretend to be covering up *V*s, like they think they're supervillains. They could be pretending to be heroes, of course, but that doesn't fit with their beating people up in the hallway. The whole glove thing is stupid because real supervillains don't use them—that would be too obvious—myself excluded, of course. I'm going to get one of those fake thumbprints as soon as funds allow. Maybe when I get back home, Mom will be so proud of me for surviving my time at Gordon's that she'll contribute to my thumbprint fund.

A girl with a green stripe in her hair giggles at Amelia's poser comment. Everyone but Amelia struggles with their impression of me, trying to decide if they think I'm as weird as she does, or if they can forgive my supposed poser status if it means me staying and them getting to inhale my teenage-boy hormones a little longer.

Sorry, girls, but I came to disappoint.

"Amelia," I say, scooting uncomfortably close to her, "I want to tell you something." I reach into my front jeans pocket and pull out a folded-up black sock with lace around the cuff. It's clearly Amelia's—it even matches the pair she's wearing now. I grip it tightly in my hand and slide it under my nose, taking a deep whiff. Luckily, it's clean.

Amelia watches in horror, then looks to her friends, her expression half asking for their help and half trying to assure them she has no idea what's going on. "Where did you get that?!" she shrieks, so loud that the people at the next table look over.

"From my pants." I let my eyes defocus in fake ecstasy and sigh, content.

Everyone watches, not daring to move, their faces pale, as if they've just witnessed something obscene.

"I wanted to tell you, Amelia, that I'm *really* glad you're my sister. And that we're going to be living together." I take another whiff of the sock.

"What the hell are you doing?!" Amelia wrenches it away from me.

Everyone else at the table decides that I am, in fact, too

weird. They pick up their lunches and leap back from the table.

"We're just going to … leave you two alone," the green stripe girl says.

"Guys, wait!" When they don't come back, Amelia glares at me. If *she* had laser eyes, I'd be dead right now. "What is wrong with you?!"

With everyone else gone, I toss the sock on the table and scoot away from Amelia, getting my personal space back. "I have a proposition to make."

"Not marriage, I hope. You're such a loser." She folds her arms and turns partially away from me.

Ugh. Marriage to Amelia? Not my first choice, and even if she didn't have her sparkling personality, there's always the fact that our children would only have three grandparents. "I wouldn't want to ruin our friendship," I tell her. "Plus, you know I don't do farm animals."

Her mouth falls open so far, I can count her fillings. "Why don't you just go—"

She holds back from telling me what I can go do with myself, probably thinking about the sock and not wanting to encourage me. She screws up her mouth, clenching her teeth as she struggles to regain composure.

"Listen," I say, now that I have her complete attention, "you don't like me, and I don't like you."

She looks offended when I say I don't like her, though she was perfectly happy to jump on the bandwagon and nod when I mentioned she had the same feeling for me.

"Nothing against your family or anything, but I'd rather gouge my own eyes out with a seafood pick than spend any more time with them than I have to."

"Screw you, Damien."

"I thought you'd see it that way. I think we can work something out. Gordon thinks he's going to give me 'superhero lessons,' and one of those involves flying. Now, between you and me, we both know I'm a supervillain—"

She scoffs. "Check your hand, genius. An *X* doesn't make you a villain."

"This?" I rub my gloved fingers across my thumb. "This is going to change."

Amelia rolls her eyes. She puts her chin in her hands. "You turned sixteen before me, and now you're going to fly before me. You suck."

"But I'm not a superhero, and I'm not going to be. I've got the power to be whoever I want." I jab my finger into the table with each word to emphasize my point. "I. Am. A. Super. Villain."

She breathes a heavy sigh and shrugs. "Fine, whatever, but Dad thinks you've got his ability." Her eyes dart over to me, judging my reaction. "Alex was right—he was talking about it last night and again this morning, before he left for work. Before you were even up," she adds, as if I should feel ashamed of my laziness. "He has a plan to 'jump-start' your flying lessons."

I cringe. Just the sound of *jump* makes me want to go find a corner somewhere and curl up and die. Besides, who's going to take me seriously as a supervillain if I can freaking *fly*? Even if I do get my *V*, it's a point against me. Another shameful secret for me to hide. "Can we agree we both want to make sure that when my six weeks are up,

I'm not stuck living at your house?"

She makes a face, no doubt picturing what that would mean for her. "I'm listening."

"You were the oldest, and now I'm horning in on your glory. It's really not fair. You're so close to being first—and you deserve to be, don't you think?"

She can't argue with that. She idly picks off chunks of her sandwich, rolling them into little balls of bread and goo, and waits for me to go on.

"It's already too late to be first to turn sixteen and get your letter, but I'm giving you an opportunity to make sure I'm not the first to learn to fly. Think about it. What other rites of passage are there? None, and with your help, we're going to make sure you don't miss out on yours."

Amelia mulls it over. "What's in it for you?"

I smile. "As you pointed out, there's a slight, teeny tiny chance that my superhero genes will, say, be a problem. And I'd rather not find out."

"What?" Her brow furrows in confusion.

I give it to her in simple terms. "Flying is superhero stuff. It's a big step in the wrong direction, and if it turns out I've inherited the ability like dear old Gordon suspects, I might *never* get out of your house. I'm also the oldest—it's likely they'll give me your room in the attic, since it's the biggest. You'll have to share with Jessica for the rest of your life." Lies, all lies. I've seen the attic stairs. They're steep and rickety and the railing is falling off. There's no way in hell I'd ever step foot in that attic, even if it meant sleeping in Alex's cramped little room until I die, but Amelia doesn't need to know that.

Amelia takes a deep breath. She shuts her eyes, like she knows she's going to regret this, and says, "Fine. Tell me what I have to do."

CHAPTER 6

"**Y**ou want to tell me about this?" Gordon asks, holding up the magazine I picked up on my way home from school.

It's nothing dirty, just a gadgetry catalog for the technologically savvy villain or hero. Though the way Gordon holds it away from himself with two fingers, you'd think it was diseased. I decided saving up for a fake thumbprint is going to take too long, and I need it now. They've got one in there that uses state-of-the-art technology to not only hide your real thumbprint but to holographically project either a *V* or an *H* onto it. It's even got a remote control for easy programming. At $3,000, it's probably out of my price range, so I'll probably have to get the one that's not much more than a cheap flap of rubber, but I'll have to check Gordon's bank records first. Did I mention this new thumbprint is a present from my dear new father? Who was kind enough to loan me his credit card, even if he doesn't know it yet? He's missed an awful lot of birthdays. I figure he owes me. I'll also have to go to the library and get on the Internet—a "luxury-not-a-privilege" they don't have here at the Tines house—to check customer reviews before ordering. "It's a catalog," I tell him. "They have some good deals."

Gordon sits next to me on the couch. I'm sitting on the end, so there's not really anywhere for me to go, but I scoot over anyway, pressing myself into the arm. He might technically be my dad, but I've only known him a few days, and that doesn't give him the right to invade my personal space.

Gordon opens up the catalog to the page with the thumbprints, where I jotted down some notes about the ones I want. "I hope you're not thinking of ordering one of these."

Uh, did you read my notes? "I have a problem. I'm trying to fix it." Also, does he really think I have that kind of money, or is he on to me?

Amelia comes tromping down the attic stairs. They wobble and creak under her weight. Someday they're going to collapse underneath her, and then she's going to be sorry she chose to live on the second story. Her eyes dart over to me and Gordon, but she rushes past us into the kitchen, no doubt to stuff her face only an hour after dinner. Alex is playing in his room and Jessica's already gone to bed, and I can hear the clinking and splashing noises of Helen washing the dishes.

Gordon's brow furrows and his chin looks extra square and stern. I think about what Sarah Kink said, about me looking like him, and I hope it's not true. Kat and I have spent a lot of time heckling his show—we would have noticed a resemblance, right? Kat would have told me if I looked like some superhero. She would have teased me about it and never let me live it down.

"Damien," Gordon says, "I'd like to have a talk with you."

Oh, boy. Our first heart-to-heart, father-and-son time. I fold my hands together and blink at him. "Please, gracious father, bestow your wisdom on me. Wait." I hold up a finger. "Let me get something to write with."

I pretend to look around for a pen, but he doesn't wait for me. "Nobody should hide what they are, especially heroes. It's dishonest."

I try not to smile, or worse, bust up laughing. *"I'm* not a hero." I'm a villain. Villains are known for their dishonesty, in case he hadn't noticed.

"You're half hero. That *X* could turn into an *H*. I don't want you to get used to hiding it." He gestures at my gloves, which he tried to get me to take off at dinner. His excuse then was something about it being rude to eat with them on.

"I'll tell you what," I say. "I'll compromise. When it's a *V*, I'll be open about it."

He sighs and flips through the catalog. "I know plenty of heroes hide what they are, and I don't agree with it. I'm not talking about secret identities. Hiding from your enemies can be important. But just because my neighbors know Gordon Tines is a superhero doesn't mean they know I'm the Crimson Flash. You see?"

He's lost me. I shake my head.

"Golden City can be a dangerous town, and knowing there are heroes around makes people feel safe. It's not right to hide that."

I drum my fingers on the edge of the couch. "I'm not a hero, and even if I was, I wouldn't drop everything to save anyone. So for me, showing off an *H* would be false advertisement. And you know what else?" I shift my position, so I'm half facing him. I wave my hand at the catalog. "I hate to break this to you, but anyone can *look* like they have an *H*, for a price. And even if someone has an *H* legitimately, because their mom and dad had *H*s and all their parents before them, it doesn't necessarily make them a good person. Whatever that is. So if people on the street are going to be stupid enough to trust anyone showing off their *H*, that's their problem, not mine."

Gordon scratches his chin. "You're right. Having an *H* doesn't make you a hero. But I think having an *H* obligates someone to become one. Do you understand, son?"

One side of my face twitches when he calls me that. "That's a nice theory, but that's not reality. Just because someone inherits an *H* on their thumb doesn't mean they're naturally 'good.' I saw this news story once about this hero guy. The Miracle Worker. He could heal people with his hands. He healed thousands of people and saved hundreds of lives over the years, and on top of that spent most of his free time volunteering at children's hospitals and libraries. Then he almost went to jail for beating his wife. Turns out he was healing her after each bout so no one would know. He would have gone to prison for it, too, if everyone didn't have such a hard time believing he was a bad guy, despite the evidence against him. There were pictures and the wife testified, and I think one of the neighbors did, too. That's the real difference between having an *H* or a *V*. A *V* would have gotten him time in prison, no matter how many hours he spent volunteering. And a *V* is going to get me into Vilmore and means I won't have to be ashamed to have bare hands in public. That's all—the rest is up to me."

Amelia comes out of the kitchen, holding a bag of microwave popcorn. She stares at us and picks the popcorn pieces out of the bag, one by one, and drops them in her mouth.

Gordon has a look of horror on his face, and not because his daughter is clogging her arteries with fake movie-theater-flavored butter. "Is that what you think superheroes are like?"

I shrug. "I'm just saying, nobody's good or bad all of the time. You've got a show for little kids, where you teach them right from wrong and how to be safe on the beach and stuff. But on the episode about riding the subway? Yeah, you left out a few things. Like what not to do with supervillains in the bathroom." I wink at him and nudge him with my elbow.

Amelia frowns, and then her eyes go wide. She coughs and nearly chokes on a piece of popcorn, like it hadn't occurred to her yet that me being Gordon's kid means he did it with someone who isn't Helen. "Oh, my God," she says. "I have to tell Tiffany."

"Amelia, this is a private family matter!" Gordon calls after her as she runs up the wobbly attic stairs. "I'd like to keep it that way!"

"Sure, Dad. No problem." She crosses her fingers. "I promise I won't tell her it was with a supervillain."

Gordon slides a hand over his forehead. He looks up at the attic, then pulls his attention back to me. Apparently I'm more important than keeping Amelia from gossiping with her friends about things that aren't any of her business.

"My point," I say, getting back to our conversation, "is that even you mess up sometimes. Nobody's perfect. Nobody's born good or bad, it's just … something you pick up as you go along."

"And you've picked up villainy."

"Right. Now you're getting it. I—"

Amelia interrupts me, running back down the stairs. She's out of breath and panting when she gets to the bottom, but she still has the energy to glare at me. She's holding something, and it takes me a second to make out the severed remains of a stuffed blue bunny. *"You."* Her voice burns with pure rage and her hands are shaking. "You did this. It's not bad enough that you had to come stay here with us and go to school with me and embarrass me in front of my friends! You have to take my stuff and destroy it, you sick freak, and then hide it in my bed for me to find!" Amelia takes a deep breath and looks to Gordon for help. "Dad, why did you have to bring him here?" She's nearly in tears.

Gordon doesn't bother answering her, turning his attention to me instead. His tone is calm but accusing. "Damien, I understand if you're having trouble adjusting, but there's no reason to take that out on your sister."

"Uh … sorry to disappoint both of you, but I didn't do it." This is what I have to look forward to in a house full of superheroes. Every time something goes wrong, they blame the villain.

"You're lying!" Amelia shouts, and she's actually crying now. "I've had Blue Bunnykins *forever*. Dad gave him to me for Easter when I was three, and you murdered him!"

"I thought you didn't approve of kids' toys? And, like I said, I *didn't* do it." I clearly enunciate the word *didn't*, in case she's hard of hearing, as she seems to be. And if I had done it, I wouldn't have hidden it in her bed, as that would involve going upstairs.

She scoffs. "Why should I believe you?" She shakes her head before I can answer, glares at Gordon, and then stomps her way back up to the attic.

"Damien," Gordon says, once she's gone, "you should apologize to your sister."

"Half sister, and what for? Some superhero you are if you can't tell I'm innocent. How many other innocent parties have you put in jail just for having *V*s on their thumbs? That's kind of letterist."

"Whether you did it or not, she's obviously upset, and an apology from you would help smooth things over and make this transition easier for both of you."

"Are you serious?"

"Maybe you should wait until tomorrow, when she's calmed down some."

I ignore him and pretend I didn't hear that little bit of idiocy. Apologizing for something I had nothing to do with? Not going to happen. I clear my throat. "As I was saying before the interruption, I like villainy, and I like things how they were before you dragged me here. I want to be accepted by other supervillains. I want to go to Vilmore. I want a supervillain girlfriend. You know what they say: supervillains have more fun." I lean in close and stage whisper, "It's true, isn't it? You've had both—you can tell me."

Gordon stands up, flailing his arms in frustration. "This conversation is over."

"Good. I'll still be wearing my gloves and hiding my *X*." And wearing my new thumbprint, when it arrives. I should probably have it sent to Mom's house, since the prints are custom made and take four to six weeks for delivery. I'm sure I'll be back home before then. At this rate, it's not going to take long to prove I'm not a hero.

"We'll discuss it more later, but in the meantime, I want you to think about something. Other people's actions might not determine what letter they get, but yours will. You've got options. You could be accepted by either heroes or villains, depending on the choices you make. I just hope you make the right ones."

X·X·X

Sarah comes to school the next day wearing a gigantic pair of sci-fi-looking goggles. They're attached to a big metal helmet she has strapped onto her head. She looks like she meant to dress up as a robot but forgot the rest of her costume. The "goggles" part looks more like the eyepieces from some high-tech pair of binoculars, and they extend a couple inches from her head.

I hear people yelling "Freak!" in the hall before she comes into math class. When she walks through the door, people giggle, and one person erupts in a snorting fit. Marty and Jill come in behind her.

Marty shoves Sarah out of his way. "Watch it, mental case."

Jill sticks her tongue out at Sarah, flicking it in a perverted gesture. Then she goes back to idly playing with her nose ring.

"Hey, *Marty*," Sarah says. She's not fazed at all by him pushing her and calling her names. "Turn around."

He turns automatically, before he realizes he's done her bidding.

Sarah presses a button on the side of her robot helmet. A little red light flickers to life in the middle of her forehead. She looks him up and down, pausing at his crotch, a slow smile spreading over her face. "That's what I thought."

Marty mutters about how they shouldn't have to put up with people like her, and he and Jill take their places with the rest of their group.

Sarah sits down next to me. She folds her hands together on her desk and grins.

Mrs. Log jumps when she enters the classroom and catches sight of Sarah's headgear. "Oh, my," she says, clamping a hand over her chest. "That's quite the ..." She trails off and hurries to the front of the room, probably wondering, like everyone else here except me, what neuron stopped firing in Sarah's brain to make her act like a nut job. Me, I don't care if Sarah's crazy. I like her better that way. It's more interesting.

Mrs. Log asks us to pass our papers to the front, whatever that means. Sarah gets a piece of notebook paper out of her bag, with math scribbles all over it, and hands it to the person in front of her. She has to get up to do it, since there's a barrier of at least one empty desk between us and the rest of the class in every direction.

I yawn and lay my head against my arm. Another sleepless night on Alex's hardwood floor, with Jessica crying for hours in the other room and Helen and Gordon taking turns trying to quiet her down. I would say Jessica is no longer my favorite, except that Alex also snores. And his arm has a tendency to fall off the bed and hit me in the face while he's sleeping. And Amelia? She's not even in the running.

I intend to close my eyes for just a second, but I must doze off, because when I open them again, everyone else has a graphing calculator on their desk and Mrs. Log is talking about how to use the tangent button. Last I knew, she was reviewing how to solve for x when there was more than one variable in the equation.

I blink, thinking about going back to sleep, when I notice Sarah staring at me through her giant headgear contraption, the little red light blinking on her forehead. She doesn't have her notebook out this time.

"What are you doing?" I mutter, putting my head back down.

"Looking through your clothes." One side of her mouth

twitches into a grin as she continues to have her visual way with me.

I sit up and hold my hand out to her, tapping my finger to my palm and glancing up at the clock. "This isn't a free show. How long have you been watching? Ten minutes? That's going to cost, oh, about …" I tally up what I think that's worth, then give her a nice discount. "Twenty bucks." It's a steal.

Sarah laughs, but then her expression melts into one of pure shock, and her eyes focus on my hand and don't look away.

"Keep looking," I say. "The meter's only going up."

Sarah suddenly pulls the contraption off her head and sets it on her desk. She pushes the little button on the side and the light fades out. Her cheeks go pink, and she can't look at me.

Now she gets modest?

"Don't you want to know what this is?" Sarah asks, her head bent forward in shame, her eyes sliding toward me, then flicking back to front and center.

"X-ray goggles. Glasses. Whatever. A little clunky on the aesthetics, but otherwise—"

"Damien!" Mrs. Log whaps a ruler against the metal edge of the whiteboard. "Could you *please* not talk in class? Now, where were we?"

Not talk in class? What kind of nonsense is that? What the hell else are we supposed to do?

"Otherwise what?" Sarah asks after a minute of silence to appease Mrs. Log, keeping her voice low. She seems eager for my opinion all of a sudden.

I shrug. "Decent."

She doesn't have her glasses on, on account of having just been wearing the goggles, but even without their magnification, I can see how much her eyes light up. *"Decent."* She repeats the word to herself, as if it was a precious gift I'd just handed her and told her never to let anything happen to.

"As for the twenty bucks," I say, getting back to business, "since it was your first offense, how about you buy me lunch and we call it even?"

X·X·X

"Wow." I drag my feet down the aisles at Helen's antique shop downtown, unable to stop gaping at her collection. Not everything here is actually an antique, but it's all superhero and supervillain related.

A proud smile creeps across Gordon's face as he gives me the tour. Which you'd think wouldn't take very long, since the shop isn't that big, except that I have to stop at every item and gawk for five minutes; I can't believe the stuff she's got.

I point to a recliner in the corner. It's made of purple leather and has a chunk of one of the arm's missing. The price tag on it is, like everything here, disgustingly more than I could ever afford. "That's Professor Doomsworth's chair! He wouldn't leave it for a *month* before he died. He was a little, you know ..." I spin my finger next to my head, indicating he was crazy. "Oh, and that's the spot where Gregorio the Necromanticore blasted Doomsworth's

99

hand off, and that's—"

"Yes, Damien," Gordon says, setting a hand on my shoulder and steering me on to the next one. "We know."

I only get excited about the supervillain stuff and don't really know anything about the hero artifacts, but Gordon seems to enjoy showing off the store to me anyway. We pass half a broken magician's wand, the black kind with the white tip, and I'm like, "Is that ... is *that*—"

"Part of it," Gordon says. "Come on. The best is in the back."

"And that's the shooter the Marbler choked on. Mom says she was at the game when it happened, but she was a little kid at the time."

Gordon winces when I mention Mom and picks up the pace, leading me around the *L* shape of the store and into the back section.

I drool at the sight of even more cool stuff. "And over there, that's—"

"Damien." Gordon taps me on the shoulder to get my attention and points to a ring under a glass case.

I recognize it immediately and press my hands and face against the glass, unable to resist getting as close as possible. Alarms blare and red lights flare overhead as soon as I do. A camera flashes, practically blinding me.

"Get back!" Gordon shouts. He jerks me away from it just as Helen hurries over to us. I'd say she ran, but it's not what I would call running, what with her limp and all.

I'm still seeing spots from the flash, but I notice a little panel open up beneath the case, revealing a nozzle that sprays out some weird mist. Gordon pulls me back farther and warns me not to breathe it in. He sounds ashamed when he says, "It's, um, a supervillain deterrent. Puts them to sleep." He scratches the side of his head. "Since you're half villain, you might be susceptible."

Helen pushes a series of buttons on a keypad on the wall. The little panel closes, and the alarm stops blaring. "Sorry about that," she says, but I can tell she's proud her security system would have stopped me.

"That's the ring," I say, forgetting to cover my mouth and nose against the mist. It's a gold ring with a ruby in the middle. It has *BB + CM* engraved on it. Bart the Blacksmith and his wife, Cissy Miles. I know all about it, and not just because the man was a legend but because he was Kat's grandfather. He had the power to imbue the metals he forged with special abilities. He was notorious for making chains that could bind superheroes'—or supervillains'—powers, for making innocent-looking jewelry that could warp your mind or make you do his bidding, and for forging bullets that could take down *anyone*, no matter what their special ability. They say that when his wife died, he took the ring he'd originally made for her, melted it down, and forged this. It's supposed to keep the wearer free from heartache. He *never* took it off, not for anything, until the day he died. Nobody knows whether it worked or not because when he bit the big one twenty years ago, the ring was never found. And now here it is.

It's the only item in the store without a price tag, though I don't know how you could put a price on it—it's too valuable.

Helen watches me taking it in, her expression shifting from pride to melancholy. I yawn, suddenly tired and feeling the effects of the antivillain mist kick in, and wobble a little on my feet. I'm about to ask if the ring really works when she says, "I earned that ring." The corners of her mouth almost twitch into a smile, then sag back down. "With my superspeed, I was the fastest, the only one who could get out of there in time to"—she licks her lips, her eyes shining—"to save everyone."

I shift my weight uncomfortably, trying to keep my eyes open and wondering about Helen's limp and if she got it in the fight. "Is that how you, um ...?" I glance down at her feet, then away again.

"Got this limp?" She shoots me a half grin, but she still looks really worn out. "By the time we got the go-ahead from Headquarters, Bart knew we were coming. He was waiting for us when we raided his workshop. He was going to blow it all up and take us and him with it, rather than get captured. One of us had to stay inside to try and stop him, to at least stall him, while the rest of the crew got out. I was the fastest. I thought I could get away in time. I thought—" She chokes up a little and clears her throat. "I'm lucky to be alive. None of us thought about the consequences of Bart's workshop blowing up. We didn't think about the effect the explosives would have on some of his creations. But even if we had ... You know he crafted jewelry that inhibited a person's power? Made it so they couldn't use it at all?"

I swallow and nod, not wanting to think about where this is going.

Helen shrugs. "I was the fastest, now I'm not. Sometimes I wonder whether I made the right choice. Maybe I didn't need to stay; maybe we all could have gotten out anyway. But maybe not. And when I come down here and look at this ring and remember my friends are safe and he's not going to hurt anyone anymore, I know it was worth it. I know I'd do it all over again if I had to."

I don't even have a power yet, but I can't imagine losing one. Especially while trying to defeat someone in Kat's family. An awkward pause hangs in the air, but I have one more question, and I know I have to ask now or miss my chance. "How ... how did you get the ring?" I picture her prying it off his cold dead finger, but then I remember he died in an explosion.

Helen smiles. Not, like, a happy smile. It's kind of sad, but still hopeful. "He took it off," she says. "Before he hit the detonator. He said he wanted to remember his wife in death. He didn't want to die masking the pain of her loss. He was only human, after all, and the ring is a reminder of that, too. That's why I took it. I wanted to remember."

She stops and looks at me, like she's expecting me to say something. Like she wants me to tell her yeah, villains are people, too.

Luckily, Gordon's phone rings, rescuing me from Helen, and he answers it. As he listens to the voice on the other side, his gaze falls to me. His jaw sets and his eyebrows furrow. "Yes, yes," he mutters. "I'll see to it." He grips his phone so hard, I'm surprised he doesn't break it. "Damien," he says, sucking in a deep breath through clenched teeth, "that was the school. We need to talk."

<h1 style="text-align:center">X·X·X</h1>

Gordon sighs across the dining table. "Did you or did you not put scorpions in those kids' backpacks?"

He means Marty and Jill. I told them they made my list. "You know I don't like to brag."

"The school has reason to suspect that you did."

"They can't prove anything. I have it all under control." I fold my hands and flash him a reassuring smile.

"You sent them to the *hospital*." Gordon trips over his chair, he gets up so quickly. He clenches his fists and paces the length of the table. "How is that having it under control?!"

"They only went to get checked out. Besides, they weren't *real* scorpions—just clever robots with stingers. They might be really itchy for a couple weeks, but it's not like they're going to die. I know what I'm doing. This is only phase one—"

"Phase one? Dear God." He slides a hand over his forehead and through his hair. "This is not an acceptable way to behave, young man!"

"Says you." I screw up my eyebrows at him.

"Don't you dare ..." He takes a deep breath to calm himself. "They didn't deserve what you did."

I say it very slowly, so maybe it'll sink through his thick skull. "Yes. They. Did." Anger boils up inside me— how can he be so stupid?—and I have to make an effort to squelch it down. This is why I hate superheroes. They might seem all right for a while, but only on the surface; deep down, they're all deranged.

Gordon is about to yell at me some more, but my tone at least must have gotten through to him, because he seems to realize how serious I am. "Listen, Damien, let's say they *did* deserve it. ..." He rubs his temples, like I'm giving him a headache. He slumps down in the chair across from me. "I'm not saying they did, but even so, superheroes can't act this way. The sooner you learn that, the easier life will be for you."

This man is completely insane. I hope it's not hereditary. "Who said I was a superhero? I don't see how letting people bully my friends is going to make life anything but hard, no matter what I am."

"You could have told the proper authorities."

"Psh." I roll my eyes at him. *"Nobody* cares what they do. They think they're so cool, that they can get away with anything, but they can't push me around. *I* care."

"You could have told me."

"It's not a problem. I took care of it."

Gordon pounds his fists into the table in frustration. "You're missing the point! Putting other kids in the hospital, even for a checkup, is *not* okay. Not ever. Listen, son, any decent superhero is going to sign the League Treaty. Maybe you'll be thinking about it when you're eighteen or so, when you're getting ready to start your career. If you don't sign, no one's going to trust you. They're not going to have a guarantee that your methods are safe. The League makes sure everyone follows the same rules, the same moral code of conduct—"

"You keep talking like I'm a hero, but I'm not." I lean back in my chair. "I don't have to abide by your useless mumbo jumbo."

"It's not *useless*. That's what I'm trying to tell you. You might think you're a villain, but there's got to be more to you than that. You're *my* son, and that means you've got hero potential, Damien. You need to consider the possibility."

I press my fingertips together. "And what happens when some bad guy comes along who you can't beat with your precious League rules? What then?"

Gordon sputters, trying to come up with a real answer, getting angrier and angrier when he can't. Finally he says, "We work together. We find a way. But we *don't* break our code. It's what binds us together, what separates the heroes from the vi—" He stops. His mouth thins into a tight line. "You can put your faith in the code, in the Treaty."

"Well," I say, "I put my faith in me."

He shuts his eyes, the anger seeping out of him, too exhausted to keep it up. "I can see what your mother meant," he mutters. "Relentless." He shakes his head. "You're going to have to change."

"I won't. Let me ask you one more question." I look him straight in the eyes. I pretend I don't notice they're the exact same green color as mine. "Would Helen still have her powers if you'd all played by my rules instead of yours?"

CHAPTER 7

Sarah presses forward, forcing me against the wall outside the school, and whispers in my ear. It's only been a little over twenty-four hours since she looked at me through her X-ray goggles, but I guess she must have liked what she saw.

Normally, I would find a situation where a girl like Sarah has her hands on my chest and her tongue practically in my ear a bit seductive. Maybe a lot seductive, depending on what happens next.

People are swarming out of the school, running to catch buses and scattering in every direction to walk home with their friends. Nobody notices the couple of freaks invading each other's personal space, but I don't expect they would. Any temptation to mess with us evaporated after what happened to Jill and Marty.

When she speaks, I know one thing's for sure: Sarah plastering herself against me has everything to do with what she saw through my clothes with her X-ray goggles yesterday. It's just not what I want it to be. Sarah whispers the words so softly that, even if we weren't the only people around, only I could hear them, and they do everything to ruin the mood: "Make me your sidekick."

I freeze up. My jaw goes slack. An outside observer might think she just said something more appealing, judging from my reaction.

My hands tremble as I place them on Sarah's wrists and push her away. Sidekick? Is she nuts? "No way."

"You haven't already got one, do you?" She looks into my eyes, hopeful and earnest.

"That's not the point." I feel my expression go sour.

"I already know your secret," Sarah says, and I'm glad she recognizes that that's what it is. "I saw your X, and that can't be helped now. Unless ..." She pauses, looking off into the distance. She shakes her head. "No, I'd rather not go through all that. The machine isn't stable yet."

"You can't be my sidekick. The position is closed."

"You already have someone?"

"It was never open. No offense."

"Ah, I see." She nods. "You work alone."

"I—Yeah, something like that."

"You're cute, Damien. And I like the way you hold your pen."

"Er, thanks." I don't know what that has to do with anything. "I like your creative use of tinfoil." The school grounds are empty now, so there's no one else around to overhear when I say, "But if you know what an X means, you know I'm not really a superhero."

Sarah's face lights up. "I didn't know what it meant for

sure. Not really … Everybody says there's a third letter, but nobody's ever actually *seen* it."

If she's trying to make me feel like a freak, she's doing a good job. "Now you have. You can sell your story to the tabloids. Tell them you're having my alien baby while you're at it."

"I was up until three in the morning last night doing research on the Internet. About Xs."

She did seem kind of tired in math today, but I chalked it up to Mrs. Log droning on and on about solving for x in terms of y. Which I guess shouldn't have been so boring for me, because when it comes to my X, I'd really like to know *why*. As in, why me.

Not that I want Sarah to think she knows more than I do about my own thumb, or that I'm interested in her research, but I can't help being curious. I scratch the side of my face and don't look at her. "Up until three? There must have been a lot of Wikipedia entries to read." I sound a little snotty when I say that, so she knows I don't approve of her online resources, because I don't want her thinking she knows more about this than I do. All I've read is the article Mom gave me—I couldn't bring myself to search the Internet. There are probably whole forums where people can report their supposed sightings of people like me. Okay, maybe not, but I wasn't ready to know what was out there either way.

Sarah sighs. "It was hard to find any real information. But I know it means you're half hero."

"And half villain."

"You can still get an *H*. You won't have the X forever."

"Half *villain*, Sarah."

"So? You live with heroes—just because your genes have some *V* in them doesn't have to mean anything."

She's right about me living with heroes, but she doesn't know it's only been for the past week. "You know what my being half villain means? One of your heroes messed up and did it with the enemy."

"It could have been a forbidden romance. Something dangerous and romantic and—"

"It wasn't. My dad, the superhero? He didn't even know her."

She breathes in deep and stares at her shoes. "Everyone makes mistakes. I did. That's why I need your help. I screwed everything up, and now I need to fix it."

"Okay, but I'm not your man. I'm *not* a superhero." I shut my eyes and will her to say she needs a villain instead. I could do that. Except that she's got the Crimson Flash's chin *memorized*—she doesn't want a villain. "You know what an *X* means, right?"

"So you don't have your *H* yet and you're not an official hero. It's okay, I'm desperate. I'll take what I can get. My dad's in trouble. I did something I shouldn't have, got mixed up with the wrong people with this invention I was working on, and he took the fall. It's completely my fault, and I have to get him back!" Sarah punches her fist into her empty palm. "And I'm running out of time."

"I bet the Crimson Flash would help you. Maybe you should ask *him*."

She wrings her hands together. "You don't know the people I'm up against."

I might, actually. That's part of the problem.

"They're supervillains. They'll see someone like the Crimson Flash coming a mile away. They're expecting something like that. I need an unknown. What? Don't look at me like that, Damien, you *are* an unknown, aren't you? I've never heard of you."

"Heard of what? You don't even know what my superhero name supposedly is—how would you know if you'd heard it or not? But you haven't because it *doesn't exist*, because I'm *not* a hero. Look, Sarah, I put robotic scorpions in Marty's and Jill's backpacks. I'm not a shining example of morality."

"That doesn't count—they had it coming." She shrugs. "Robin Hood stole from the rich, right? I don't care if you only have an *X*. It's not like you're some kind of villain or anything."

"I'm sorry, Sarah." My chest feels tight and sweat prickles up and down my back. I can't take up superheroing, not now. I can't risk getting caught and having to live in the Tines household for the rest of my life, and the last thing I want to do is influence my *X* the wrong way and end up with an *H*. "You've got a whole town full of superheroes. Find somebody else. But if you ever want to run your hands over my body again, I'm available for parties and other recreational events."

"Oh." Sarah's shoulders slump. She looks so disappointed. That's what she gets for thinking I'm something I'm not. "I wouldn't expect you to do it for free. I could do your homework for a month or ... if that's not enough, I could do it for the rest of the year."

"No, thanks." I could care less about this homework stuff.

"Please, Damien. I'll do anything."

"Anything?" My ears perk up at that.

"Well, maybe not *anything.*" Sarah glares at me, her glasses sliding down her nose. She sighs and waves her hand, dismissing the whole idea. She folds her arms and turns her shoulder to me. "Never mind," she says. "Forget the whole thing. You're right, you're not a hero, so I shouldn't have asked."

She's about to walk away, all disappointed and sullen. "Sarah, wait."

She looks over her shoulder, hope sparking in her eyes. "You'll do it?!"

"I'll … I'll think about it."

She smiles at me, beaming like I said yes instead of something noncommittal. She throws her arms around me and hugs me before running off down the street.

X·X·X

"Ready for the big day?" Gordon chuckles on his way past the breakfast table on Saturday morning, grabbing an orange and digging into it with his thumb to peel it.

Due to some sort of nightmarish birthday sleepover— thankfully at someone else's house—where a bunch of eight-year-olds gathered last night to torture somebody else's family, I actually had Alex's room to myself, so I know it's not from grogginess that I have no idea what Gordon's talking about.

Amelia munches on her cereal across the table from me. She pours so little milk on it that the cereal might as well be dry. She told me milk makes you fat. Though she didn't seem to care about all the butter she was hogging down last night. I think her ratio is about half a pound of lard per dinner roll.

Gordon accidentally sprays me with his orange as he peels it. The sharp smell of citrus fills the room. "Amelia told me how much you're looking forward to it."

A very bad, gut-wrenching feeling creeps its way through me. I laugh. "That Amelia," I say. "She's such a kidder." I glare at her.

She stifles a snicker.

Gordon ruffles my hair with his orange-juice hands. "I remember how excited I was the first time I flew. Course, I'd already done it by your age. I didn't sleep for weeks afterward."

This wasn't the plan. Amelia was supposed to give him the fake article I wrote about how people with Xs don't have powers. I even made up lab reports with graphs and everything, showing how mixing the H and V viruses renders the victim—er, patient—superpower-less. I spent hours on that, and I even went through all the trouble of sneaking into the computer labs at school and Photoshopping it to look like it came from a real newspaper. Amelia was supposed to tell Gordon about the interesting article she read. She was supposed to leave it lying around where he could see it and talk it up like forcing me to discover my power would actually be harmful to my health. I could have given him the fake article myself, but he'd never believe it, coming from me. It'd be way too suspicious. I should have picked Alex to help me out, except he's too young to be reading scholarly articles and photocopying them for others to enjoy.

Amelia stuffs another spoonful of bran flakes in her fat, lying mouth. *Crunch, crunch.* She has the gall to smile at me. And talk with her mouth full. "I'm *so* jealous." She says it without her usual groan. Bits of brown flakes stick to her teeth. I can see why the boys flock to her.

"Actually, Gordon," I say, "I have a lot of this ... 'homework' to do today."

He shoots me a proud grin, like his glorious influence is finally getting through to me. "You have my permission to do it tomorrow."

"Can't." I fold my hands together and look up at the sky. "Church tomorrow. All day." I stepped inside a church once, when it was raining really hard and I couldn't get my umbrella open. It smelled like old people, and every little noise I made echoed really loudly. I remember everyone in the pews turning to stare at me funny, but that could have been because I interrupted their service. You know, by jumping up and down and screaming that God was burning me.

Gordon claps me on the back and laughs. "We're only going for the morning service. You'll have all afternoon."

Oh, God. They actually go to church? And they think they're dragging me with them?!

"Looks like you're free," Amelia says. Bits of her cereal fall out of her mouth and into her bowl as she moos.

The front door opens. An overstimulated Alex

stampedes past Helen.

"Look what I got!" Alex bounces up and down in front of me and blows on a noisemaker. It lashes out and whips me in the face. He reaches into a small plastic bag with balloons printed on it and pulls out a yellow Jolly Rancher. "For you," he says, carefully setting it on the table in front of me. Then he zooms off to his room.

It's lemon flavor. I stare at the candy and don't touch it. I have a feeling I'm already going to regret having eaten breakfast.

"Better get ready," Gordon says as he goes into the other room to greet Helen. "We've got a busy day ahead of us."

Once he's out of earshot, I lean forward and jab my finger into the table in front of Amelia. "We had a deal. I thought you didn't want me to fly first?"

She cackles to herself. I'm supposed to be the black sheep here, yet no one notices the embodiment of pure evil living in their house, right under their noses. "That was before you killed Blue Bunnykins. If you hate flying so much, maybe you'll just leave. It's worth it."

"I can't leave—my mom made a deal. Tell him to call it off!"

She shrugs. "Can't. He's so excited about it. Plus, maybe you won't come back in one piece."

The blood drains out of my entire body. I don't know where it goes, only that I feel cold and tingly all over. "What are your friends going to think when I show them your underwear at lunch on Monday? The ones that say *I love Robert March* on them?" I didn't even have to write

115

that on there—Amelia already did, complete with a big red heart on the butt. Robert March plays the tuba, badly, in the school band and has a lot of freckles. He spends all of lunch playing trading-card games with his geeky friends. The same way Amelia's table has yet to have a boy other than me grace it with his presence, Robert's table is equally lacking in the girl department, but that might be because they have a cloud of *odeur de gym socks* hovering over them.

Amelia goes completely pink. I've heard her tell her friends she likes the same blond football player they all spend every moment of every day gushing over. I know because she talks to them on the phone for about ten hours a night about it. I wonder what her friends would think if they knew her secret true love.

"You won't." Amelia pulls herself together and gives me a snotty know-it-all look that twists up her nose in such a way that I can see inside her nostrils. "You'll be too busy sitting with your *girlfriend*."

She means Sarah, who is not my girlfriend. Even if I kind of liked the way she hugged me the other day. I'm not over Kat, and that hug was given under false pretenses. If Sarah knew what a horrible person I really was, I don't think she'd be so keen to beg for my help.

"Plus," Amelia says, "I'm not going to let you have them."

"Too late." I sit back in my chair. "I've already hidden them somewhere in the house, and only I know where they are." I spotted them in the clean laundry when Helen was folding them the other night. I thought I'd better keep my options open and seized the opportunity.

Amelia sticks her lower lip out in a sneer-pout, her cereal forgotten. "I hate you," she says.

"Then tell Gordon to call it off."

But she shuts her mouth and doesn't say another word, not even when Gordon comes lumbering back in and claims this is going to be the best day of my life.

CHAPTER 8

Kidnapped. I've been kidnapped by a madman in tights and a cape. We're on the roof of *the tallest building in Golden City*. There's us, the little room that houses the stairwell, and nothing but roof and a long drop in every direction. I cling to the stairwell house, the one we just came through. Too bad the door is now locked, thanks to Gordon, who didn't think we'd need to go back that way.

I do not have words for what I want to do to Gordon, my loving father, right now. He's dressed as the Crimson Flash, the world's moralest superhero, and no one thought to stop him as he dragged a sixteen-year-old boy through the streets of Golden City, going, "It's okay to be nervous. I was my first time, too. It's hard to take the plunge, but before you know it, you're going to be enjoying the ride." Why couldn't anybody have taken that out of context and saved me? I wonder what his precious League Treaty's rules are on hauling people up to the top of Golden City

Banking and Finances, the tallest building in town—known more for the number of people who commit suicide by flinging themselves off the top than it is for its banking skills—and throwing them to their doom?

I hate Amelia. Hate her so much.

"Come on, Damien." The Crimson Flash's cape whips around in the wind. He holds his hand out to me.

Screw him. You know what he can do with this whole flying thing? He can take it and shove it up his kitten-saving ass. Put that on TV. Hey, kids, you know what your hero *really* does? *Tortures people.* He thinks he's so much better than supervillains, but at least my mom wouldn't try to kill me. Accidentally nick me with her lasers once in a while—and maybe sometimes on purpose, sure—but not this.

Gordon grabs my arm. "This is the only way."

"How can you be certain I have the ability?" I have to shout to be heard over the wind. "I could die. Mom's not going to be happy about that. You think you don't get along with her now? Wait until you have to tell her you're the reason her only son's never going to walk again. Wait until you have to ask her if I wanted to be cremated or not, because I probably should be, given the state of the body."

He takes a deep breath. He acts like he's trying to get a little kid to ride their bike without training wheels for the first time. "I won't let you get hurt. You just have to trust me, Damien."

"Oh, I'm sorry, am I putting you out for not *trusting* you when you're about to throw me off a freaking building?"

He bends down so we're at eye level. I'm not that much shorter than him, but the way I'm cringing and hugging the wall makes it hard to stand up straight. "Damien," he says, "I'm certain you have the power." His voice sounds like it's on fire, he's so damned *sure* and so noble about it, even though he has no real reason to think that. "My father had it before me, and his father before him. You come from a long line of fliers. I know you're a little reluctant to ..." He puts a hand on my shoulder. I jump at his touch, that's how skittish I am. "I'm not stupid," he says. "I know what this means for you. If you can fly, well, then that might mean you'll grow up to be a superhero."

"Villain all the way. Don't try and talk me out of it." I barely know what I'm saying, I just hope he'll shut the hell up and let me go home. And not in a box, if you know what I mean. I could just tell Gordon about my fears about being up here, but he probably wouldn't listen, he's so set on me following in his tight-wearing footsteps. Plus, the last thing in the world I'm going to do is admit to Gordon I'm afraid of *anything*, let alone that I have a phobia about heights. It's personal information. He's only known me a little over a week—he hasn't earned the right to know. I'll just have to talk him out of it.

"Even if you don't become a hero, villains aren't going to take you seriously if you can fly. I hate to say this, but even Marianna—"

"You leave her out of this. Mom doesn't care about my thumb or my abilities or any of that. That's all you and your cape-fearing family." Except that Mom would love it if I got a *V*. She'd probably cry her eyes out for days if I screwed up and somehow got an *H*.

Gordon chews his lip, his head bent. "There comes a time when you have to face the truth. You're half hero, whether you like it or not." He grabs me and drags me toward the edge.

I shut my eyes and dig my heels into the floor. I squint at him and the approaching ledge and feel my breakfast coming up. My insides are weak, like I've lived off of Jell-O my whole life. I want to be dead. I want my life to stop right here and fade into nothingness. I shout at Gordon, spouting off random, barely coherent nonsense. Mostly about how much I hate Amelia, peppered with such classics as "I'll never forgive you!" and "You're going to regret this!"

I'm dizzy and panicked and I think I might be foaming at the mouth. This is my worst nightmare. I must say something about that in my ramblings, because suddenly Gordon stops. He says, all serious and worried, "Why didn't you tell me you had a fear of—"

And then it's too late, because the ledge lurches out from under me. I'm hurtling through space and it isn't exhilarating or wonderful or anything other than *terrifying*. Gordon makes to dive down after me, but his cape whips in front of his face and gets caught on his head.

I laugh. Ha ha. I'm going to die and maybe he'll disown Amelia for her lying treachery, but probably not. Maybe my mom will murder Gordon, or maybe she'll end up back in the sack with him. It's not like they were anything but enemies *before*—why should this be different? They'll replace me, and maybe Helen will find out and divorce

Gordon, and won't he be sorry when he doesn't get to push Amelia off a building in a couple months?

Rows and rows of windows rush past me. Everything's a blur. I'm going to die—I'm going to freaking *die*. Gordon finally gets the cape off his head and dives after me. He speeds through the air, pulling his arms in close to his body. He's gaining on me, but he's not going to make it.

The look of horror on Gordon's face tells me the ground is getting too close. His mouth twists in agony, his eyes squeeze shut, like he can't stand to watch. He forces them open again, reaching his arm out to me. Even though there's only about ten feet between us, and the gap is closing, he seems impossibly far away.

I hear cars and smell their exhaust and the hot dogs from the vendor on the corner. I hear screams and oohs and ahhs and this is it. And then ...

I just stop. Suspended in the air. I feel like my heart stops, too, but then it's pounding in my chest so hard it hurts. I can't move. Then I drop the last couple of feet and land on the ground. I turn over and throw up, right in the middle of the street. Cars honk at me, and a taxi driver sticks his head out the window and yells at me to get out of the way. My mouth tastes bitter and sour and some of the puke goes up my nose and it burns like hell.

Gordon lands on the ground next to me. He puts his hand between my shoulder blades, but I push him off. "Don't touch me!" Then I'm flailing my arms and screaming obscenities at him, not even sure what I'm saying or where it comes from. Mothers standing on the streets cover up their kids' ears and hurry them along past us. The taxi driver shuts up and listens. He might be taking notes.

"Think you can push me off a ledge, you toad-licking, slime-swallowing, chicken-choking, gizzard-loving, orphan-tasting—"

"Damien!" The Crimson Flash looks around at all the bystanders, embarrassed, and tries to pull me out of the street.

I tear myself away from him, stumbling backward into traffic, which is conveniently still stopped, with everyone gaping at me.

"Damien, wait! I—I didn't know! You didn't tell me you were afraid of heights!"

"I'm not afraid of anything!" It's obviously a lie, but it sounds good to me.

Gordon hurries after me. "Everything's going to be okay," he says in a soothing voice, trying to calm me down. "You flew. You actually flew!"

I mutter what he can go do to himself.

He makes a disgusted face but reaches out to me again. "Damien, I'm sorry. I didn't know—how could I?"

Gee, I don't know, maybe if he wasn't so dead set on pushing people off buildings, he'd realize how crazy that is?!

Gordon shuts his eyes. He looks concerned, but I don't know if he's actually worried about *me* or all the people staring at us. "Let's go home, son. We can talk about this."

I want to scream at the crowd that the Crimson Flash, their hero, just tried to kill me. But then there'd be reporters and mobs of people asking questions, and I'm not in the mood for that today. "Let's get one thing straight," I tell Gordon, my voice low but burning with anger. "Your house? *Not* my home. Don't ever call it that again if you know what's good for you. And even if it was, last time I went somewhere with you, I almost wound up dead. So thanks, but no thanks."

He starts to protest, but then I shout at the crowd that the Crimson Flash is practicing his stunt work for his upcoming movie, and that he's answering questions and signing free movie posters. A mob of people rush him, even though he's still standing in the middle of the street, and it isn't hard for me to slip away.

X·X·X

The first thing I hear when I get to Mom's house is the sound of kissing. I hope my grandparents are over, renewing their love for each other, but no. A champagne bottle pops, then fizzes, and Mom says from the living room, "To us."

"To us," Taylor's voice repeats as their glasses clink together.

They can't see me skulking in the hallway, and apparently they were too preoccupied to hear me come in. I peek past the corner, thinking I can't get any more traumatized today than I already am. Mom is sitting on the couch with Taylor Lewis, the dean of Vilmore, the prestigious secondary school for villains in training. The one Kat and I are supposed to go to this fall, assuming one of us isn't disqualified for not having a *V*.

Taylor has a scraggly beard and blond hair with dark roots. He puts his champagne glass to his lips but doesn't drink. He sets it back on the table. "You're not going to tell me, are you?"

Mom downs her whole glass. "It was a long time ago. I was young and … no."

"So, in other words, you're not going to tell me what other villain swept you off your feet?"

"That's not exactly how it happened. There was no sweeping—just one night while I was young and stupid."

More like desperate. Taylor's in for a big surprise if he ever finds out about Mom's subway adventure.

She grins at him. "But while Damien's at his … with his other family, *we've* got the whole house to ourselves."

Uh-huh. What was all that stuff about living with Gordon being a big opportunity for me? More like an opportunity for her to have her boyfriend over without me getting in the way. I like Taylor okay and everything, but I don't like having to listen to him and my mom call each other stupid names like "honeybuns" and "sugar lemon," and I *don't* want to know what they do behind closed doors. Or doors that are only mostly closed. But I can guess, and having him spend the night at our house kind of creeps me out. Now they've got six weeks of bliss while I'm stuck in a hellhole full of superheroes.

Mom sets her glass down on the coffee table. "Imagine what it'll be like next year, when he's off at school. The house will be so empty!"

"At *my* school, Marianna." Taylor half groans, half laughs. "Causing all sorts of trouble, no doubt."

Ha. That scamp. What a rascal that Damien must be.

"The admissions process is nearly over," Taylor says. "The deadline is coming up. I ought to be making the final decisions within the next couple weeks. I'll definitely have them done by the first of April. I was … ah, wondering if Damien might find time to talk to me. I don't want to show special treatment, but I'd like to do an interview, if you don't mind."

What's wrong with special treatment? I have absolutely no objections to him interviewing me to see how great I am. Maybe he wants to start me in the advanced classes.

"I'm sure we can arrange something," Mom says. A timer dings in the kitchen and she gets up to check on it.

Taylor corks the champagne bottle and sets it on the other side of the table, away from Mom's glass. She hurries back in, a giant metal pot steaming between her potholder-covered hands. She nearly drops it on the table. Slowly, she pulls back the lid and waves her hand over the pot to waft the smell toward her nose. "Ahhh. Another perfect batch. Now if only you could get Dr. Kink's device working."

Dr. Kink? As in Sarah's father, who got kidnapped by supervillains? And are they talking about the same hypno device that I sort of, uh, broke? Nah. Probably all a coincidence.

Taylor rubs his temples. "Don't remind me. I'm not planning on doing any more testing until we get more answers out of him. He swore to me he'd repaired the device last time, and you know how that turned out. I don't want another Ruthersford incident. Your potion worked beautifully, of course, made the whole town susceptible to the effects of Dr. Kink's device, but ultimately he must not have adjusted it right, because things didn't go as planned. The trigger word turned the people of Ruthersford into a mindless, raging mob, instead of properly submitting to mind control. I almost didn't get out of there. Luckily, I chose a trigger word not likely to be used too often so close to Vilmore. And even if someone does say it, you know how they feel about superheroes around there. No one will care."

"Don't let it discourage you, honeybuns. It's not your fault. If Damien had been more careful in my lab …" She takes a deep breath to calm herself and shakes her head. "The device is the last piece of the puzzle, and once we have it working, everything will go exactly as planned. We'll be making big names for ourselves in no time."

"*If* we can get it working." Taylor sips his champagne. "Dr. Kink was in tears today, tinkering around with the device with a tiny screwdriver, but he couldn't make it work. I honestly believe the man's had some kind of breakdown since he published those articles and made the prototype. He's not the same. Some days, he tells me he doesn't know anything about the invention at all and begs me to let him go free. Still …" Taylor sets the glass down and drops his arms at his sides. "The students have been quite useful in getting him to talk. I told you I took on a couple of promising TAs from the Advanced Torture Techniques class? Henrietta Stone is still a little timid, but you should see Peter Heath."

Ah, good old Pete.

"He's extremely enthusiastic, and his methods are ..." Taylor's eye twitches. "I think he'll find himself very at home in a torture chamber someday, if he chooses to go that route. If we need an assistant in the final stages of the plan, I think he'd do quite nicely. Lots of ambition, that boy."

I have ambition, too. Just because I maybe broke their stupid hypno device, they're going to pick Pete to help them with their evil plans? It's one thing for them not to want me in the house while they make out, but choosing Pete over me? That hurts.

"But enough business," Taylor says. He reaches into his pocket. "Marianna, we need to talk about something important, something I've been thinking about for quite some time now, but I didn't want to bring it up with Damien around. It's nothing against him, I just wasn't sure how he'd react, and ... I want this to be a happy occasion." Taylor swallows and pulls a small, black velvet box out of his pocket. He flips it open to reveal a glittering diamond ring. "Marianna Locke, you're the best partner in crime a villain could have. No matter how many hypno devices get broken, and even if all our schemes come to nothing, I want to spend the rest of my life with you. What I'm trying to say is, will you marry me?"

Mom shrieks with joy. She puts her hands to her face, gaping at Taylor. "Yes, of course!" He slips the ring on her finger and puts his scraggly bearded mouth over hers. I'm so disgusted, I can't see straight.

I feel sick, and like the ground just dropped out from under me. The memory of falling off the tallest building in

Golden City flashes through my head, and I relive that horror on top of this one. I can't stand it. I step out into view, ruining their moment. It takes Mom a second to notice me, but when she does, she looks pretty freaked. She pushes Taylor off her. "Damien! Sweetie, what are you doing here?!" She moves to press the lid back over the container of hypno potion.

I put my hands in the pockets of my sweatshirt and look around, as if I've never seen the place. "Last I checked, I thought I lived here."

"Damien," Mom says, scrambling to her feet, "you're supposed to be at Gordon's, not creeping around the house."

"I have to come home, Mom. You can't make me stay with those people!"

"Just a moment, Damien. It's not safe for you, with ..." Mom glances at the pot containing the hypno potion, then at Taylor. "You're young, and you don't want to breathe in nasty chemicals with those healthy lungs of yours, right?" She laughs nervously, then grabs her potholders and carts the potion off into the other room, so the superhero half of me doesn't get poisoned by it or whatever.

Leaving me alone with her boyfriend. I mean *fiancé*. I stand there in my hooded sweatshirt with my hands in my pockets, the perfect picture of a sullen teenager, staring down Taylor Lewis.

"So," he says, "are you excited to have your *V*?" I guess Mom didn't want him to know about her shameful tryst with a superhero. He tries to laugh good naturedly, but the tension in the room is too high. When I don't respond, he goes on. "Damien, I want you to know I love your mother very much. I've thought a lot about this—it wasn't spur of the moment—and I never meant for you to find out this way."

"How *did* you want me to find out? When I was off at school, where my freaking out about it couldn't bother you in your love nest?" I'm so mad, I'm tempted to tell him who my father really is, just to spite Mom.

Taylor's mouth hangs open. He struggles to find something else to say to me. "I'm going to be your stepfather. I'd hoped that would be good news to you."

"At least you're a supervillain," I mutter.

"What?"

"Nothing." I turn away from him and wait for Mom to come back. When she does, she's got this big, fake smile plastered across her face. Or maybe it's not so fake, because when she smiles at Taylor, it looks pretty real. I guess it's only fake when it's for me.

"Damien, sweetie, can I have a *word* with you?" She shoos me into her bedroom. The room she's no doubt shared with Taylor many times since she shipped me off to Gordon's. Her bed isn't made, and it's obvious both sides have been used lately. Great. I kick some of her dirty laundry out of my way on the floor.

Mom shuts the door. She can't help beaming at the ring on her finger. "Isn't this exciting?"

I scowl at her messy bed. "I hope you're using protection, Mom. The last thing I want right now is another sibling."

She acts like she doesn't hear me. She's got this

selective-hearing condition that acts up now and then. "I want you to be happy for me."

"Sure. Whatever." Not exactly enthusiastic. Maybe she should try me again on a day when I *haven't* just been thrown off a building. "Look, I need to come home. I promise I won't get in your and Taylor's way."

"It's only a little while longer," Mom says, putting her hands on my shoulders and giving them a squeeze.

"Like five weeks—"

"It'll fly right by. It's a learning experience. Studying the enemy in their own home. Think how much further ahead you'll be than the other students when you start at Vilmore."

My shoulders slump. All I want to do is go home, but I don't know where that is anymore. "You're only saying that to get rid of me. You want the house all to yourself. How's Taylor going to like having a stepson who's half *superhero*, huh? He didn't know all the facts when he popped the question. Maybe if you tell him the truth, he'll change his mind. He's going to find out when I go to Vilmore next year."

Mom glares at me, her lasers charging in her eyes. "Damien Locke. You *don't* have to be happy for me, but you do have to accept that I can make my own choices. Taylor makes me happy, and he's going to be your stepfather, whether you like it or not."

"You're hiding things from him, and you think it's a good idea to get married?"

Mom's lasers die down, her anger replaced with a smug look. "Have you told Kat yet?"

Touché. "Kat's not my girlfriend. It's different."

"I know this is going to be difficult for you, especially with all the other changes and new people in your life, but you're going to have to face the fact that I'm not going to stay single forever, and Taylor and I are in love."

"Were you even going to invite me to the wedding? Or were you going to elope before I got back?"

"How should I know? He *just* proposed—we haven't made plans yet."

"Right." That makes me feel so much better.

"You should probably go now, Damien. Was there anything else you needed?"

"I'm not going back to them. Gordon tried to kill me. That lousy cape flapper tried to—"

"Then I guess it really is good supervillain training, isn't it?" Mom smiles at me. An "I'm older and smarter than you" smile. "I'm sorry, but you can't come home yet. Taylor and I are involved—"

"I can see that."

"—in some very important work. We can't be bothered."

"By someone who's only half villain."

"It's the superhero half that's a problem. I don't know how the hypno potion would affect you, and I don't want to find out. Plus, I don't want to have to worry about what to tell Taylor, concerning your *X*. We've got a lot of work to do, and I can't be distracted." A gleam off her new diamond ring catches her attention. "At least, not any more than I'm going to be." She grins, then opens the door and steers me out. She walks me through the living room and the hallway, to the front door.

Mom leans forward and hugs me. I'm taller than her, but I don't remember when that happened. "Take care of yourself, all right, sweetie? And for God's sakes, eat more, will you? I can feel your ribs."

"Sure, Mom. Whatever you say."

"Oh, and Damien? One more thing. Next time you visit? Call first."

Then she shuts the door in my face.

X·X·X

When I get back to Gordon's that evening, the first thing I notice is that someone has snipped Mr. Wiggles in half. *Someone*, who is a fat, lying bitch with shallow friends and no way to attract boys, has cut him in two, right under his little guitar, and left him for me to find on the dining room table.

Alex and three of his liveliest friends come screaming in from the kitchen. They whirl past me, each of them touching my leg like a goalpost as they continue on into the other room. I don't feel them, I don't feel anything.

The top of Amelia's head appears from around the corner in the kitchen. She gasps and pulls back into hiding.

"Honey?" Helen calls from the other room. "Is that Damien? Your father's been looking all over for him!"

Amelia doesn't answer her. She ventures into the dining room and bites her lip. "I'm sorry, Damien," she says. "I thought you killed Blue Bunnykins."

133

I don't acknowledge her presence. I gather up Mr. Wiggles's broken body, still in shock.

"But it turns out it was Alex, not you." She twirls a lock of her hair around her finger. "He was playing heroes and villains with it and got carried away, so I'm mad at him, not you, and I'm really, really—"

I turn and walk away. I don't care what her explanation is. Not today. She was so quick to blame the villain before. She didn't believe me about not doing it, so why should I believe her about feeling bad for what she's done?

Amelia trails after me as I try to get away from her.

Alex and his friends stomp around, shrieking and slamming Alex's door.

Helen calls out to Amelia from the other room, asking her again if I'm home.

I step into the bathroom, the only place where I can be alone in the whole house, and close the door only inches from Amelia's face. I don't know what she thought she was going to do—follow me in? I lock the door before slumping down against the wall and sliding to the linoleum. My eyes water, and I lean my head back to keep the tears from falling.

"Damien?!" Amelia pounds her fists against the door, her voice shrill and getting frustrated. "I said I was sorry!"

Mr. Wiggles will dance no more. She ruined the only thing in this house that was any sort of comfort to me, the only thing that was really *mine*.

"Fine, don't talk to me!" Amelia shouts. "You're the one who came here and acted like a jerk. Maybe if you were a little nicer, I would have believed you in the first place and this wouldn't have happened."

Or if she hadn't been so quick to point the finger at me.

I hear footsteps, then Helen's voice asks, "What is going on?"

Amelia pounds on the door again. "Damien! Talk to me already!" When I don't respond, she makes a huffing noise and tells Helen, "He's being really emo. I apologized and everything, and he won't say *anything.*"

"Then he might not want to talk," Helen says. "Maybe you should leave him alone for a while?"

"Mom, I'm going to get through to him. I'm—"

"Amelia." I hear mumbling mixed with scolding, then some groaning from Amelia, and then, finally, the sound of them leaving. I can still hear Alex and his friends storming through the house, but otherwise I'm alone, and it's quiet.

I hug Mr. Wiggles to my chest. I thought finding out my father was a superhero was the worst it was going to get, but that doesn't even come close to today. A couple of tears streak down my cheeks as I get out my phone.

Kat answers after only one ring. "Hey, Damien!" We haven't talked since the day I told her I didn't want to get back together. She sounds nervous at first, but then excited and relieved. "It's so good to hear from you. I thought, when you didn't call or come over again ... Anyway, what's up?"

I wipe my face on my sleeve. I half expected Kat to hang up on me, still upset about the other day, but no. I guess she's over it, and we're cool. My best friend is still there for me, even if everything else sucks. And maybe that's really all she should be—my best friend. It sounds good. I could live with that. "Oh, nothing much," I tell her. "I just wanted to hear your voice."

CHAPTER 9

Monday afternoon, Sarah and I share an armrest on the train. We're supposed to be in school, but instead we're traveling to Vilmore, to find Sarah's father. I know, I know, I wasn't going to get involved in this. But I figure since I was the one who broke the hypno device, causing my mom and Taylor to kidnap Dr. Kink, I owe her one. I won't call it a rescue. That sounds like we're doing a good deed. I don't have anything against "good deeds" in general, only when they make me seem ... heroic. In the superhero sense. If I was out superheroing, and the news got back to Gordon and Helen, Gordon might take that as evidence that I have superhero potential, and then he'd make me stay with him forever.

Well, he might. Depending on how he reacts to the dead baby spiders I injected into his toothpaste, or the inchworms I dropped in his shampoo bottle. I have yet to discover what Gordon's biggest fear is, but I'm hoping it's the worms.

Even if what I'm doing does count as superheroing in Gordon's book, I can console myself with the fact that ditching school and running off on my own to do it doesn't mesh well with his precious rules. Not only did I leave school without permission and without telling anybody, but I found the money for this trip lying around in Gordon's wallet.

Sarah looks over and smiles at me. She thinks I'm a good person, a wannabe superhero trying to fight off my half-villain status. That's the impression I get from the way she talks about how great I am for doing this, and how awful it is I only have an *X*, but how cool it'll be when I finally get the *H* I deserve. Yeah, right.

I should set her straight. I really should. But then she wouldn't want me to help her, and, to be honest, I'm her best bet for getting her dad back. So it's for her own good that I'm not telling her the truth, and not because I'm selfish and want her to keep talking about how great and wonderful I am. Honest.

Sarah leans across the armrest, her eyes huge behind her glasses. She's wearing a pink turtleneck sweater with a cartoony cow on the front, mooing in Japanese. "What's your superhero name going to be?"

"I told you, I'm not a superhero. This isn't a superhero mission." I wave away the idea with a flick of my hand.

She raises a finger in protest. "A rescue is a type one mission, according to the superhero handbook. That's the highest rank a mission can have."

"Let's not think of it as a mission. That sounds so ... complicated. This is going to be no problem. Easy peasy, right?" Maybe not on her own, but with me here, we should be able to get in and get out and be home in time for dinner. Well, a late dinner—midnight snacks at the worst.

I can't wait to see Gordon's face when he wants to know where I was all night. He'll already be suspicious that I was up to no good—telling him I was out spending the money I stole from him at villain-themed strip clubs is going to be awesome. Especially when I tell him it was minors night and I got all my drinks for free.

A grin spreads across my face, and I almost share my after-mission plans with Sarah. But then I remember she thinks this is a sanctioned trip, all on the up and up, and that she probably wouldn't appreciate me lying to and stealing from my own dad. So instead I tell her, "It's more like we're just two teenagers, casually skipping school and enjoying a train ride together through the country, with plans to help someone out while we're, you know, there. No big deal. Not anything that requires any superhero antics."

Sarah chews her lip, then says, "But it'd be easier for me to come up with a sidekick name if I knew what you were going to call yourself."

"You're not my sidekick. Can I borrow those?" I point to her glasses.

She blinks and hands them to me. I put them on and instantly feel like puking, but I stick it out, trying to look off to the side and not through the lenses. I want to know how long she'll let me wear them before asking for them back. I stare out the window, but we're past the city and there's nothing to see but grass and cows. Fields and fields of them.

I shut my eyes and start to drift off. I know I'm falling asleep because I suddenly feel like I'm plummeting from a million stories up and jolt awake. I don't think I've slept more than five minutes straight since Saturday. I hope Gordon likes his worms. I'd hate to have to start messing with the family food supplies. Maybe fish eggs will mysteriously appear in the milk, or maggots in the ice cream. That'll get Amelia—and hopefully several friends— next time she decides to pig out.

I look outside, peering over the edge of Sarah's glasses. Still more grass. I lean my head on my hand, propping my elbow against the window, and sigh. "Deviant Demon."

Sarah shakes her head and laughs like I've just said something in another language, like the cow on her sweater. "You can't call yourself that. You sound like a super*villain*."

Let's see ... Fraidy Flier and Freak Girl? "How about Locke and Keynk?"

She snorts. "I'll keep it in mind of we start up a detective agency."

"Cool Guy and Nifty Girl. That's my final offer."

Sarah leans over, her hand on my arm. She looks like a pink-and-yellow blob through her glasses. I feel dizzy and sick from looking through them. Sarah moves in close, but I can't make out her expression through the blur. She grabs her glasses off my face and puts them on. Her eyes flick up and down, studying my reaction as she whispers, "What about Renegade X?"

Did it get hot in here, or is that just her? My chest tightens. Renegade X. It sounds *really cool*. I grind my teeth. I lick my lips and say, "I think it's been done before."

My arm hurts where her fingers dig into it. She lets go. "You're wrong. I checked." She sighs in frustration as she folds her arms across her chest and stares into the aisle.

Great. There goes my entertainment. I pull my phone out of my pocket and check the time. A little after two thirty. Perfect—the Crimson Flash is having a special afternoon Q&A session. *Live.* This is a once-a-month feature, so maybe it's not really all that special, but Kat and I have taken advantage of it several times. The studio doesn't even accept calls from her phone number anymore. Luckily, mine hasn't been blacklisted yet.

I lean toward the window, away from Sarah, who's still being all huffy about me not wanting to be Renegade X— not that I don't want to be, because it's a cool name, but, like I've told her a thousand times, I'm not a superhero— and pick the studio's number out of my contacts list. It rings.

"Hey, there, Honorary Safety Member," Gordon's voice says. "The Crimson Flash is here to answer your question. There's no challenge too big, no injustice too small—"

"Yeah, I have a safety question." This always works better when Kat does the talking, what with her voice not having changed and it being easier to sound, you know, the appropriate age for this show. This time around I'm more worried Gordon will recognize my voice before I get to the good stuff. Not that there's actually an official age limit, and wouldn't Gordon be thrilled if he thought teens loved his show as much as little kids?

Sarah glances over at me, her eyebrows bunched up in a quizzical expression, but then something farther down the aisle catches her attention.

"If I'm in a subway bathroom, and I meet a girl I like, do I still need to use protection? Or will the germs in the bathroom give us nasty enough infections that we'll both end up sterile?"

Silence. Then Gordon laughs awkwardly. I've never heard anything more forced in my life. "This better not be who I think it is," he says, and I can hear the fake smile in his voice.

"So that's a no, then?"

Gordon diverts my question onto the Safety Kids. "What do we think about safety?" he asks them. I know he's asking them because this is a standard line of his.

And they shout back the standard response, "Always be safe!"

"So would you call pushing someone off a building safe? Or is that a—"

The line goes dead—took them long enough; I'm surprised I was on the air as long as I was—and then Sarah nudges me with her elbow. "Damien!" she whispers, pointing to a middle-aged man making his way down the aisle. "Do you see who that is?"

He looks a little familiar, but I can't place him. Before I can shake my head no, she says, "Meet me in the bathroom in thirty seconds," then runs off.

X·X·X

I knock on the bathroom door. At the other end of the train car, the middle-aged man opens his coat to reveal a red supervillain outfit underneath. His chest has the letters *TB* on it, plus a picture of jacks. Not the kind you use on a car, but the kind kids play with. And the *TB* doesn't stand for *tuberculosis*, either. This is Jack the Toy Boy.

Erg. His name makes him sound more like a porn star than a supervillain. I met him at the Christmas party Mom threw last year. I don't know if she even invited him. He kept hounding Kat to show him where the coat closet was, *alone,* until she shapeshifted into a six-foot-tall burly guy.

Just for the record, this isn't the type of supervillain I want to be. I prefer to be the calm genius type, not a creepy soap dropper.

Pedophilia Man pulls out a handful of jacks and lets out a peal of maniacal laughter as Sarah opens the bathroom door for me and I slide in.

"God, it stinks in here." And the floor is inexplicably wet. All over.

The sink digs into my back, and my knee jabs into Sarah's thigh. I have to hold my arms up and twist my torso to fit in the room.

I hear the muffled screams of the people in the train as Jack shouts at them. "Don't move, and nobody gets hurt! *Too badly."* He laughs. He sounds like a hyena on crack.

Jack busted out of prison only about six months ago, after getting captured by his superhero arch nemesis, the Bold Defender. He's not even a well-known hero—I only heard of him because when Jack got captured, everyone kept making fun of how he'd said the Bold Defender was going to be easy to defeat. I bet getting caught by him was really embarrassing, but not as embarrassing as taking two years to find a way to make a jailbreak. Since then, I hear he's been trying *way* too hard to prove himself to other supervillains. As far as I know, I'm the only supervillain here, and I don't appreciate him hijacking the train and making me late for my very casual not-rescue mission.

"We have to stop him," Sarah says, now that we're both safely hiding in the bathroom. "It's a good thing we're here." She digs through her backpack and pulls out a gun. I say "gun," but I'm not really sure what it is. It's gun-*shaped*, though it looks more like one of those toys for toddlers where you can push buttons and have it make silly sounds. It's a big, clunky piece of white plastic, a little too round in places to look like a real weapon. It has three buttons on the top, like a trumpet, only they're different colors—blue, red, and yellow—with blinking lights underneath them. Wires hang off it, and I wouldn't be surprised if she told me its guts were all tinfoil and duct tape.

"I made you something," she says.

"Aw, you shouldn't have." The way she points it at me makes me a little nervous. I'd back up, but there's nowhere to go.

"It's not fully tested, but I used my most up-to-date research, so there shouldn't be any unpredictable side effects."

"Unpredictable? Side effects? Sarah, you just said three

of my least favorite words in one sentence."

Sarah ignores me, fiddling with her invention, sliding panels around to reveal more buttons. She holds her finger to the trigger and closes one eye, aiming for my heart. "It only works for superheroes. Well, someone with superhero DNA. I wanted to make it so it only responded to your specific DNA, but I'm not there yet."

She fires, and I jump, banging my elbow hard against the wall. Other than injuring myself, nothing happens.

"See?" she says. "This way, bad guys can't take it from you in a fight. It's completely useless."

Great. A useless gun. Add that to my useless power of flight, and I think we've really got something. "So, what does it do? Is it like a homemade raygun or something?"

"It has a variety of settings. I'll explain later—you have to trust me."

"Fine, but I can't go out there," I tell her, jerking my head toward—and bonking it against—the door. "I know him—I mean, he might ... I need a disguise."

She grins and rummages around in her bag. "You mean something like *this*?" She pulls out a very sleek superhero costume. It's black and dark green and has a silvery *X* on the front. It could be for a supervillain, or a vigilante hero. There's even a mask that goes with it, which is a good thing, because if it was my *body* I didn't want anyone to recognize, I have a feeling I'd be out of luck. It looks like the type of skintight outfit where people are going to be able to count my ribs. Next time I want the kind with the muscle shapes built in.

"Did you make this?" I ask, gaping at it. Okay, I can't

help it. Renegade X is a cool name, and this costume rocks.

"I had it done." Sarah looks a little ashamed at her confession, even though it's pretty normal to go to a specialty shop instead of making your own. Though our high school apparently has a costume club that Amelia was a member of for about two seconds, before she found out they were a bunch of snobs. Read: the club was all skinny girls who thought she was fat. "But," Sarah adds, "I designed it myself. Now hurry up and put it on!"

Outside, I hear Jack laughing after one of his explosive toys goes off. He seems to be making his way down the aisle. He's probably got a big sack with a dollar sign on it that he's forcing people to dump all their jewelry in. I hope he doesn't try the bathroom.

I stare at Sarah.

"What?" she says.

I nod toward the door. I make a shooing motion with both hands.

Her mouth hangs open in shock. "You want me to go out there? With the *terrorist*?!"

"Well, there's not enough room to breathe in here—how am I supposed to change clothes?"

She taps her chin. "I don't know, but people have sex in these things all the time, so I think we can manage."

"No, they don't!" I feel my face heat up, and not because I'm trapped in a small space with a girl telling me to take my clothes off. "That's just a myth, Sarah. Ha ha. I can't believe you were fooled by, um, an urban legend."

"It's not an urban legend. Don't be so naïve, Damien. I

don't know the statistics, but it must happen all the time."

"Well, I don't *know* anyone who's done it, do you?" And I don't know anyone who was conceived in a public bathroom either, because things like that don't happen. No, they do not.

"Come on, Damien," Sarah says. "We don't have a lot of time, and it's not like I haven't seen it all before. You weren't so shy when I had X-ray glasses, and that wasn't even an emergency!"

She has a point. This is no time for modesty. I get undressed, but it's a nightmare, and not because Sarah's here. This place is so gross. I don't want to touch anything, I don't want my clothes to touch anything, and every time I move, I slam into something. And I'm in a hurry, what with all the poor, innocent people getting exploited in the other room. Maybe if I take long enough getting dressed, Jack will have finished looting everyone and have escaped, and I won't have to stop him. We can just sit down again and enjoy the ride. But also the longer I take getting dressed, the longer I have to be in this bathroom. Ugh.

Sarah stuffs my clothes into her bag as I hand them to her. She closes her eyes when I get down to my underwear, which I suppose is considerate of her. Maybe she's afraid I'll make her buy me another lunch.

I get the costume on pretty quickly, all things considered, and pull the mask on over my face. It covers my whole head and has tinted green plastic over the eyes, so I'm completely hidden. No goggles required, though I have to say, the ones I had at my birthday rocked pretty hard. I'd wear them anyway if I had them with me.

I look myself over in the mirror. What I can see looks wicked awesome. Until I hold up the gun Sarah made me, and then I'm not sure if I'm cool or just a loser in a cheap costume. "Okay," I say, "you wait here." She might not need to hide from this guy like I do, but that doesn't mean she wants him recognizing her in the future.

"I don't think so." Sarah pulls her sweater off, revealing a sidekick costume underneath. It's black and blue and has a theta on the front. "You're looking at the Cosine Kid." She pulls a blue mask over her eyes and positions her glasses in front of it.

I narrow my eyes at her, my hand already on the door. "I thought you hadn't made up a name yet."

She shrugs. "It wasn't written in stone."

"Just spandex." I glance down at the big silver X on my own costume, the one I thought was so cool, and realize it has nothing to do with the letter on my thumb. "You named me after a variable, didn't you?"

Sarah ignores me. She throws the door open and shoves me into the aisle. "Come on. We have a bad guy to catch."

X·X·X

"Catching bad guys" definitely sounds like superhero work, if you put it that way. I'm not "catching" Jack; I'm getting him out of my way. He's a loser and a crappy supervillain, but I'm not looking to hand him over to the police or to get credit for this or to ever have anyone mention it again. *Ever.* He's hijacking the train and slowing us down, and I want to get this non-rescue mission over as quickly as possible. Simple as that.

I point the gun Sarah made me at Jack the Toy Boy. I still don't understand what it does, if anything, but it's all I've got. "Stop right there!" I say.

Everyone on the train lets out a collective gasp-wail and ducks in their seats, covering their heads with their hands.

Jack half grins, half makes a face like he just ate month-old seafood. He looks a little like he's going to cry. He tosses his explosive jacks idly in one hand, holding his bag o' loot in the other. "You want me?" he says, making like he's going to drop all the jacks on the floor, which would end in lots of booming noises and fire.

I start toward him and shout, "No!" though really I was answering his question, not responding to him almost dropping the jacks. No, I don't want anything to do with him, ever.

"Then come and get me!" Jack shrieks, and he throws the jacks straight at me.

"Renegade!" Sarah shouts. "Fire!"

My hand shakes as I pull the trigger, not expecting it to do anything. I squeeze my eyes almost shut, resisting the urge to keep them safe from explosions enough to see what happens. Which at first seems like nothing. The gun doesn't shoot or make noise or do anything. It could be an overly elaborate dog whistle, for all I know.

And then the jacks speed up, racing toward us. We're the only people on the train stupid enough not to duck. This is it, we're going to die, and then—

The jacks stick to the gun. I'm shaking all over, staring in disbelief. Jack's eyes get wide, realizing he's about to get hauled back to prison by yet another superhero.

Jack drops his loot bag and runs. I chase after him through the other train cars. Passengers scream as we go by. Someone shouts, "He's robbing the train!"

Gee, thanks. I hadn't realized. I pull the trigger again, aiming at Jack. Sarah screams, "No!" and grabs my arm, but she's too late.

Everything happens in slow motion. The jacks that were conveniently stuck to the gun and not exploding go shooting in every direction. I grab Sarah and fling us both to the floor. I hear the jacks go off, and debris rains down on us.

"He's trying to kill us all!" Jack screams, pointing his finger at me.

Nobody looks hurt. There are some scrapes and bruises, but I don't see anyone gushing blood. Covered in dust and maybe not as dry in the pants department as they'd like, but otherwise okay. Some of the seats have holes in them, the ceiling has chunks blown out of it, and a couple of kids are wailing. Nothing permanent.

I get up, and everyone is staring at me like *I'm* the maniac here. Don't they see Jack over there, with his obvious picture of *jacks* on his *supervillain* costume?

Wait. Jack has his coat closed up again, so you can't see that part. You can't see that he's wearing a costume at all. And then there's me, looking really bad-ass and holding a gun that I've apparently just fired. At everyone, at the same time.

Damn.

I try to hold my hands up in a peaceful gesture, but it looks like I'm waving the gun around.

When someone asks me what my demands are, I scream at them to stop the train.

CHAPTER 10

I had to wave my gun around a bit more, but eventually I got the train to stop and let us off. Unfortunately, that meant it dropped us off in the middle of nowhere, but Sarah and I had no choice but to make a break for it. We stopped to change back into our regular clothes, hoping it would be enough to fool any authorities who might be looking for us. Because we hijacked a train. Even though they let us go, that was because I was holding some crazy gun Sarah made, and I'm pretty sure they're going to report my supposed crimes. Just a hunch.

Now, an hour later, Sarah and I drag ourselves into some Podunk town, tired and sweating and maybe even *lost*. I have a general idea of where we must be, but I couldn't tell you how to get home from here. Or to Vilmore.

The town is a one-horse kind of place, except instead of one horse they have one *car*. It's painted like a police car and sits in the middle of town, at the only intersection. I guess it's there so travelers will slow down and obey the ten-miles-per-hour speed limit.

"Truth or dare," Sarah says. We've been playing for the past fifteen minutes or so to pass the time, and Truth or Dare is apparently Sarah's favorite game, because no matter which one someone picks, it results in good data. I'd never played before, but I can already see plenty of ways to use it to make people uncomfortable. Sarah tells me girls play this game a lot, especially at get-togethers. I can't wait until Thursday night when Amelia has what she calls "one of her famous slumber parties." And people on the train thought I was evil.

"Truth."

Sarah takes a deep breath and thinks about it. She slips on a patch of mud on the ground, but luckily I grab her arm and keep her from falling. I'm quite the hero. "What's the most embarrassing thing that ever happened to you?" she says.

"I caught my girlfriend making out with my best friend."

Sarah's spine stiffens. "Your girlfriend."

"At my birthday party. On my bed. We're not together now," I mutter, thinking about how Kat and I are friends, nothing more, and about how I keep having to remind myself that's a good thing. "It was a year ago, and she'd just gotten her shapeshifting power—"

"Shapeshifting?" Sarah raises an eyebrow and scrunches up her nose. "What is she, a *supervillain*?"

"Ha. Ha. *No*." I rub the back of my neck and wish I hadn't said anything. "What I meant was, she thought she wanted to be somebody else. To be *with* somebody else, I guess."

"You're using the past tense." The way Sarah says that, I feel like I'm in an interrogation room, with the hot lights shining on me. "She *thought* she wanted to be with somebody else. That implies she doesn't think that anymore." If Sarah's tone didn't sound so accusing, I'd think she was trying to help sort things out between me and Kat. "So she wants to be with you."

"Uh ..." Oh, how I miss the simple times when I saved Sarah from getting her pants muddy. Those were the days, thirty seconds ago, before I mistakenly opened up this can of worms. I can see that this Truth or Dare game has more potential to make people uncomfortable than I thought. "Yeah, well, she realizes what she missed out on, now that it's too late."

I shut up after that, and Sarah doesn't ask any more questions about my love life. Instead she purses her lips and looks deep in thought. Neither of us says anything until we reach the middle of town, where there's a helpful sign that says Vilmore is another twenty miles away. Which is just wonderful. I already want to die from fatigue, and it's getting dark. So much for getting home for dinner.

Sarah sags against the sign and rubs her shoulders where the straps of her backpack dig into her. "Easy peasy, right? No problem?"

"Right. Because now that we're in town, we should be able to find some kind of transportation. A ride, if you will."

We're standing next to the town police car. I peer in the window and notice it has the keys in the ignition. I guess nobody worries about it getting stolen. Maybe nobody here would know what to do with it anyway. "A ride," Sarah says, sounding doubtful.

"Maybe a bus comes through here or something. These people have to have some way of leaving. ..." As I say it, I think about those stories you hear where someone's car breaks down in some nowhere town, and they don't have the money to fix it and leave, so they end up living there. Until they die.

I shudder. "Come on." I lead Sarah across the street and into a nearby diner called May's. The diner is half full with the dinnertime crowd. The locals sit hunched over their food, but they all turn and stare when we come in. It's a small town with no tourist attractions—they must not get very many visitors. I ignore them and stride up to the counter. The woman behind it has a pot of coffee and a rag glued to either hand. Her scraggly brown hair hangs in stringy clumps around her face. I can't tell how old she is. Her body says she couldn't be much more than thirty, but her wrinkled and haggard face says nothing under fifty. Her name tag reads, DELORES.

I slide onto an empty stool, and Sarah sits next to me.

"What can I get for you?" Delores asks. She has hard, beady eyes that look over me and Sarah with curiosity.

"We're a little lost," I say. "We got separated from our field trip. The bus stopped for everyone to go to the bathroom, and then they ... *left without us*." I hide my eyes with the back of my arm and shake my head. "We're looking for a way to get to Vilmore. That's the closest train stop."

Delores's jaw moves like she's chewing actual food, even though I'm pretty sure her mouth is empty. Her eyes wander from me to Sarah and back again. "It's polite to order first before asking for information."

"Yeah, fine." I was hungry anyway. I point to the nearest pie display. "I'll take a slice of that."

"Two," Sarah says.

Delores shuffles over to the pie and shovels out two pieces of lemon meringue. She dumps them on a couple of plates and slides them in front of us.

"Great," I say, digging in. I grin at her, doing my best to look lost, scared, and unbelievably charming. "Can you tell us when the next bus leaves?"

The whole diner busts up laughing. Even dried-up old Delores cracks a smile. "Kid," she says, "a bus hasn't come through here since I was five years old."

One side of my face twitches. I exchange a glance with Sarah. "I'm guessing I was right about Vilmore having the nearest train stop?"

Delores nods. "I could give you a ride, but I don't get off until two in the morning. And you'd have to order a lot more food first."

Sarah eats the meringue off her pie before cutting into the lemon. "Easy peasy," she mutters.

"I'll take them," a woman in the far corner says. "If you two help me clear out my truck, you can ride in the back. Your parents will be wondering where you are, no doubt. I remember when Angela didn't come home from a field trip once. I was *so* worried, I just about died."

"Thanks," I say. I smile at Sarah. *See? No problem.*

Delores scratches out a bill on a pad of paper and slaps it down in front of me. "That'll be five dollars even."

I feel around my back pockets, but apparently I don't have my wallet on me. It must have fallen out in Sarah's bag. She digs around in her backpack, reaching farther and farther into it, until I think she's going to disappear inside it altogether. She frowns and checks the outside pockets. "I can't find our wallets," she whispers. "We must have lost them on the train."

I lean over and talk out the side of my mouth. "Write them a check."

"I don't have checks!"

Delores is getting suspicious by now, squinting at us and shaking her head.

"It seems we have a slight problem," I tell her. "You see, we must have left our money on the bus, with our schoolmates."

Delores's lip lifts in a snarl. "You mean you can't pay?"

I swallow. "Yeah. That's about it."

"But," Sarah says, getting out a pen and one of her notebooks, "we'd be happy to mail the money to you. Just give me your address."

"This ain't no free lunch," Delores growls.

"No, no, it's okay." I hate myself for what I'm about to do. I hold up my right hand and stick out my thumb, giving her a good look at my *X*. "I don't have an *H* right now, but I'm a superhero in training, see? My dad's the Crimson Flash. You can trust me—"

Delores slams her coffeepot down on the counter, shattering it and spraying hot coffee everywhere.

I notice out of the corner of my eye that the other patrons in the diner are no longer hunched over their meals; they're on their feet and creeping toward us.

"Superhero." Delores's eyes glaze over and her face twists in rage. Her arm shoots out across the counter. She grabs the neck of my sweatshirt with her gnarled claw. "Superhero," she repeats, as if it's the most disgusting phrase she's ever heard.

Her grip tightens. I struggle to get away. Sarah reaches over and unzips my sweatshirt, and I slip out of it, leaving it in Delores's clutches.

The customers are closing in behind us. They all chant, "Superhero," under their breath.

"It was only a concoction of basic ingredients," Sarah wails. "Mostly flour and eggs and lemon juice!"

"In other words," I say, "it was just pie!"

The goodly diner patrons grasp at us with their hands. Sarah reaches into her bag, pulls out the gun, and pushes a bunch of buttons on the side. "Here!" she says, shoving it into my hands.

I have no idea what I'm supposed to do with it, so I point it toward the ceiling and pull the trigger.

"Close your eyes!" Sarah shouts.

I do, just in time to see the super-bright light that flashes across the room from the safe side of my eyelids. When I open my eyes, I see spots, but I'm doing better than everyone else, who can only blink and run into each other.

Sarah and I seize our opportunity to get the hell out of there.

"It won't stop them for long," Sarah says, hurrying out of the diner.

We don't bother to look both ways as we run across the street. Already I hear the chant of "Superhero!" behind us.

I make a beeline for the cop-car look-alike. "You drive!"

"Are you batty? I can't drive!"

"Neither can I!" What would I need to drive for? Traffic in Golden City is awful, there's nowhere to park, and Mom doesn't even own a car.

Sarah rolls her eyes at me. "Get in." She tosses me her bag.

It's heavy. I grab it and scramble into the passenger side, slamming the door shut behind me. I hurry to roll up the window and lock the door.

Sarah jumps into the driver's seat. She closes her eyes and takes a deep breath, holding her hands out flat, waving them over the steering wheel, then the radio, then the parking brake. She looks more like she's having a séance than getting ready to drive the stupid thing.

The mob is already plowing through the diner door, lurching across the street toward us like zombies. "Sarah. Now would be a good time to start the car."

"I'm getting there." She opens her eyes and buckles her seat belt. Then she carefully adjusts the rearview mirror, then the one on the side.

"That's not going to be very useful if the lynch mob tears us apart."

Sarah switches on the headlights. She puts her foot on the pedal, testing the distance. She purses her lips in a frown and moves her seat forward a couple notches. Then back one. Then forward again.

"Sarah!"

"Okay," she says. "I'm ready."

Just as she says it, a superhero-hating diner customer snaps our antenna off. He pounds on the window. I hold the gun and point it at him, but I don't dare shoot it. You never know what it's going to do.

Sarah takes more deep breaths. She turns the key. The engine sputters and dies. "Hmm," she says, peering at the dashboard.

More diner zombies pound on the door. Their nails screech against the window. Pretty soon they're going to start rocking the car. Delores jumps onto the hood, splaying herself against the windshield. She presses our bill against the glass and points at it.

"Oh, wait," Sarah says, in a "silly me" voice. "I have to hold the gas in." She does and the car starts and we move backward with a jerk. "Oops. Reverse."

I cover my eyes as Sarah makes the car go forward and Delores leaps off the hood. The car lurches a couple feet. Then a couple more. Sarah presses her foot in all the way, and the car takes off, speeding down the road. The dust we raise behind us blots out the mob.

Every time Sarah moves the wheel at all, the whole car swerves to the side of the street. She grazes a telephone pole and knocks off my side mirror.

She cringes. "Sorry!"

"Maybe you should slow down!" I shout over the roar of the engine.

We pass a sign that says, NOW LEAVING RUTHERSFORD! and has a smiley face graffiti-painted over the *o*. The name sounds familiar, and I wonder where I've heard it before.

Sarah holds her arms out straight, her hands frozen on the wheel. She doesn't take her foot off the pedal. "It's under control."

My stomach disagrees. And so does the tree zooming up in front of us. "Sarah!"

"Got it!" She turns the wheel. We skid into a 360-degree turn. And another one. We're both screaming. And then we're not spinning anymore, but racing downhill, backward. Sarah slams her foot on the brake. We slow, but not enough. I look behind me, then forward again, not wanting my neck to be twisted when we crash.

I remember to keep my muscles relaxed as the car smashes into a tree, rear end first. There's the sickening crunch of metal and a horrible, jarring feeling as the back of my head hits the headrest.

I'm shaken *and* stirred, and I have to fight the urge to puke up my lemon meringue pie, but otherwise I'm okay.

My heart pounds as I look over to see if Sarah's all right. I hold my hand out to her, but she doesn't notice. She's too busy poking at the contents of her bag, which spilled open during the crash.

She reaches down and picks up her wallet off the floor. "Look at that," she says, beaming at it. "I guess we had them the whole time."

161

"What did I tell you?" I say, secretly thinking about strangling her. "Piece of cake."

CHAPTER 11

When we get to Vilmore, I call up everyone I know who goes to school here. Five people, but I don't get ahold of any of them.

"I used to hang with a bad crowd," I tell Sarah when she raises her eyebrows at me.

"Oh, right," she says. "Since you spent all that time at Eastwood as a delinquent." She laughs to herself.

"I told you I'm half supervillain." I grin, making it seem less serious than it is.

Sarah smiles, then just looks worried. "How *are* we going to get in?"

All the outside doors at Vilmore open for supervillains only. As in, real supervillains, which means not me. You have to have a thumbprint with a *V* on it to get in anywhere important. I bite my lip and sigh. "There's one more person I can call." My shoulders slump in defeat as I dial Pete's number.

He knows it's me when he picks up. "Damien!"

I find it suspicious that he sounds happy to hear from me. Then again, he sounds like he's been drinking. Maybe he's too inebriated to remember he hates me. I tell him I'm on campus and I want to come see him.

"Great. Come on up, man. I'm having a party." He laughs. It's been about two weeks since my birthday—maybe he's celebrating getting over all the itchy pustules. "With you here, it'll be just like old times."

There's something sinister about the way he says it, and chills twitch up and down my back as I hang up. On second thought, maybe he *does* remember he hates me.

I smile at Sarah anyway. "What did I tell you? *Easy.*" I ask her to wait for me outside the main office building while I make my way to Pete's dorm. Things will be less complicated the less I have to explain to him. Pete lets me up when I get there. He lives on the second floor, so I only have to maneuver one staircase. I can hear the party as I walk down the hall. Even if I didn't know which room was his, I could guess it's the one with the open door and the loud music.

"Look who's here!" Pete shouts when I appear in the doorway.

No one I recognize. I wonder what he meant by "just like old times." There are four guys sitting around in the common room Pete shares with a couple other people—probably *these* people—all four wearing pajama sets they bought at the student store: T-shirts and sweatpants with big *V*s on them. Nobody looks familiar. Three of them look up when I come in and raise their drinks at me, though I can tell by their expressions that they have no idea who I am, either.

The fourth one is too busy making out with the redhead in his lap to care. Okay, that's not true. His eyes flick over to me for a second, probably to see if I'm female. Then the girl sticking her tongue down his throat notices me. She shoves herself off him and stumbles, falling down once, then steadying herself with the coffee table. She smiles at me. She has wavy red hair, green eyes, and a short leather skirt and fishnet stockings. "Damien!"

It's not the sound of her voice but the way she says my name that makes me want to throw up. My heart stops beating. "Kat."

She morphs into herself, short straight black hair, clear blue eyes, and a thin nose.

Pete is sitting on the arm of his couch. Laughing. He has half-circle pockmark scars all over him. I warned him not to scratch.

I catch Kat in my arms as she flops against me. The guy I stole her from glares at us.

"Kat," I say as she wraps her arms around me and slides to the floor, resting her face against my knee, "what are you doing here?"

"What does it look like she's doing here?" Pete says. "Having a good time without you."

One of the bedroom doors in the back opens up, and two girls in tight clothes and another guy in rumpled Vilmore pajamas strut out. The girls give Kat a dirty look when they see her on her knees.

"Why did you even invite her?" one of them says, her

tone as snobby as possible. She flicks her curly blond hair behind her shoulder. She sits next to Pete and shakes her head. The second one sneers at me.

Yeah, I bet they don't like the girl who changes into whatever a guy wants her to be for the next five minutes.

"I invited her cousin, not her," Pete says. "I told Julie to come *alone*. Girl never listens."

"Kat ..." I glare at Pete, then get my arms under Kat's and drag her to her feet. Those rippling muscles I don't have would come in handy right about now. "You shouldn't be here."

"Julie ditched me," Kat whines. "She said it would be a fun party, and I could forget about ... about you. She didn't say Pete would be here. Not you, either." Kat's eyes fill with tears. She touches my face, sliding her hands down my cheeks. "I always loved your ears," she says. "And your nose. And your ... eyebrows."

Forget about me? "Let's talk about it later. You have to go home."

"No!" Kat shouts. She reminds me of my two-year-old half sister, Jessica. Great. A really hot sixteen-year-old girl with the mental powers of a toddler in a room full of drunken college guys. And if she's not hot enough for them, she can turn herself into anything they want her to be.

Kat drapes her arm over my shoulders and pulls me down with her into an armchair. She licks the side of my face and tries to stick her hands down my pants.

"Kat, don't." I grab her wrists.

Conversation continues like normal around us—nobody

cares what we're doing. The guy who made out with Kat goes off into a bedroom with one of the other girls. I hear two of the guys cough the word *slut* as soon as they're gone.

It's a tight fit with both me and Kat in the chair, and we're even cozier than when we'd hang out on her bed and watch TV, both secretly wishing we could do more than that. Only now I'm freaked because I caught her drunk at a party, making out with some guy. To forget about me, 'cause I told her it was never going to happen. "Kat," I say, my voice shaking, "tell me you only made out. Not ... not anything more than that."

Kat glares at me. "Why? You're not my boyfriend. You don't care."

That was the plan. In hindsight, I can see how it might be flawed. Her not being my girlfriend doesn't make me any less pissed to find her here. Except this time around, it's not cheating, because I turned her down—I said it was never going to happen. We're close, but I said we were only friends-close, meaning I don't have a right to be jealous. Some crappy plan that was.

"I'm your friend," I tell her. "You shouldn't be doing this."

Kat wraps her arms around my neck and rests her head on my shoulder. "Damien," she says, "we were supposed to get *married.*"

Whoa. This is news to me. She sounds serious about it, but that could be the booze talking.

"Looks like somebody won't be wearing white," the blond girl mutters. Everybody laughs. So much for not paying attention to us.

I move to stand up, dumping Kat off me. She tries to hold on, but I'm too wily and coordinated for her. "Don't go!" she wails, reaching after me and almost falling off the chair.

I tell her I'll be back. I tell everyone else that if they touch her while I'm gone, they can ask Pete what will happen to them. Then I step into the hall and call Kat's mom. I have a nice chat with her about the horrible teenage travesties her daughter is getting herself into, keeping an eye on Kat through the open doorway.

I sigh as I hang up and rejoin the party. I look over at Kat, who seems pretty out of it. Good—that way she won't witness what I'm about to do.

Instead of settling back down with her, I head straight for Pete. I stand in front of him, twiddling my thumbs and not making eye contact.

Pete smirks. "Looks like I'm not the only one your girl will ditch you for. Guess she'd rather be having a good time with *anyone* than hanging out with you."

I am *so* a good time. As Pete is about to find out. "Pete,"

I say, my throat constricting, "I have to tell you something. I can't wait any longer. I want to apologize."

Pete sets his drink down and folds his arms. "Here it comes. I've been waiting all year for this."

I lick my lips. "I was jealous. Back when you and Kat … you know."

"Keep talkin'."

I glance around the room at everyone, like them being

168

present makes me really nervous. "And that thing with the invitation ..." I stare at my shoes. There's mud caked around the edges. "I couldn't stand the idea of you being with anybody else. I wanted to make it so no one would want you. Not Kat and not *Vanessa*." I sneer at her name. I don't know if any of the girls here are "Vanessa," but I get the feeling Pete's steady girlfriend wouldn't be invited to this kind of party.

Pete uncrosses his arms. He looks around the room, like he's wondering if everybody else heard the same thing he did. "What?"

I speak really quietly. I make quick eye contact with him, then look away. "It's you, Pete. You're the one I've always ... I didn't want anyone else to have you! We were so close, and then *she* came along." I glare at Kat, who's asleep and has no idea what I'm saying. "She led us both astray." Then I slide my hand over Pete's knee. "It's been so lonely without you this year, Pete."

"Oh, no. You are *not* doin' this."

Oh, yes, I am. I force so much emotion into my voice that tears spring up in my eyes. "I've had to hold back all these feelings for you. I just want to know you don't hate me!"

Pete swears under his breath. He looks around the room for help, but even though everyone is staring at us, nobody offers to pull me off of him.

I lunge at Pete, knocking him off the arm of the couch. Pete scrambles to his feet and backs up. "Damien, man, this isn't cool."

I hold my arms out and walk toward him, like I'm

going to hug him. Pete runs out of space and ends up doubling back and hitting the edge of the couch. He topples over it and lands on the cushions below. The blond girl makes a face and scoots as far away as possible. Until I chase after Pete and join him on the couch. Then she jumps up and moves to the other side of the room.

"Pete, Pete!" I moan, sliding my hands under his shirt.

He knees me in the stomach, holding me off as I struggle to get closer to him. He's a lot stronger than me. "Damien, I'm serious!"

"Just tell me you don't hate me!"

"I don't hate you! Now get off of me!"

I stop struggling and dive for his belt buckle. Pete takes the bait and sits up to stop me. I've got him right where I want him. Now that he's close enough, I grab his chin with both hands. I put my lips on his and kiss him before he has a chance to fight me off. The kiss involves tongues. Or at least my tongue—Pete's doing his best not to reciprocate.

When Pete finally manages to push me away, everyone in the room but Kat is watching us with wide eyes and undivided attention.

Pete is silent. I can't tell if he feels violated, newly smitten, or if he feels sorry for me and our love that can never be.

"Pete," I say, sounding guilty, "I have another confession to make."

Pete nods, too dazed to answer.

A grin creeps across my face. "I threw up earlier." Okay, so I only *almost* threw up, when stomach and lemon meringue fought it out after the car crash, but Pete doesn't have to know that.

Pete's nostrils flare and a vein twitches on his forehead. "Damien, you freaking *psycho*!"

I take it that's my cue to get off of him before he gets physical. And not like I just did, but in more unpleasant ways, like those of the painful beating variety.

All his other guests giggle and snicker at us.

"That's it," Pete shouts, getting to his feet, "everybody out! *Now!*"

"I live here, man," one of the guys mutters. But he gets up and shuffles off to one of the bedrooms.

I flop down in the chair with Kat.

Pete shoos everybody else out and slams the door. He turns off the music. Then he glares at me. "That means you, too, you psychotic little bastard."

I put my arm around Kat and glare right back at him. "I'm not going anywhere. Unless you want to be the one to explain to her parents how you got her drunk and let her make out with your friends." I smile at him. "Don't mess with me, Pete. You never win."

Pete grunts and storms out of his own dorm room.

I settle in with Kat. She moans and leans her head against my chest. She and I are very cozy as I hunker down, ready to wait the forty minutes it'll take her parents to get here.

$$X \cdot X \cdot X$$

It isn't until an hour later that I go to find Sarah. I have a big wet puddle of drool on my shirt—Kat's, not mine—and two guest passes I swiped from Pete's bulletin board for prospective students and visiting younger siblings who haven't gotten their *Vs* yet. The school puts a couple up in every dorm room with important phone numbers and reminders about Parents' Day.

At first I think Sarah is watching a couple of dogs chasing each other across the lawn. She's sitting on a bench, under a lamppost, scribbling away in her notebook. Then I see it's the couple groping each other behind a tree, not the dogs, that's caught her interest.

I thump down on the bench next to her. I rub my arms, feeling the cold after being inside for so long. It's the middle of March, so it's not exactly winter, but it's not exactly warm out yet, either.

"Was it easy peasy?" Sarah asks.

"Just like everything else." I hand her one of the passes. We have to call an 800 number to activate them, but then they should get us wherever we want to go, as long as it isn't into one of the dorms. Which is fine by me.

We use the guest cards to get into the main building and head up to Taylor's office. I pretend to be really tired to hide my, er … reluctance to go up the stairs at a normal pace. It's not hard to fake. I stick close to the wall and cling to the inside railing—they have it on both sides here —and act like I have to haul myself up out of fatigue. Sarah thinks I'm cool, even if she also thinks I'm some kind of wannabe superhero. How awesome would she think I was if she knew I can barely get up the stairs? Yeah, I didn't think so.

We get to the office door marked T. M. Lewis, Dean of Vilmore University, and go in.

Taylor's office smells like spiced apple cider. I wonder if my house will smell like that when he moves in. *If* he moves in. What if he expects us to move to his house when he and Mom get married? No way. Mom would never move her lab. Course, she'd never sleep with a superhero, either.

There's a bookshelf on one side of Taylor's office, a large desk in the middle, and a coat rack over in the far corner, along with three filing cabinets. A large book lies open on the desk, next to Taylor's laptop. It looks like a logbook, with a list of names of all the supervillain kids who applied to go to Vilmore. Some of the names have stars by them, depending on how likely they are to get in. It's getting late in the submissions process, and Taylor should be making the final decisions and sending out notices soon. Some of the names have already been stamped with ACCEPT or REJECT. My name is at the top of the page. It only has three out of five stars, and it doesn't have an acceptance stamp yet, which is odd. Next to my name, it says, *Very smart, shows much aptitude for success in villainy, but might not be Vilmore material.*

What?! I double-check to make sure I read the note next to my name and not someone else's. I can't believe it. Taylor's dating—no, *marrying*—my mom. That means he's not allowed to say I'm not Vilmore material. I'm excellent material. Has he been drinking Mom's punch? Think of the strain it's going to cause on their relationship if he doesn't let me in. And if in their selfish marital bliss they're too distracted to care that I'm miserable? I'll make them care. I'll have plenty of time for it.

There's another note scrawled in the margin of the page, explaining the first one. It says:

Damien is clever but lacks a certain ruthlessness. I believe he has potential, but Vilmore may not be the place to harness it. Marianna tells me he once freed all twenty of her lab rats when he learned she was going to inject them with a possibly fatal concoction. This Weakness on its own is not enough to condemn him. However, if he wishes to do well at Vilmore, he'll find there's no place for that kind of sympathy here. On the other hand, he's committed several villainous acts that I find quite interesting—the three-day Black Plague scare at City Hall, the moths in the butterfly exhibit—all ambitious for his age, but ultimately small-time and frivolous.

I take quick, deep breaths. That's not fair. That's *so* not fair. The lab-rat incident was years ago. Okay, only two, but if Mom didn't want me to get upset about her murdering them, she shouldn't have made them out to be my pets. Did she mention that little fact when she was sharing embarrassing anecdotes about me? The other applicants could have freed thousands of lab rats, only Taylor doesn't know about it because there wasn't a check box for that on the application. And I think I learned my lesson when one of them crawled into my bed and nibbled my toes. I mistakenly thought the rats and I were friends.

What's wrong with that? Taylor said I was ambitious—that has to count for something. And if he thinks my villainous acts are too frivolous, I can kick it up a notch. Bigger, better, more … ruthless. Either way, Taylor and I are going to have a talk. Hopefully it will involve me showing him a thorough list of my villainous exploits and explaining to him why I'm Vilmore material incarnate, instead of me getting on my knees and begging him to let me in, because if I don't get into this school, I will die. End of story. And if I have to, I'll explain to him that if he wants to keep doing my mom, he's going to find a place for me at Vilmore, because I'm not as sympathetic as he thinks.

"Are you okay?" Sarah's staring at me, her forehead wrinkled in concern. "Your breathing definitely sounds off."

"I'm fine."

She comes closer and points at the book. "What's that?"

I slam it shut before she can read my name on the list. The last thing I want right now is Sarah finding out I applied to go to school here. "Santa's naughty-or-nice list. Nothing about your dad."

She chews her lip and stares at the floor when I mention him. She jumps when I put my hand on her shoulder. "It's okay," I say. "We'll find him. No problem."

"Right." Sarah nods, mumbles something about checking out the coat rack, and slips out of my grasp.

I sit down at the desk, shoving the admissions book farther to the side and pulling Taylor's laptop closer. I flip it open and push a button to wake it up. "Hey, Sarah," I say, "what exactly did you do that got your dad in trouble?"

Sarah turns pink. She wrings her hands together. "Oh, that. Well, I made this invention and published some articles about it—"

Footsteps echo in the hall, cutting her off. They come closer and stop in front of the door.

Sarah and I look at each other. I shut the laptop and motion that we should hide, and we glance around the room, frantic, but there's nowhere to go. I duck down under the desk and Sarah crawls in beside me just as the door opens.

I know it's Taylor because I hear him humming to himself. My heart beats too hard and too fast in my chest. The laptop spins down and goes silent, and I will Taylor not to notice the sudden change. I feel a little dizzy at the thought of coming all this way and getting caught. Sarah bites her thumbnail, cringing every time Taylor takes a step nearer to our hiding place.

He picks up a coffee mug, then sets it back down. He mutters to himself about working too much. His footsteps come around the side of the desk.

I don't know about Sarah, but I'm holding my breath. And praying. Everything about tonight has been anything but easy, and now Taylor's going to settle in for a rousing bout of late-night paperwork and find us. And then we're going to have a lot of explaining to do.

Taylor pulls out his desk chair. Sarah breathes in too sharply, too audibly. I'm sure this is it. Taylor starts to sit down, and then ...

His phone rings. He answers it. "Hello, sugar lemon." "Sugar lemon" is my mom. And totally nauseating. "Ah … just about to do some paperwork."

Just about to decide I should get into Vilmore, he means. If he knows what's good for him.

"No, I got the message and took care of it—Ruthersford is back to normal. I brought the raging mob out from under the mind control. I guess we were wrong about no one saying our trigger word."

Ruthersford? As in the town full of crazies Sarah and I just escaped from? Now I know why it sounded familiar— it's the same place Taylor was talking about testing Mom's hypno potion on. Whatever bugs Mom's still trying to work out with her potion, it's obviously pretty powerful.

Taylor sighs. "You're right, Marianna, I work much too hard. No, I won't this time—I'll be home in less than an hour. I promise."

Home? He'd better mean his home, not ours.

He hangs up and shoves the chair under the desk, almost crushing my hand. He stomps off, then comes back and grabs the admissions book. So much for marking my name with an ACCEPT stamp while he's not looking. How would that be for a villainous act? The door slams shut, but neither of us can move until we're sure he's gone.

I feel like I woke up from a bad dream. I take a deep breath.

"Damien," Sarah says, leaning over me, "I have a very important question to ask you."

She's shaking. I probably am, too. I raise an eyebrow, thinking tonight can't get any worse.

"Do you have a girlfriend?" She says it so intensely that I think it must have something to do with our mission.

Do I have a girlfriend? Let me think. ... *No*, no I don't. Not after I told her I only wanted to be friends and then she made out with some guy at a party. "No, why?"

Sarah kisses me. On the mouth. Her lips meet mine and I close my eyes and put my arms around her without thinking about it. She smells like vanilla and sweat. I lean back, pulling her closer and trying not to think about all the more important things we should be doing, like saving —er, liberating—her dad. But Taylor's obviously going "home" to sugar lemon, not off to harass anybody. I figure Sarah's dad's safe enough and we've got time.

Suddenly everything seems so simple. Sarah's kissing me, and I'm kissing her back and wondering why I didn't think of this before. This is the girl who came up with a name like Renegade X, and her tongue is touching mine, and she's not like Kat at all. She wouldn't ever change herself to be what people want—I've seen her at school; I know these things. And she *likes* that I have an X on my thumb, even if I hate it. She—

I pull away from her. "Sarah, what are you doing?"

"Taking notes." She has her notebook spread out on the floor beside us, and she's writing like mad in it. While making out with me. "I'm getting good data." When I stare at her, she says, "You're obviously more experienced than I am, and you seemed like a good candidate to try this experiment with. Since I'd never kissed anyone before. And now seemed like an ideal time for results—I've read that human beings feel a heightened sense of passion after narrowly escaping danger. And this time we don't have any zombies chasing us." She pushes her glasses farther up her nose and kisses me again.

I don't kiss back. "Experiment?" That sounds awfully cold and not like she actually, you know, wants me or anything. Like I'm just a bunch of numbers for her to crunch and put in her database.

Sarah gives up and writes more in her notebook. "That's what I said. I don't have anyone to compare you to, but you seem pleasing enough. If this session goes well, I might be interested in trying more complicated experiments with you. As long as I'm getting good data."

I'll give her good data all right. "Experiments? Like dating? There's a place on Twenty-sixth Street, downtown, with the snottiest waiters. I'd be happy if the lady could join me in some troublemaking and snarking back at them. I've even been known to make the chef cry, on very special occasions." I hold my arm out, like I'm going to escort her there right now.

"Oh, well, um ..." Sarah takes shallow breaths and counts on her fingers, finding an excuse not to meet my eyes. She grabs her pen and focuses all her attention on her notebook, but doesn't write anything. "Don't be ridiculous." She forces out a laugh and shakes her head. "We can't go out."

"We can stay in, then." I picture bringing her over to the Tines house. And Amelia making fun of me for having a girlfriend, but that's only because no boys will ever touch her.

"Damien." She sighs. "We can't get involved."

"What do you call this?"

"If we're going to work together, we have to maintain a professional relationship. As sidekick and superhero—"

I glare at her. "You're not my sidekick. I'm not a superhero. There's nothing professional going on. You *like* me, right?"

Her whole face turns pink, and she avoids the question. "This can never be more than an experiment."

"So, you're only interested in me as a human lab rat?"

"No! I didn't say *that*."

If she says she wants me because I look like the Crimson Flash, I'm going home. "Do you like me or not?"

She doesn't answer, lost in thought or at least pretending to be. She taps the back end of her pen against her chin. "I planned to lose my virginity on top of the Empire State Building, but you're afraid of heights." She sucks air in through her teeth and makes a face. "I suppose that I can make an exception, because I'd rather it was with y—" She clams up. Her cheeks redden and her voice gets shrill and she talks really fast when she says, "I mean, there'll be plenty time for landmarks later!"

"Whoa, you want to …?" My mind spins—did she just say she wanted to do what I think she said, with *me*? And did she also say I was afraid of tall buildings? Anger and a sense of betrayal push away any thoughts about what Sarah wants to do with me in the name of good data. How long has she known? Was it that obvious? And was she just going to let me think my secret was safe while really she knew? "Who said I'm afraid of heights?!" I move to stand up, forgetting I'm under a desk and bonking my head.

"Don't pretend—it's obvious." Sarah hurries after me as I crawl out from under the desk, not even stopping to grab her notebook first. "You're always late for all of your classes that aren't on the ground floor because you wait until the halls are clear to go up the stairs. I know, because I have PE when you have English, and I see you trying to go up them when I'm going from the locker room to the gym. You demonstrate classic signs of fear. Sweating, trembling in the extremities, and difficulty breathing."

"Maybe I'm that out of shape. Maybe I have asthma. Did you ever think of that?" I grit my teeth and open up Taylor's laptop again.

She shakes her head. "I've also seen you in *your* PE class. I sit next to the window in Japanese, and I have a good view of the track. You seem fine then. So what day works for you? I think if we meet regularly, we can be at the final stage in another two months. Maybe less."

The laptop finishes waking up. I shove the desk chair out of the way, not bothering to sit down, and start up the "find" function and search the files for any mention of Dr. Kink. "Aren't you worried about sav—about helping your dad?"

"Are you kidding? I'm a complete mess! Can't you tell?" She peers at me through her glasses, studying my face like she thinks I might be joking. "Research calms me down."

Yeah, sure it does. I don't like feeling betrayed and used—I've gone through enough of that with Kat—and

Sarah doesn't even *like* me; I'm just another research project to her. I clench my fists as the search results pop up on the computer. "I'm *not* your science experiment."

Sarah sighs, then pushes me out of the way to get a better look at the screen. "You're being unreasonable."

I pretend I didn't hear her and glance over her shoulder. Most of the results are copies of articles Dr. Kink wrote. One of the files is labeled *Guest Check-in*. Right. "Try that one," I say, pointing at the screen.

Sarah double-clicks, and a spreadsheet opens up. She searches for "Kink" and it jumps to his entry. His "check-in" is dated a little under two weeks ago, right after someone, uh, knocked over a certain hypno device in their mom's lab. It says he's staying in Basement Suite Four.

"The basement," Sarah whispers. "That sounds—"

Dangerous, ominous, and not exactly the five-star hotel the check-in file would have us believe? "We can get a key from the main office down the hall. No—"

"Don't say 'no problem.' And you *are* being unreasonable, you know." She gets up from the desk and adjusts her glasses, glaring at me. "We could learn a lot from each other. I realize I'm inexperienced, but I believe the results could be pleasing enough for both of us."

She might not know how to flatter a guy, but she does have a point. I've spent all this time chasing Kat, only to turn her down when I find out she wants me. Everything with Kat has gotten so complicated, and it seems like no matter what I do to avoid it, I'm going to get hurt. She's dangerous, and Sarah seems pretty safe in comparison. And I like Sarah well enough. She's interesting and thinks

I'm cool, and I can't say I'm not tempted by the idea of "experimenting" with her. An easy relationship? One that only involves fooling around? Kat and I aren't together, we're over—she proved that at the party earlier—so I'm free to do whatever I want. And right now, all I want is to fill Sarah's notebook with plenty of good data.

I take both of Sarah's hands in mine. "Here's the deal. Neither of us messes around with anybody else."

She nods. "But it can't be more than that. You're not my boyfriend."

"Done." Good thing I don't want to be, or my feelings might be hurt. I let go of her and hold my hand out to shake on it. She spits in her palm first, even though I didn't. When we've sealed the deal, Sarah grabs her bag and her notebook from under the desk, and I wipe her spit on the side of my pant leg. She throws her backpack over one shoulder and we head for the door.

"Oh, and Sarah?" I say, stopping her before we go into the hall. "One more condition."

"Yes, Renegade?"

"I choose the experiments."

CHAPTER 12

We stop by the main office—which is deserted at this time of night—and grab the key to Dr. Kink's room. By the time we get to the basement, Sarah's got practically a whole rulebook written up for our "non-dating" experiments. It's like the tabletop RPG version of messing around.

It's great. The more rules she adds, the more excited I am about this, but I'm not going to tell her that. I get the feeling she likes thinking I'm upset about it, like the rules cramp my style or something.

"And if we meet at my house," Sarah says, "you're my lab partner."

"And if you come over to *my* house, I'm telling everyone you're a hooker I picked up on Saint Street. You're in training, so I get a discount, like getting your hair cut by student barbers."

Sarah scowls. "I'm not writing that one down. If we go

to any dances—"

I wag my finger at her as we round the last corner. "Ah ah ah. Dances is dating."

"Please. Everybody only goes to dances for five minutes to get their pictures taken, then goes somewhere to make out. Plus, dancing is physical. It's part of the experience."

"How are you going to explain going to dances with your lab partner?"

Sarah grins at me. "I'll tell everyone you couldn't find anybody else. I have a pink dress, so don't wear anything that clashes with that."

Oh, man, if we ever go to one of those things, I'm showing up in a red-and-yellow zoot suit with green polka dots and no pants. But I'll bring her a corsage, of course. "Define 'clash.'"

But Sarah isn't listening because we're there. She slams her notebook shut and shouts, "Daddy?" at the door marked *B4*. She doesn't even ask me for the key I grabbed from the office, just fishes it out of my pocket without my permission—what are the rules on that?—and shoves it in the lock. There's a click, and the knob turns, and I feel a wonderful sense of relief because tonight is finally *over*.

It's after midnight and I've skipped school, hijacked a train, and stolen a car. I'm going to be in so much trouble when I get home. But Gordon can go ahead and yell at me, because I will be asleep.

It's not over. The door swings open to reveal a dark, cramped little room. There's a tile floor, and a bed in the corner with only a thin white sheet and a pillow to match. A sickeningly sweet smell, like there's meat rotting under the bed or something, mixes with the chemical scent of floor cleaner. It's definitely not what I'd call a suite, though it's thankfully not as gruesome as I was picturing either. Just ... awful, and not somewhere I'd want find anyone I knew. Speaking of not finding anyone, there's no Dr. Kink. I don't know if that's a good thing or a bad thing. It could mean they let him go already. But ... probably not.

Sarah runs in, panic twisting her face. She grabs something off the floor and holds it up for me. "This is the tie I got him for Christmas." It's red and green—the only real colors in the room—and has actual tiny Christmas lights on it. Sarah flips the switch to turn them on, but they must have burned out. "He was wearing this the day he disappeared," she says.

"He's been gone since December?"

"No. Since last weekend."

I don't ask who wears Christmas lights in March. And I don't mention what a coincidence it is that her father disappeared *after* I broke Sarah's hypno device. After seeing Sarah's handiwork on the gun she made me, I'm sure that that garage-sale-reject contraption Mom had in her lab was pure Sarah. It could be a case of "like father, like daughter," but I'm pretty certain inventing that device is what Sarah did to get her dad in trouble. She mentioned publishing some articles, and Taylor said it was like Dr. Kink didn't understand his own invention. I'm putting two and two together, and it looks like Mom and Taylor got the wrong Kink.

I put my hand on Sarah's shoulder. Is comforting her in

the rulebook? "Come on, Sarah. It's late, and he's not here."

She shrugs me off and runs to the bed in the corner, searching the sheet and checking under the mattress. "There has to be some clue. He'd know I'd try to find him —he wouldn't ... he wouldn't just disappear!" Sarah stops and takes a long, slow breath, shutting her eyes and tilting her head back a little. She looks like she's trying not to cry. When she gets ahold of herself, she says, "I know what you're thinking, but he's not dead. He can't be."

I shove my hands in my pockets. "They probably wouldn't kill him. They want him to fix the—" I catch myself and shut up before I reveal I know a lot more than Sarah's told me. "I mean, they probably need him for something, so ..."

She shakes her head. "You don't know supervillains. They're ruthless and ... and they don't care who they hurt or how much."

Right. She's upset, so I ignore how offensive she's being. I feel a twinge of guilt for agreeing to do "experiments" with her, since right now she sounds just like everybody else. A hero worshiper who thinks all villains are pure evil. Like we're not people with homes and families and stuff. Does her not wanting to go out with me for reals have to do with the fact that I'm only half hero? I guess in her mind it's okay to use villains.

"Don't look at me like that," she says. "Your X means you're only half villain, and you were raised by the Crimson Flash. I didn't mean *you*."

Okay, that's it. Do I really act like I was raised by that

cape-wearing idiot? Do I rescue orphans or help little old ladies cross the street? No, I do not. "Sarah, I think we've seen enough. He's not here, and it's time to go."

"We can't leave. This is my fault. It was my invention that got him here. I wrote some articles about it, but I didn't think anyone would take them seriously if they were by someone still in high school, so I put his name on them. Then someone stole my invention, and then they kidnapped him!"

"What are you doing in here?!" A girl about our age appears in the doorway. She's got curly brown hair and blue eyes and a security badge that reads HENRIETTA STONE. She's casually holding a raygun that's about to slip from her fingers, along with a bag of Cheetos and a Cherry Coke Zero. As the seriousness of the situation dawns on her, she drops her snacks and adjusts her grip on the gun, wavering between pointing it at me and at Sarah. "I go on a vending-machine run for *five* minutes, and this is what happens." She mutters under her breath about being "*so screwed.*"

She's screwed? What about us? We're the ones with the weapon pointed at us.

"If you're looking for Dr. Kink," Henrietta says, "he's busy in the torture chamber." She starts to laugh, then chews her lip. "Hey. You." She focuses the gun on Sarah. "I've seen a picture of you in his wallet. You're—"

I fake like I'm going to rush past her, to take the heat off of Sarah and keep her from asking more questions. It works. Henrietta aims the raygun at me. She stands so her feet are shoulder-length apart, kicking her Cheetos and soda out of her way on the floor. Her hands shake, but we're still too close for that to make me feel better.

Henrietta fires at me. I don't know if her finger slipped or if she meant for it to happen. I duck, narrowly avoiding the beam of green light that *zaps* through the room. I smell burning hair and realize my evasion wasn't 100 percent successful. The ray hits the wall behind me, sending chunks of plaster flying through the air and spewing dust everywhere. Henrietta gapes at us, stunned by her own actions. Sarah rummages through her bag, but I grab her arm and shout, "Run!"

We push past Henrietta, shoving her to the ground, and my foot lands on the Cheetos with a satisfying crunch. I almost slip on the bag, but I recover and keep moving.

Behind us, Henrietta swears and takes a walkie-talkie off of her belt. "Pete!" she shrieks. "I need backup! Hello?" She makes a frustrated noise to rival one of Amelia's. "He's never around," she mutters, then screams at the top of her lungs, "Security! Security breach in the basement corridor!"

I hear doors open in several directions. Crap. Sarah pulls me into a side hallway. She stops to catch her breath and digs through her bag until she finds the gun she made. "Did you hear her?" she says. "The torture chamber! We have to get him out of there!"

"Sarah, listen to me." I'm breathing hard, almost too much to talk. "The bad guys will be here any second. They're going to catch us, and then *we'll* be in the torture chamber." Well, I won't, but Sarah doesn't need to know that. I don't want her getting hurt, and I don't want my mom or Taylor finding out I was here. "There's another way. We don't have to do this."

Sarah fiddles with the panels on the gun, sliding them around and pushing the buttons on top. She does it in a sequence of blue, red, yellow. "Here. This should give them a taste of their own medicine. Aim for the heart."

I hold my hands up to ward off the gun when she tries to give it to me. "Are you crazy? I'm not going to kill anybody!"

"It's okay, you're half villain. You can do it."

Is she nuts? I thought she wanted me to be a hero? And what does she think we villains do, just go around slaughtering people? There she goes with her offensive stereotypes again. Plus, there are a lot of bad guys coming for us and only one of me. Brute force isn't my style, and it isn't going to get us out of this.

Footsteps come tromping down the hall, at least three or four sets of them. Someone shouts, "Found 'em!" and then more people join in the chase.

I grab the gun from Sarah, and we both take off running. "Sarah," I gasp, "you have to trust me."

We turn down another hallway, only to find it blocked by three more members of Vilmore security. All packing rayguns. We leap out of the way just as all three fire at us. There's a loud exploding sound as the rays hit the wall. If we get caught, I have a feeling my tuition's going to have some added expenses tacked on. Assuming all this doesn't completely ruin my chances of getting in.

"We're not going to find your dad like this," I tell Sarah, wishing I didn't have to talk and run at the same time.

"We can't leave him here!" She stumbles on the carpet as another raygun blast misses her foot, blowing a hole in the floor.

We hit a dead end. Sort of. We reach the elevator, and I punch the up button over and over.

There are about ten security guards, plus Henrietta, closing in on us.

"Use your weapon, Renegade!" Sarah shouts. "Shoot them!"

I hold the gun up, but I don't want to use it. "Cosine, if I told you I could get your dad out of here but we'd have to leave right now, would you believe me?"

Sarah looks to the elevator doors, which are still closed, and to the Vilmore security force. The security guard closest to the front eyes the gun I'm holding, in all its garage-sale chic, and he actually smiles. A smug, nasty smile that sends unpleasant shivers up my spine.

Sarah grabs my shoulder. "Do something!"

"Do you believe me?!"

"Yes! Anything, just get us out of here!"

I swallow and aim the gun. The security guards go tense but don't shoot. Henrietta hangs out near the back, ducking behind them. There's no way I could shoot them all before they took us down, *if* I was crazy enough to listen to Sarah. It's easy for her to tell me to do the dirty work. She sees me as a hero, but I'm half villain when it's convenient.

In one quick motion, I point the gun at the ceiling and fire. A blue laser flashes. Huge chunks of plaster and wood and debris rain down on the security guards. A couple crumple to the ground, buried in ceiling remains. The others cough and wipe at their eyes to get the dust out. The elevator doors ding open. I shove Sarah through and push the button for the ground floor as fast as I can.

X·X·X

I surprise Helen when I drag myself into the house at almost two thirty a.m. Once we got out of the elevator, Sarah and I were able to evade Vilmore security long enough to get off campus and find our way to the train station. The last train didn't leave until after one, hence my late arrival back at the Tines house. I was hoping I could sneak in unnoticed, since Amelia tells me we're not allowed out after nine on a school night. But after hijacking a train, stealing a car, and causing massive damage to my future alma mater, coming home late is the least of my crimes. Helen's sitting at the dining room table in her pajamas, reading a book. She gasps when I open the door and puts a hand over her heart.

"Oh, Damien, you startled me."

"I didn't think you'd be up." To catch me sneaking in at all hours of the night, which is apparently frowned upon. Mom wouldn't care when I was out. She has a tendency to get cranky if I wake her up at ungodly hours or disturb her lab time, but that's it.

"I couldn't sleep, so—" Helen sets her book down, her brows furrowing. "Hey, you all right there? You look exhausted. What happened to the sleepover?"

Apparently she didn't get the memo about what a horrible, misbehaving stepson I am. I stand in the doorway, my mouth gaping open, not sure what to say.

"Things didn't go so well at Joe's, huh?"

Joe? Who the hell is Joe? I play along and shake my head.

"Amelia said you were staying over. I figured your phone call to Gordon earlier might have had something to do with you wanting to be scarce tonight." She sighs. "What happened? You change your mind, kid?"

"Oh, well ..." I scratch the side of my head and tromp into the kitchen. I haven't eaten anything since the lemon meringue, and that was hours ago. "Joe and I got in a fight."

"What?" She heaves herself up from her chair. "About what?"

Judging by her level of surprise, she must be under the impression that I'm some kind of saint, despite knowing about my phone call to Gordon. I guess acting out against my dad who recently tried to kill me is one thing, getting in a fight with a supposed sleepover buddy is another. I grab a box of crackers from the cupboard. I stuff some into my mouth as I say, "Well, he didn't like it when I kissed him."

Helen pales. She stops in her tracks, too shocked to come comfort me. She blinks a couple of times. "You kissed him."

Cracker crumbs spill from my mouth. "To see what it was like."

"How was it?"

I shrug. "I've had better."

Helen laughs and pats me on the shoulder. "Guys are jerks."

"Oh yes. Down with Joe. Good riddance to him." I chug down a glass of water to go with all the crackers. Maybe tomorrow I'll eat something real. After I've slept.

"Gordon wasn't too happy you were going to stay out on a school night, especially after your phone call, but I told him you needed space and it was good you were making friends. I won't tell him it didn't work out if you won't."

I promise her I won't say anything. She says good night, chuckling to herself over my exploits, and goes to bed.

I turn out the lights and flop down on the couch. I'm already half asleep when I hear the attic stairs creak, and then Amelia pokes me in the shoulder. *"Psst. Damien."*

I open my eyes, which is a mistake because she has a flashlight. I squint and shield my face with my arm. "Put that away." I ward off her flashlight, covering the bright end with my hand. It glows red, but at least I'm not blind.

Amelia points it at the floor. She kneels down beside me and whispers, "There was a message on the machine, from the school. About you not showing up today. I erased it."

"Ah, for me? You shouldn't have." So much sarcasm oozes out of my voice, even someone as thick as Amelia could pick up on it.

"I told Mom you were at a friend's house. So you wouldn't get in trouble for not coming home."

"Oh, great. Too bad none of that makes up for what you did. Dr. Wiggles finally got his degree, only so you could kill him."

"I said I was sorry." Her voice is tight and small. "I thought …"

"You thought I'd forgive you if you covered for me?" I raise myself up on one arm. "I thought you wanted me out of here? You could have done us both a favor and let me get in trouble." Okay, I am kind of glad she did what she did, because I've had enough hassle tonight—I didn't need to deal with Gordon getting mad at me for coming home late, too. But on the plus side, if Gordon got mad enough to kick me out, Mom would have to take me back early.

"I shouldn't have done that to Dr. Wiggles," Amelia goes on. "I got carried away, because I was mad. I should have believed you about Blue Bunnykins. I've caught Alex playing with him before, but …" She scrapes her fingernail against the rim of the flashlight. Her eyes shift back and forth, too guilty to meet mine. "I didn't blame you because you're a supervillain. I did it because I was jealous, okay? I jumped to conclusions."

"You got me thrown off a building." Does she expect me to let that go? Because she says she's sorry?

"I didn't know Dad was going to—"

"Oh, I think you did."

"Okay. I didn't know you'd take it so badly."

I glare at her.

"I didn't know you were almost going to die!" Her eyes meet mine for the first time in this conversation. She sets her flashlight down on the floor, so the glow from the light creeps around the edge of the couch. "I thought you'd tell Dad you didn't want to do it, and then he'd see how you don't belong with us. How he shouldn't have brought you here."

"And then he'd see how great you are, since you're chomping at the bit to get your flying power going?"

"Dad told us what happened, how he couldn't save you and thought you weren't going to make it. First, I was mad at you for not saying no. You didn't *have* to try and fly. You went on and on about how you were a villain and didn't have flying power, so I thought you were stupid for going along with it. But then I was mad at myself for betraying you. You're my brother, and"—she grits her teeth and sucks it up—"and maybe you wouldn't be so bad, if I got to know you. So I'm glad you're not dead."

"Thanks." I think. "I want you to know, Amelia, that I feel the exact same way."

A hint of a smile plays across her lips.

"I'm glad I'm not dead, too."

The smile wilts. "Ha ha." She punches me in the shoulder. Then she lowers her voice, talking so quietly that I can barely hear her. "Did you really kiss a *boy*?"

"Wouldn't you like to know?"

She's silent for a while. I'm drifting off when she says, "Damien … I … I tried to fix Dr. Wiggles for you. I taped him back together, but he's not the same." Her voice gets higher and louder the longer she goes on. "I really am sorry! I sewed up Blue Bunnykins—he's all right—but Dr. Wiggles is really dead! I killed him!"

"Shh." I reach out and poke her cheek. "It's okay." It's

going to be. I think. I'm too tired to fully assess how I feel about her apology and her confession of not hating my guts. "Sleep now. Grovel later."

Amelia gets up and hovers over me. She keeps making sounds like she wants to say something else. Finally she says, "Damien ... do you hate me because I'm a superhero?"

If I wasn't already half asleep, I might tell her that her being a superhero is the least of the reasons she's given me not to like her. Instead, all I manage to do is mumble, "No."

"Good," she says, sounding like she means it.

And I don't know what happens after that, because I'm finally asleep.

CHAPTER 13

"I'm *so* glad you didn't let me come home," I tell Mom Tuesday morning before school. I'm sitting at the dining table, forging a note from Gordon, saying to forgive my absence yesterday, since I was too busy recovering from a nasty fall I had this weekend. One that left me emotionally scarred for life and that was all his fault.

"What?" Mom yawns on the other end of the phone. She wasn't awake when I called. Not the first five times anyway.

"I was having trouble adjusting at first"—I pause to get the flare on the *G* of Gordon's name right—"but now everything's great. All I needed to do was give it some time."

"Damien, it's *six a.m.*"

"Did you know superheroes get up early? I've been up since five—can't wait to start the day, you know?" I got

198

up twenty minutes ago, and only because the rest of the house was awake, stomping around while I was trying to sleep. I had to race Amelia and shove her out of the way to get a turn in the bathroom, and when I looked in the mirror … my hair was lopsided. Because someone had to shoot at me with a raygun. That first blast from Henrietta singed off the ends of my hair on one side. It could be worse—there could be a bald spot or a racing stripe instead of only being uneven, but still. This is the thanks I get for helping out Sarah. And it's not over.

"Mom, you'll never believe how many nice superhero girls I've met. They're totally hot and extra friendly. Three hero girls want me to call them tonight. One might want to go all the way, but I'm okay with that. I can see myself settling down with her, having some kids." I put the finishing touches on my fake note from Gordon and give it a second to dry.

"Damien," Mom growls. She knows I'm saying these things to piss her off, but that doesn't mean it's not working. "What happened to Kat?"

"You see, the thing about Kat is she's not what I'd call 'my type' anymore. All that villainy." And, you know, taking up with other guys. "She's—"

"Would one of these new girls happen to be Dr. Kink's daughter?"

Whoa. How does she do that? "I'm afraid I don't know what you're talking about." Plus, Sarah's not a superhero. "Must be the generation gap. Could you use hipper slang?"

Gordon wanders through the room, all dressed for work in his cape and leotard. I stuff the note I forged into my pocket before he can see it. He glares at me. "We need to have a talk," he says. "About appropriate use of Q and A sessions."

I point to the phone, indicating I can't be bothered.

He clenches his fists and seems like he's going to have it out with me right there, whether I'm on the phone or not, but then he takes a deep breath, gets ahold of himself, and continues on into the kitchen.

Mom's tone is serious business. "Taylor got a phone call last night. Two kids broke into the room where they were holding Dr. Kink at Vilmore. One of them turned out to be his daughter. Messy blond hair and glasses. Does that ring any bells, sweetie? Because the other description sounded a lot like a certain, beloved son of mine who I know would never betray me like that."

"No bells are going off. Honestly. But since you brought it up, I've been doing a little Internet research. Dr. Kink is a biologist, not a … hypno-device maker. I think your problem with him is you might have gotten confused. It was probably a different Dr. Kink who wrote those articles and made the prototype."

"We found it in his house."

"Probably his cousin or a sibling, then. Or someone could have stashed it to make it look like it was his. Either way, I think you've got the wrong guy."

Mom sighs. "You know, that's very astute of you. Taylor and I, we were starting to think the same thing."

Gordon's phone rings. I hear him answer it in the kitchen with a groggy, "Hello?"

"So you're going to let him go, right?"

"Damien, he's not a lab rat. We can't go around letting *everyone* go."

"But, Mom, he's not the right guy. He has a life to live, biology students to teach. Maybe he can still go back to that, if you didn't mess him up too much."

"I don't know, Damien. His daughter knows where we kept him. It could be a liability."

"But it's already a liability then, so letting him go doesn't change anything. Plus, what's she going to do, go to the police? You can cover it up. Dr. Kink's still a brilliant scientist. You wouldn't want to kill off someone in the profession, would you?"

"Well ..." I think I have her. "We'll see." Typical Mom answer. "You really don't know this Sarah Kink girl?"

"Never heard of her." I'm totally not on a two-month plan for getting into her pants. A plan she came up with, not me. I said I was going to choose the experiments, but that one can definitely stay.

"Are you sure? Because, if it was you last night—"

"It wasn't! I was singing folk songs with my new family after eating dinner together, and then we all hugged for an hour. I was way too busy to break into Vilmore to find some guy I've never met with a girl I don't even know."

"Good, sweetie, because I remember the lab-rat incident, and I wouldn't want to repeat it. Behavior like that isn't conducive to making the history books as a first-rate supervillain, and it's *not* going to turn your X into a V. Taylor and I have put a lot of work into this project, and if this girl is part of the puzzle—"

I miss what Mom says next because Gordon suddenly

shouts from the kitchen, "What?! Dear God! No, I was about to go to work, but of course it can wait. This is serious." He hangs up, runs his hands through his hair, and then marches up to me at the dining table.

"What was that, Mom? I couldn't hear you. Someone wasn't respecting my personal audio bubble—"

"Hang up," Gordon says.

"Hold on," I tell him.

"Damien, hang up the phone *now*."

"Is that man telling you what to do?" Mom says. "Because you tell him from me that he's not going to order my son around!"

Gordon reaches over and rips my phone out of my hand and flips it shut. "Come on—let's go."

He tries to grab my wrist, but I pull away from him. "Oh no. Last time I went anywhere with you, you pushed me off a building. I'm staying put."

"It's an emergency." Gordon motions for me to get out of the chair. "We need everyone we can get, even you."

"Wow, even *me*? I'm so honored." For the record, emergencies aren't my thing. It was poor word choice on Gordon's part, because he could have told me he wanted to take me out for ice cream or to get me my own puppy. Something he might imagine was pleasant and that I might conceivably go for. Dragging me out of the house at six in the morning to go to some emergency that I presume has nothing to do with me or anyone I care about? Try again.

"I'm not giving you a choice," Gordon says. "I hate to do this the hard way, but we don't have time to argue."

He lifts the back two legs of my chair off the ground and tilts it to one side, so I slide off. He grabs my arm so I don't fall and drags me out to the car. "Come on, son—it's time you found out what superheroes are really like."

X·X·X

This big superhero emergency Gordon's dragged me to at almost the crack of dawn is a burning apartment building. Four stories of spewing flames light up the dark morning. Clouds of black smoke fill the sky. Bystanders gather around the scene, sipping their lattes and pointing up at the building. The police motion for them to keep back, while the fire department and a couple of superheroes fight to stop the flames.

Gordon parks the car, badly, on the far side of the street and tears his seat belt off. I'm tempted to stay right here. What the hell is he thinking, bringing me to a dangerous scene like this? I'm all ready with my spiel about staying in the car, instead of getting within burning-to-death-range, but Gordon doesn't say anything to me. He brought me here to help, or so he said, but he flings open the door and jumps out without closing it. He leaves the keys in the ignition. I'm surprised he turned the car off.

"I'm just going to stay here," I mutter to no one. "No, it's okay, you go ahead. I'll watch."

Gordon runs across the street—*not* looking both ways first, like he teaches kids on TV—and gets to work, only pausing to check with one of the firefighters. There's a superhero with freeze breath using his power on the ground floor, but that doesn't do anything for the upper stories. The firefighters hurry to get a ladder up, while Gordon takes to the air and zooms up the side of the building and into a fourth-story window. Another hero with super strength helps the firefighters with the hose. I watch as a couple others catch Gordon's insanity and run inside the burning building.

If Gordon really wanted me to help, why'd he ditch me? Maybe when he got here, he decided I was a useless supervillain and the best thing to do was to get going before I could ask questions and get in the way.

Flames shoot out of the same window Gordon flew through only half a minute ago. My heart stops. I've only known the guy a couple weeks, and I *don't* care that he's technically my dad, but cold fear runs up and down my spine anyway and leaves me shaking. I fumble to get my seat belt off and think about how mad I am at my father. Who might be dead now. Thanks a lot, Gordon. You not only push me off a building, but you bring me to this gigantic bonfire so you can get yourself killed. Great. I suppose he expects me to deliver the news to his now-fatherless family, since I was a witness and everything.

I get out of the car and stumble across the street, dazed and silently cursing Gordon for getting me into this mess. I feel the heat from the fire, making me sweat as I get closer. He'd better not be dead. I haven't paid him back enough for the whole flying-lesson thing. It's only been a couple days—he hasn't even discovered the worms in his shampoo yet.

I push my way to the front of the crowd. I try to move

past, but a policeman holds his hand up, signaling for me not to come any closer. "Sorry, kid. You'd better stay back."

"I'm with the Crimson Flash." The words fall out of my mouth before I have time to remember I'm ashamed to be associated with him. "He's my dad."

The policeman looks me over. I can tell he's about to say no anyway, when Gordon bursts out of a *third*-story window, carrying two small children. His face is smudged with ash and his cape's a little tattered, but he's alive. He sets the kids down, and a couple of paramedics rush to their aid. I picture what it would be like to be trapped high up in a fire, with no way to get down, and nothing to do but wait for the flames to kill you. My palms clam up and an overwhelming burst of terror jolts me into action. I push past the policeman and make a run for it. He moves to come after me, but Gordon motions that it's okay.

The guy with the freeze breath is up on the ladder now, blowing ice into the second-story windows. He looks dizzy, like he's been taking too many deep breaths. As I'm thinking that, he loses his balance and topples to the ground. He lands with a heavy thud. I imagine falling and feel like I'm going to throw up.

"Okay," I tell Gordon, "I'm here." He should be happy I got out of the car, and he didn't even have to nag me about it. I'm doing what he brought me here for, unasked. "What do you want me to—"

He doesn't stick around to tell me what to do, or even to say, "Oops, sorry I scared you, son, what with rushing into that burning building and all."

As Gordon flies back into the building, I feel abandoned and alone. I'm standing in the middle of a bunch of commotion, because the Crimson Flash told a police officer it was okay for me to be past the line of ordinary citizens. He shouldn't have done that. He shouldn't have brought me here to help and then run off without telling me what to do. I stand here, getting in the way, utterly useless and totally overwhelmed by all of this. The flames crackle, and the crowd makes "ooh" and "aah" noises every time a superhero uses their power or drags a victim out of the burning building.

The freeze guy gets off the ground and climbs back up the ladder. One of his arms is bleeding and is bent funny. He doesn't look any steadier than he did before, but that's not stopping him.

There's a loud crash, and then two more superheroes come running out of the apartment building. They're empty-handed. They stop to catch their breath. Gordon zooms outside again, a cat clinging to his shoulder with all its claws, the end of his cape catching on fire as flames bust out another window. I guess he's lucky if all he has to worry about is his cape and getting mauled by a housecat. He's about to go in for more when a fireman stops him. I run over to them and hear something about the structure not being sound and it getting too dangerous. Gordon nods and joins the other superheroes. I trail after him like a lost puppy. I don't know if he remembers I'm here.

"The kids think there's one more in there," a superhero in a bright green spandex outfit says. "Second story, but we couldn't find them." The front of his costume proclaims him ACE QUICKSPEED. Guess what his power is.

Gordon bites his lip. "Jeff tells me the building's not sound. We can't risk it. Not on a 'maybe.' When we get the flames out, we'll send in a team—"

"So you're going to let that kid die?!" This is me talking, and not one of the superheroes, like you'd expect. *I'm* a lousy, no-good villain, and I think they should go back in. They're supposed to be the good guys, and they're acting like letting some kid burn to death is okay. So much for superheroes being brave and, well, *heroes*.

All three of them stare at me. Like they didn't notice I existed until this point. Even Gordon looks shocked by my presence. He scratches the side of his head.

"You can't wait," I tell him. "That kid'll be dead by the time you get the fire out. Plus, the structure's not getting any sounder."

Gordon puts his hands on my shoulders. "Damien, listen, there's nothing we can do. We don't know if anyone's still in there, the building's about to collapse, and it's likely whoever we send in won't make it back out. If I knew for sure there was someone in there, that would be a different story, but as is …" He shakes his head.

I gape at him in shock. "You're supposed to be a superhero! You can't say that!"

"Damien, calm down. Sometimes these things happen."

"But somebody could be trapped. What if it was 'maybe' Jessica in there, or Alex?" Or even Amelia. "Wouldn't you want someone to save them?"

The three superheroes all share nervous looks.

"Is this what superheroes *really* do?" I ask. "Stand around whining about how dangerous it is?"

Gordon's eyebrows come together. "I don't like this part of the job any more than you do, but that's how it is. Being a hero means having to make hard choices. Sometimes the hardest choices involve letting other people get hurt."

"Don't worry," the other superhero mutters. He's wearing a blue costume with a picture of a raindrop on the front. "The kid's from a family of supervillains. Might do everybody more good if we don't go in."

I'm seriously the only one who reacts to that. Gordon says, "Damien, he didn't mean it," when my eyes go wide and I glare at the guy so hard, I think I might burn a hole through him even without laser eyes. But other than that, nobody says anything because nobody cares.

"That's why you're not going in?!" I shout. I might hate superheroes, and I might not be keen on rescue missions, but there's no way I'm going to stand around not even trying. Gordon's insanity must be hereditary, because I turn and run toward the burning building. The one that's about to fall apart and that the superheroes are afraid to go into.

"Damien, no!" Gordon calls after me, but I barely hear him.

A blast of heat hits me in the face when I get close to the building. I ignore it and hurl myself through the open doorway. The heat's overwhelming and smoke burns my lungs, choking me. I cough, and my eyes water, and it's hot as hell in here, and I can't tell where I'm going.

Everything's on fire. Beams from the ceiling have fallen down in places. One of them blocks the end of the hallway, but luckily not the stairs. They said second story. Great.

I gather up all my courage. There's no time to worry about my phobia. I tell myself I'm probably going to die anyway, so it doesn't matter. I feel sick all over and lightheaded as I force myself up the stairs. It's only one set, just up to the second story, and then I'm home free. Still stuck inside a burning deathtrap, but now's not the time to think about that. My lungs ache and I stop for a coughing fit. The stairs creak, and the boards a couple steps down from where I'm standing crack and fall, succumbing to the flames. It doesn't take any more motivation than that to get my legs moving. I hurry the rest of the way to the second-story landing, ignoring the searing pain in my lungs.

I turn down a hallway, hoping this is right. I struggle to find enough breath to call out, "Is anybody here?!"

No one answers, but I hear an explosion of flame, and then a scream down another hallway. I run toward the sound. As soon as I take a step, a beam falls where I was standing. The idea that I narrowly avoided getting crushed and burned to death crosses my mind, and so does the fact that my way out is now blocked, but I make myself focus on getting to whoever's still in here.

I call out again when I reach the end of the hall. A shrill, little-kid voice screams for help, and I turn to the room on my left. The door's open, but a hole in the floor separates me from the little girl huddled on the other side of the room. She's Alex's age and wearing a pink nightgown, clutching a teddy bear for dear life. I can hardly breathe now from the smoke, and the burning in my lungs is wearing me out.

"I'm coming!" I shout. It takes a lot more effort than it should and starts me coughing. The little girl looks up at me just in time to pass out from lack of oxygen and slump against the wall.

I'm getting really dizzy, and my vision is going dim. There's a giant, flaming hole in the floor, and there's no way I can get to her. I wonder why I even came in here. And then I hear Gordon's voice, shouting, "Damien!" and suddenly he's grabbing my arm. He tries to pull me away from the scene.

I don't have a lot of strength left, but I manage to dig my heels into the floor just enough to stop him. "She's still in there," I croak.

Without hesitating, Gordon rushes in and flies over the gaping hole. He grabs the girl, limp under one arm, and gets out right as the ceiling collapses and the window bursts. He shouts, "Hold on!" and grabs me around the waist before flying all three of us to safety.

Once we're outside, he sets me down and hands the little girl to the paramedics. Then he grabs my shoulders and looks like he's going to yell at me. Instead, he pulls me to him and hugs me. It's when he lets go that the yelling starts.

"What did you think you were doing?! Damien, you could have been killed! Do you understand me?"

I try to talk but end up coughing instead. When the

coughing fit is over, I say, "You weren't going to save her because she's a villain. You think she's better off dead, that society's better off without people like her. Like me."

"I didn't say that."

"You went along with it."

"No. Damien, it wasn't safe. You proved that. What would I have done if you'd gotten yourself killed?"

"What would you tell Mom, you mean." I kick at a pebble on the ground. I'm tired of arguing with him. I wander, dazed, across the street and climb into the passenger seat of the car.

Gordon follows me and gets in the driver's seat. He doesn't turn the car on. "I'm so mad at you right now," he says. "You disobeyed me, and you could have gotten seriously hurt, if not worse. But I want you to know, I'm also proud of you. You did what you thought was right." He puts his hands on the steering wheel, even though he's not actually driving, and stares out the front window. "I respect that. It's … more than I would have done at your age. I know that probably doesn't mean much, coming from a superhero, and … you don't seem to care at all that I'm your father, other than to ridicule me for it. But I hope, someday, you can get something out of it."

I remember how useless I felt throughout all of this, and especially standing on the edge of that gaping hole that separated me from that kid. It occurs to me now that I'm even more useless than I thought, because I can *fly*. A lot of good that power does me. Even if I *wanted* to act like some superhero and use it—like to, say, help a little girl from a burning building instead of standing there like an idiot—how useful would it be if I could only get a couple inches off the ground before having a panic attack? But Gordon wasn't useless. He could have left me there. He could have saved only me and not her, but he came through in the end. I catch myself thinking maybe he's not so bad, and that I don't mind him being my dad as much as I thought.

"Well," I mutter, half hoping he won't hear me, "it might mean something."

X·X·X

Making out with Sarah in front of the spandex kids' lockers during lunch on Wednesday isn't what I originally had in mind for phase two of my plan, but it seems to be working really well. And not just on the spandex kids— everyone who passes us is grossed out.

"Oh, my God," I hear Jill mutter when she shows up for lunch, the heels of her shoes clicking on the floor. The spandex kids are too cool to eat in the cafeteria with everyone else. They prefer to sit in the hall near their lockers and make fun of anyone who walks by.

Jill's and Marty's lockers are right next to each other. Sarah and I are pressed up against both, so neither of them can get to their stuff. We're also standing right where they usually sit to eat.

I feel Sarah go a little tense when she hears Jill's voice, but she doesn't stop kissing me. She slides her tongue against mine. Her mouth tastes like spearmint gum.

"Ew, gross, it's the dork brigade," Marty says. "Get rid

of 'em, Wes."

I hear some mutterings of reluctance and glance over Sarah's shoulder. Jill and Marty and three other members of their spandex posse are keeping their distance from us while still trying to seem menacing, looks of pure disgust on their faces. They're all holding lunch trays full of breaded mystery meat and fake mashed potatoes.

I close my eyes and moan a little, pulling Sarah closer to me. I can almost feel the wave of revulsion pass over our audience.

"Isn't that the kid that got you with the scorpions?" someone, presumably Wes, asks. He doesn't sound like he's coming to get rid of us anytime soon.

"So?" Marty says. "He's a loser. Don't tell me you're afraid?"

"Like you're not," Wes mutters. "I heard he's, like, an actual supervillain or something."

"He's not cool enough to be a supervillain. Plus, I'm not scared even if he is."

"They're going to make me vomit, and I haven't even eaten yet," Jill says, sounding extra snotty, probably to make up for the fact that she doesn't want to be the one to try and stop us. "We can't eat with them here, so somebody get moving."

I'm not sure if she's talking to us or to her posse.

"I'm not touching them," Wes says.

"Like they can't hear us talking about them," someone else adds.

I slide my hands under Sarah's shirt, and she reaches for the waist of my jeans.

Various shouts of "Ew!" and phrases such as "Losers shouldn't breed!" escape the spandex kids.

"My food's getting cold," Jill whines, her heels clicking against the floor as she turns to leave.

"Let's go," Marty says. He takes a step toward us and adds, "But these freaks better not be here tomorrow if they know what's good for them!"

I smile as I listen to them leave, waiting until I'm sure they're gone before breaking away from Sarah. "I'd call that a success, wouldn't you?"

Her face is flushed and she takes a second to catch up on her breathing. "One hundred percent."

"And I suppose you'll want to write down all the good data I—"

Sarah reaches up and caresses the side of my face. There's something sensual about it, and it's definitely *not* the way you'd touch someone who's only a "lab partner," even if you did just make out with them. Then she kisses me, one long, slow lip-lock that says more than a whole notebook full of data.

"What was *that*?" I ask her, taking a step back. I thought Sarah didn't *like* like me, but that's not how you kiss someone you don't care about.

"Just an experiment," Sarah says, trying to shrug it off. She reaches for me again, and I move away before I have time to think about it. It leaves a weird tension hanging in the air.

We're silent, my chest tightening with every awkward breath. Then I break the ice. "We should go get lunch, before the bell rings." Totally smooth. Right.

Sarah shakes her head. "I have to go study for a geography test. You're still coming over later?"

"Yeah. Sure."

"Good," she says, picking her backpack up off the floor and hoisting it onto her shoulders. "I can't wait for you to meet Heraldo."

X·X·X

I go over to Sarah's house Wednesday afternoon, after school. There are pictures on the wall of a woman I'm guessing is Sarah's mom, but I don't see her anywhere, and she isn't in any pictures where Sarah's older than ten. Whatever happened to her, I'm guessing she's not around anymore.

I'm trying to figure out the best way to ask Sarah about it—her mom could be dead, or maybe her dad isn't the first person in the family to get captured by supervillains, and we are *not* going on any more liberation missions—when Sarah says, "Come on, I'll show you my room," and leads me down the hall.

Her room looks like a robot threw up all over it. There are piles of nuts and bolts shoved into the corners. Shoe boxes full of stripped wires and plastic knobs poke out from under the bed. Her bedspread has a real map of the night sky on it, and it looks like it's got blobs of glow-in-the-dark paint where all the stars are. There's a bookshelf against one wall, overflowing with nonfiction. There are a couple of romance novels shoved in here and there, wherever there was enough room to cram them in. One of

215

the covers has a superhero with long, wavy hair, making out with some cavegirl. I think she's a cavegirl—she's wearing a leopard skin and holding a club, but I could be jumping to conclusions. Sarah probably considers this stuff "research." Next to the bookshelf is a heap of various gadgets. They look like half-finished projects, but knowing what Sarah's end products look like, it's hard to tell.

I dump my backpack on the floor and flop down in her computer chair at her desk. She has a clunky black laptop, covered in superhero stickers. The biggest one is of the Crimson Flash. Wonderful.

"So, this is my room." Sarah talks too fast, like she's not used to having people over, and shoves her shoe boxes a little farther under the bed. "What do you think?"

I think your giant Crimson Flash sticker creeps me out, and you might want to cover it up if you want me to hang out with you. "It's cool. So, um, how's your dad?"

Sarah smiles. "He came home last night. He said they just … let him go." She chokes up, just a tiny bit, and her eyes water a little. "I don't know what happened, but I'm glad I trusted you."

"Uh-huh." Is that why she kissed me like that earlier? Or was she lying back at Vilmore when she said she didn't want me to be her boyfriend? Either way, it sounds like my "you wouldn't want to kill off a fellow scientist" argument must have gotten to Mom. I just hope she didn't tell Taylor that letting Dr. Kink go was my idea—I don't want him adding that to my list of "weaknesses."

"He's in the hospital." Sarah sits down on the edge of her bed. "The doctors say he'll be okay. He's got three broken ribs and a mashed-up finger. And a lot of stitches. He gets to come home this weekend, and then you can meet him."

Meet her dad? Was that in the rulebook?

"Just as my lab partner," Sarah adds. "He doesn't need to know what kind of experiments we're conducting. He'd be way too thrilled if he thought I had a boyfriend." She rolls her eyes.

"Speaking of experiments ..." I get up from the desk and sit next to her on her bed.

She tucks her hands under her legs and stares at her knees. I was going to put my arm around her, but now it feels too awkward with her holding so still and not looking at me. She was all over me at lunch today—why the lack of cooperation now that we're behind closed doors?

I decide we're both just nervous. Our lunchtime experiment had a purpose—we were putting on a show to annoy other people. Now that it's just us, it's, well, kind of weird. I lean closer to her, but she jumps up from the bed before I can so much as breathe on her. She picks up a gadget from the pile on the floor. "Do you want to see my new inventions?"

"Do any of them explode? Because we should probably go outside for that."

She laughs. "No. I haven't done any more work in weaponry. These are all accessories. This one"—she holds up a metal circle, about the size of a saucer, with seat-belt straps hanging off of it—"is a holographic projector."

"Oh, yeah?" Can it, say, change my thumbprint? For

less than three thousand dollars, which Gordon apparently doesn't have left on his credit card? It was practically maxed out. The most I could have gotten out of him was five hundred, and it wasn't worth it. Instead, I bought five hundred dollars' worth of subscriptions to risqué supervillain magazines in his name. He should be getting at least one a day for the next two years, with such favorites as *Hottest Villains, Girls Galore—Supervillain Edition,* and *Naughty, Not Nice,* to name a few. His subscription to *Hottest Villains* includes a special Baddest Girls of the Year issue, where they go in depth with the supervillain girls who committed the "hottest crimes." It also includes a sixteen-month calendar, swimsuit edition.

"It changes what a person looks like," Sarah says, explaining her invention to me. "What I mostly had in mind was being able to change outfits with it. Think of all the money it could save on clothes." She buckles it around her waist, tinkers around with a few buttons on the side of the seat-belt buckle, and presses the metal circle. I watch as her white T-shirt turns into a black one. Her arms look really tan and her facial features suddenly look pinched and not like Sarah at all. Then the device makes a little *zap* noise, like something's shorting out inside it. The image flickers, blinking between Sarah and the holographic projection.

"Oops," Sarah says, banging her fist on the side of the device. "I haven't quite worked out all the bugs yet."

It's neat, I guess, considering Sarah made it at home, but it doesn't compare to Kat's power.

Sarah sighs, seeing I'm not impressed. "I know it

doesn't seem like much. It can only handle simple changes so far, but I'm hoping to have it up to something more complicated before prom. I'll save money on a dress, and I won't have to go to a salon to get my hair and nails done. But I've got a couple years to work on it." She deactivates it and takes it off, reaching for another invention. "And this one—"

"Actually, maybe you could show me later. I'm here as Damien, not Renegade X."

"Don't mix business with pleasure," Sarah says. "Got it." She sits down on the bed with me. "You want to watch something?"

"Yeah, sure." Anything to make this not feel so awkward.

A dog barks outside. "Oh, that's Heraldo. Here"—she shoves her TV remote in my hand—"I have to let him in."

Sarah runs off, her footsteps echoing down the hall. I inspect her remote, but it looks store-bought, like it might actually go to her TV and not to, say, a robot in the closet who'll bust out and try to kill me as soon as I press power. I wince as my finger pushes down on the button, but the TV flickers to life, and nothing else in the room seems to do anything. I'm safe from Sarah's crazy inventions, for now.

The news is on, so I flip the channels until I get to something I recognize: *The Crimson Flash and the Safety Kids.* They show it in the mornings, and again in the afternoons in case you miss it the first time. Strangely enough, it doesn't make me think of my dad—it reminds me of Kat. That's the last thing I want right now. I'm about to conduct a serious make-out session with my new girlfriend—er, lab partner—something I got involved in so I *wouldn't* think about my ex. I hold up the remote to change the channel, but I hesitate, waiting to see which episode this is.

"Today," the Crimson Flash says, "we're going to visit the zoo. What do we think about that, Safety Kids?"

The camera pans to a dozen elementary-school children, ranging from ages six to ten, sitting on the floor, wearing little red capes. They wave noisemakers and shout, *"Yay!"* There's no standard set of Safety Kids. It's one of those shows where any kid can be on it if they sign up and are between the right ages.

I hear pounding footsteps in the hall, and then a Great Dane leaps on the bed, knocking me down and causing me to throw the remote across the room. It lands in a pile of gears. The dog pins me to the bed and licks my face. Similar to what I was hoping to do with Sarah, but *not even close.*

Sarah claps her hands. "Heraldo! Down, boy! Leave Damien alone."

Heraldo reluctantly gets off of me. He stands on the bed and walks in a circle a couple times before lying down and panting heavily in my ear. I sit up and wipe the dog slobber off my face.

"He likes you," Sarah says. Then she spies what's on the TV. The Crimson Flash is standing in front of the zebra pen at the Golden City Zoo, explaining how they use their stripes to avoid predators. "Oh, I love this show!" She bounces down on the bed next to me, grinning, as if I chose this on purpose because I knew it was her favorite. Sarah grabs my hand and leans her head against my shoulder.

Heraldo crawls forward a little, so his front legs are across mine. He puts his head down and drools.

My face is dry now, but I can smell his spit. Gross. I'm not only stuck with him, but it looks like Sarah's not changing the channel anytime soon. These experiments are supposed to be fun, so I decide to make the most of it.

"Look at that—is he wearing an honorary zookeeper badge?" I scoff at the screen. "Does he think being a superhero makes him a *zookeeper*?"

Sarah lifts her head and scowls. "Damien, he's your dad."

"Exactly. That's how I know he has no zoo training whatsoever." Kat would have taken the bait. She would have snickered and made comments about spying the superhero in its natural habitat. *You'll notice, kids, that the superhero wears bright colors to trick its enemies into believing it's poisonous. The bright colors mean,* Danger, stay away! *This, however, is a rare evolutionary flaw, as the bright colors serve only to attract the dreaded supervillain.*

Sarah looks at me like I'm speaking another language. "That's why he's only an honorary zookeeper." She adjusts herself so she's sitting up more and not leaning on me.

Heraldo's breath is hot on my knee. I'm uncomfortable, physically and emotionally, and I'm ready to go home. I wish Kat was here instead of Sarah. I'm not supposed to think that or feel that way, especially since Sarah kissed me like she really meant it earlier and invited me to her

221

house and wants me to meet her dad, but here I am, doing it anyway. I put my arm around Sarah to appease my guilt, even though she can't possibly know what I'm thinking. She smiles at me—a warm smile, like you'd be more likely to give a boyfriend than a lab partner—then turns her attention to the screen, taking the Crimson Flash's zoo trip really seriously.

X·X·X

I'm sitting upside down on the couch Thursday evening, my feet up where my head should be, and my head hanging off the edge of the cushions, talking on the phone.

"I can't believe Pete called my parents," Kat says.

"Pete's a narc. What do you expect?"

Amelia stomps through the living room, making fussing noises and straightening out the furniture. She plunks a bowl of chips down on the coffee table, steps back to get a good look, then shuffles them around until they're all at the same level while still looking "casually tossed." God forbid Amelia's friends find out how much effort she's put into making this slumber party perfect.

"Don't touch those. They're for the party," Amelia says, storming off to check that her Superhero Day streamers are straight. We get a whole day off from school for it tomorrow, hence the slumber party, especially since Amelia's the only one of her friends with any superhero heritage. She acts like it's her birthday. Her friends might not know Gordon's really the Crimson Flash, but you can bet they know Amelia's a superhero and expecting to get her *H* this year. Amelia's told all her friends—and me—that she's already applied to Heroesworth Academy for fall, since her birthday's in October and she'd just barely miss the cutoff otherwise. She's hoping they'll let her in early.

"Who's that?" Kat asks.

"I'm, um, staying with relatives."

Kat clears her throat. "Listen, Damien ... I'm not too clear on everything that happened Monday night, but I know you stopped by. At Pete's."

"Yeah, for about five minutes. Why?"

"I wanted to say I'm sorry."

"For what? Drooling on my shirt? You can buy me a new one."

"What? No. I got pretty wasted and made out with one of Pete's roommates." I can tell by the tightness in her voice that she's not looking forward to my response to that. "Julie brought me to the party," she goes on, when I don't say anything. "I didn't know it was at Pete's, just at Vilmore, and then I was so upset about ... *things* that I didn't care what I did. I wanted to have a good time."

"So you did. Good for you."

"But I didn't. I was miserable."

"Uh-huh."

"So ... I'm sorry. That I did that. Especially in front of you. It's not something that's going to happen again. I was upset, but I'm going to fix that."

"And you're telling me this because ...?" My tone is friendly, possibly even cheerful. Pretending I don't know exactly why she feels the need to apologize to me.

"Because, Damien, you're ... we ... I thought you'd be mad, but forget it, okay?" She's silent. Then, "Also, at the party, did I say anything weird?"

"Hmm. Let's see ... Other than when you stuffed a hundred bucks down my pants and told me to take off everything but my socks? No, can't think of anything."

Amelia almost falls over in shock, sloshing punch over the edges of the punch bowl she's carrying. She makes a face at me that's half revulsion and half wide-eyed terror. From my upside-down position, I can totally see up her nostrils. She sets down the punch bowl and runs into the other room, shouting, "Mom! He's not going to be here during my party, right?"

Oh, I'm going to be here. Starting up a rousing game of Truth or Dare with a bunch of fifteen-year-old girls. Amelia wants to get to know me better, right? It's perfect. The great things about siblings, I'm learning, is it turns out you can be as awful to them as you want, and they still have to put up with you.

"Har-har, Damien," Kat says. "And where did I get that kind of money?"

"A better question is, did I give you the show of your life and you can't remember it, or did I take the money and run?"

"But, seriously, I didn't say anything, did I?" She sounds awfully nervous.

"No."

Gordon comes in from the bedroom, wearing a bathrobe. His hair is wet and he keeps touching it, like he's feeling for something. He seems kind of twitchy.

"Damien," he says, "can I have a word with you?"

I put my hand over the receiving end of the phone. "Do you mind?"

"Did you put …?" He shuts his eyes and shudders. "Did you put *worms* in my shampoo?"

I guess the worms all sunk to the bottom of the bottle. That or he's waited four days to wash his hair, since I put them there on Sunday while everyone was at church. "I don't know. Pushed anyone off any buildings lately?" Saving me in a fire makes up for him trying to kill me, but it doesn't mean he's learned his lesson. Thus he will get no sympathy or apologies from me.

He plants his hands on his hips. "Damien, I was only trying to help you. If you'd just listen to me—"

I tap the side of the phone impatiently. "Can you speed this up? I've got a hot girl on the other line, and you know how those nine-hundred numbers are. The first couple minutes are cheap, and after that, they rack up the price."

He looks like he wants to throttle me. His face turns red and his forehead knits up. "I know you don't like to leave the ground. It was a little scary for me at first, too, but I think you'll find that it's not so bad. Even if you are afraid of heights, *you'll* have control. It'll be a very different experience for you once you realize you can't fall."

I don't acknowledge him, going back to my conversation with Kat. "Yeah, baby, tell me again what you'll do to me."

"What?" Kat says.

Gordon storms off, grumbling about "that boy." He's as bad as Amelia.

"Nothing."

The doorbell rings and Amelia shouts, *"I'll get it!"* She thunders to the door, glaring at me and motioning for me to *get out.*

"Hey," I say into the phone, getting a great idea, "do you want to come ov—" I stop myself. Kat doesn't know I'm living with a bunch of superheroes. She's going to find out about my *X* eventually—I'm going to tell her soon, I promise—but maybe now isn't the right time for it. It might ruin the Truth or Dare session. Plus, I don't want Amelia teasing me that Kat's my girlfriend, because as I've stated a million times before, she's not. "I mean, it's a nice day for a white wedding."

"Yeah … What are you doing tomorrow night?"

"Undressing myself at parties for money. Tonight's my trial run."

Amelia's eyes are going to burst out of her head. She drags her friend, the one with the green stripe in her hair, as fast as she can through the living room, sleeping bag and pillows in tow. "My brother's *not* going to be at the party."

"So," Kat says, "in other words, absolutely nothing?"

"Well, you know, I wasn't married to the idea."

Kat's quiet for a minute. When I don't go on, she says, "You'll never guess what I found out. You remember my grandfather? I mean, you don't *remember* him, he wasn't alive when we were born, but … you know the stories. Anyway, I found his ring! I was shopping downtown, and I went into this little antique store with all this really cool villain stuff, and it was *there*. On display, like they were really proud of it. It didn't even have a price."

I sit upright, all the blood draining from my head. She means Helen's shop. "That's … great, Kat." I don't sound like I mean it.

"Tell me you want to come with me this weekend to get it back. It's mine, right? It doesn't belong in some antique store."

"It's not even an antique." I pace the living room. Sure, Kat should have inherited the thing, but I can't help thinking of Helen and her losing her superpower and her one trophy that makes it all worthwhile. They both have a right to it.

"It's collecting dust there, like some useless trinket, and I *need* it."

"You need it, Kat?" The ring's supposed to protect the wearer from heartbreak. Maybe she should have the ring, if it'll help her get over me and I won't find her drunk at any parties, trying to forget what happened between us. Maybe we can just be friends, with neither of us wishing we were together. Maybe … maybe I don't want her mission to succeed, and not just because it means stealing from Helen's store.

Kat clears her throat. "I've been down lately. A new toy might cheer me up. Come on, Damien. *Supervillaining.* We've got our *Vs*, right?"

Right. "Am I seriously going to pass up the chance to wrea—" I was about to say "wreak havoc around town with you," but perhaps that's not the thing to say in a house full of superheroes, on the very eve of Superhero Day. "I'll be there. With wedding bells on."

"Damien!"

"What? You know you want to *marry me*."

She makes a choking sound, then starts sputtering. "I … That … Err! I can't believe you."

"Katherine Locke. It has a nice ring to it."

The doorbell goes off again, and I dip one of Amelia's chips in the punch bowl as she and her friend come barreling down the stairs. I put it in my mouth like it's the most sumptuous food I've ever eaten.

"Oh, my God," they mutter, making disgusted faces.

"Mmmmm," I moan.

"What's that?" Kat says.

"Nothing, just thinking of you on our wedding night."

The girls—there are four of them now—roll their eyes at me as they giggle past. I think I'm winning them over.

"Damien, I *want* that ring. You'll be there Friday, right?"

"Of course. Wouldn't miss it."

X·X·X

Sarah clings to my arm as we walk up the hill toward Lovers' Peak Friday afternoon, leaning her head on my shoulder. She rubs her thumb against my palm and sighs.

"Dad's coming home from the hospital tomorrow," she says. "He's taking me out for pizza, once he's feeling better. He said I could invite somebody, so I was thinking …" She lets go of me, pulling away. She sucks in her breath and stares at the ground and doesn't ask me to come with them. That would be against the rules.

Lovers' Peak is where all the cool, promiscuous teenagers go to get drunk, feel each other up, and make unwanted babies. The ones with cars park at the cliff side, and the ones without them do it in the woods or hide out in the abandoned cabin.

It's the perfect place for a Superhero Day make-out session with my not-girlfriend—dog and Crimson Flash free. We're wearing party hats, the conical cardboard kind with the elastic string you strap onto your head. I'm dressed all in vertical stripes, and Sarah's going all plaid. Most kids bring beer, but I brought sugar-free sodas—for that extra level of ridiculousness—that I planned to chug and then scream, "Woooh!" at the top of my lungs to annoy all the people supposedly cooler than me, but, alas, there's nobody here to witness it.

That's because I had to rearrange our plans. I was planning on bringing her here *tonight*, when there'd be more of an audience, but I promised Kat I'd be there for her.

"You know," Sarah says, "this violates rule number twenty-nine, no love on a ledge. That was your rule, you know, but I forgive you." She smiles at me.

"It doesn't violate it," I say, setting the sodas down and adjusting the elastic of my party hat, "because we're not going anywhere near that cliff."

We aren't going to even look at it or acknowledge its presence, as far as I'm concerned.

Sarah raises her eyebrows at me as if to say, *Oh, yeah?* She strides over to the edge to spite me and holds her arms out at her sides, taking in a deep breath. She looks

229

like a giant bird about to take flight. "Wow. You can see everything from here."

I can't watch. I turn away, surveying the cabin instead. People call it a cabin, but it's more of a shack. A dirty, filthy shack that I wouldn't want to take a black light to, if you know what I mean. The windows are broken and beer bottles spill out of the open door, like the building itself has had too much and is puking them out.

I peek behind me and flinch. Sarah's still on the ledge. I tell her to come back, and she leaps toward me, going, "Yes, sir!" She throws her arms around me, then gets uncomfortable about it and lets go.

Maybe because it was obvious she meant it, like I'm more to her than a lab partner. Or maybe it's because I didn't hug her back. Because "being more than a lab partner" makes me think of Kat, and then I feel guilty.

"Damien," Sarah says, poking at a rock with her foot, "I'm really glad you came with me the other night. Even if we didn't get Dad back right then, I'm glad I trusted you, and I'm … I had fun. *With you.*"

I swallow and don't look at her. "I don't know—I could have done without the crazy zombies."

We're silent for a minute, standing around and not touching each other. Finally Sarah asks, "Damien, is something wrong?"

I make an effort to smile. I put my arms around her. "Nothing."

I can tell she doesn't believe me, but she leans into me, resting her head against my chest, and breathes in deep. She turns her face up to kiss me.

Katherine Locke.

I break apart from Sarah, pretending I didn't notice her attempt to press her lips against mine. I was joking when I said that, about me and Kat getting married. Totally not serious. It was supposed to torture her, not me. So why can't I stop thinking about it?

Kat wasn't joking when she said she was sorry for kissing that guy. We weren't together, she didn't have to apologize, but she did.

"Actually," I say, taking my party hat off, "I think ... I think I should go home. I can't concentrate."

Sarah's mouth wilts into a frown. She observes all the garbage on the ground, all the cans and bottles and ... other things. She kicks a used condom toward the ledge. "Will you come with us? To the pizza place? You don't even have to say you're my lab partner, just my friend, or my ..." She marches over to me and looks me in the eyes. "I've been thinking. Maybe it wouldn't be so bad to have a boyfriend."

That's not what I bargained for. But so what? I wanted a new relationship, one not so complicated and painful as mine and Kat's, and I got what I wanted. Would it really be so bad, going to eat pizza with Sarah and her dad and having her introduce me as her significant other? No. It'd be okay, I guess. It's not like I have anything better to do. Though I'm not crazy about watching more Crimson Flash episodes—her *favorite* show—with her shushing me every time I start laughing. And Heraldo might like me, but I don't like his giant nose in my crotch or his hot, nasty breath in my face. He wasn't part of the deal when Sarah and I started all this.

But seriously, what else am I going to do this weekend? Sit at home and watch *Wheel of Fortune* with Amelia? "Of course I'll go with you," I say, squeezing Sarah's hand. "We still on for tonight?"

She kisses me and grins. "I'll bring my costume."

I smile back at her. "We're going to be unstoppable. The bad guys won't know what hit them."

The bad guys, of course, being me and Kat.

I told Sarah I had a hot tip about some villains who are going to rob an antique store downtown, and stopping them is a perfect opportunity for us to begin establishing ourselves. For the record, just because I'm going out superheroing tonight, on Superhero Day, it doesn't make me a superhero. I don't even *want* to go, even though it was my idea. I just happen to know that Helen's store is getting robbed tonight, by me and Kat, and maybe I don't want us to succeed. Helen could have hated me for being her husband's supervillain love child, but she didn't. And that ring is all she has left that makes her life worthwhile —er, well, and her family, I guess—and it might rightfully be Kat's, but ... Maybe I don't want Kat getting over me. So I'm playing both teams, just for tonight. It's a foolproof plan.

Sarah waves good-bye to me and wanders over to the cliff. She kicks the condom the rest of the way over the edge and watches it go down.

I hate leaving her there, where she could fall to her doom, but everyone's always assuring me they're not going to fall, like I'm being so ridiculous. I set off down the hill, leaving the sugar-free sodas for the next visitors of Lovers' Peak to chug and enjoy. I'm not even twenty feet down when I hear a bloodcurdling scream.

Crap. My heart leaps into my throat, pounding like *I'm* the one who fell off the cliff. I turn and run back the way I came. A guy wearing all black, including the ski mask on his face, shoves into me, knocking me to the ground. He keeps running. I get the feeling I should chase after him, but I have to save Sarah first.

"Damien!" Sarah's voice is shrill and sharp with fear.

I make it up to the top of the hill. My heart slips out of my throat and weighs heavy in my chest like a stone. My legs and arms tremble as I creep toward the ledge. I see Sarah's fingers, clamped to the rocky edge of the cliff for dear life. They're turning white and shaking with the strain. I see her slipping.

"Sarah! I'm coming!" I catch sight of the oh-so-wonderful view from up here and feel dizzy. I sink to my knees and crawl toward her. I see one set of fingers slip all the way, then scramble to grab the edge again.

"Damien!" Her voice is full of tears and panic. She doesn't sound like Sarah at all.

I can do this. I can fly. What did Gordon say about having control? I *can't* fall. My mind buys into it, but my body says no way, almost paralyzed with fear. Memories of falling off the tallest building in Golden City flash through my head. I can hardly breathe when I finally reach out and grab Sarah's hand. Mine are sweating. My pulse races so fast, I can barely see.

I take Sarah's other hand and pull. We work together,

and she's almost safely over the edge when she slips out of my grasp. Sarah tumbles backward, and I picture her falling really far and not getting up again. I lunge toward her before I have time to think about it. I throw my arms around her and haul her to safety.

Sarah clings to me, even after it's over. Her glasses are gone, lost over the edge. I can see her breathing hard and trying not to cry as she takes her party hat off and throws it on the ground.

I pet her poofy hair. I hold her close to me, and we cling to each other for a while, shaking and not saying anything.

Then my strength and resolve give out, and I lie flat on my back in the dirt, still trying to catch my breath. The ground reeks of stale alcohol. It's almost a welcome scent; it's familiar and it means we're not dead. Sarah lays her head on my chest and listens to my heart beating. Her hands find places to hold on to me, her fingers hooking into the belt loops on my jeans.

If somebody walked up here right now and saw us, two hot and sweaty teenagers clinging to each other on the ground, they might get the wrong idea about what just happened.

"There was a guy," Sarah says, her voice shaking. "He ..."

"He pushed you?"

"No. He tried to grab me. He pulled my arm and said I was coming with him. But then I fell, and when I screamed, he panicked and ran off."

I'm too freaked out to think about what that means. I

234

look around, but I don't see anybody. "We're safe," I say, but I can't make my heartbeat slow down or my mind stop racing.

CHAPTER 14

In tonight's scheme, I will be playing the parts of both the Midnight Marvel—the supervillain partner to the lovely Shapeshifter—*and*, simultaneously, that of Renegade X, the super cool superhero, looked up to by his brilliant sidekick, the Cosine Kid.

There are several factors that are going to make this possible. I'm wearing plain black spandex, but I've got the holographic projector Sarah used to change her T-shirt and her facial features. She doesn't know I borrowed it. All I have to do is press the button, and a big silver *X* appears on my chest and a mask appears on my face. If I press it again, the *X* changes into two *Ms*—I didn't have time to come up with anything other than the Midnight Marvel— and my mask changes into my insect goggles.

I've also got a utility belt that Sarah gave me to go with my costume. It hides the holographic projector belt quite nicely, and I can also use it to hold my gun or stash my goggles in one of the pouches.

This is going to work. Even though Helen's shop is small, it's got a lot of stuff piled up in it, and it'll be really dark in there. This would be so much easier if I had Kat's power, but really all I have to do is go, "What's that over there? I'm going to check it out, you stay here!" and run behind the junk, press a button, and voilà! I'm a new man.

Kat wants to be there at midnight. I told Sarah to meet me at the same time, in front of the bookstore down the street, so we can get organized before alerting the bad guys to our presence. It's cold out tonight, but I'm sweating as Kat and I make our way to the store. We keep to the shadows, avoiding streetlights and being really sneaky-like. I've already got the projector on, making me look like the Midnight Marvel.

Kat peeks out from behind a building to see if it's safe, and I hum "Here Comes the Bride."

"Damien!" she whispers, her cheeks going red. "Will you quit that?"

"I'd look hot in a tux, don't you think?"

"Listen, about the other night ..." She touches her fingertips together and looks away.

"Yes?" In my mind, this is where she leaps into my arms and screams, "Marry me, *please*!" and I kiss her and pull out two fake IDs and a couple plane tickets to Vegas. In reality, I feel really embarrassed for fantasizing that, and my face gets hot. Not only have I self-proclaimed Kat off-limits, but I'm involved in a series of very important experiments with Sarah. I fidget with my utility belt and lick my lips, my mouth suddenly dry. "Let's not talk about it."

"That's what I was going to say." She breathes a sigh of relief. "So you can quit teasing me. I wasn't myself."

"We're too young, anyway," I mutter.

We're quiet until we get to the store. Then Kat stands in front of the door and grins at me. "Tonight," she says, "we're real supervillains."

"Just call me Midnight."

The projector device around my waist makes a *zap* noise. I glance down just in time to see the *M*s on my chest blink back into existence.

"Whoa." Kat blinks and stares at my face. "Did your goggles just ... *flicker*?"

"That's crazy." Okay, so Sarah's invention isn't perfect, but it's all I've got. "You're imagining things, Kat. It was the streetlight that flickered."

Kat shrugs and moves to pick the lock. With her finger. She doesn't need tools.

I thought about stealing a copy of the key, in case we had to do any damage to break in—and because Kat shapeshifting her finger into a lockpick always creeps me out—but I didn't want her to get suspicious.

She opens the door and I put a hand out to stop her. I point to the doorway. "Hidden lasers," I whisper. "I did a little research earlier today. It was hard work, but I scoped out the security system for you."

Kat laughs. "Sweet-talked the owner, I bet."

I pretend to step over the invisible lasers and Kat follows me in. "I'm going to find a way to turn them off, so we can make a quick getaway. You go on ahead. And be careful. There's so much junk in here, it's an avalanche waiting to happen."

Kat gives me a thumbs-up and moves on inside the store.

As soon as her back is turned, I slip outside and hit the holographic-projector button around my middle. It hums a little as my torso fades back to black, then to displaying a big silver *X*. I can't see my face to know for sure, but I tested it enough times in the mirror to know that my goggles have changed into a mask. I take off down the street to meet Sarah at the bookstore.

"You're a little late," she says. "It's almost a quarter after midnight."

"I had trouble sneaking out. I'm here now." I did have to sneak out to do this. Gordon doesn't want me out past ten on the weekend, and even though he approves of superheroing in general, I get the feeling this mission doesn't fall into any acceptable categories.

Sarah and I rush over to the shop. "Looks like they're already here," I whisper, pointing to the open door.

Sarah nods. "Get your gun out," she says. "In case we have to immobilize the bad guys."

Uh … right. I haven't learned how to program it, and Sarah hasn't fiddled with it since she wanted me to shoot to kill. Don't think I'll be using it on Kat, thanks. I slip it out of my belt anyway. "Good thinking, Cosine. And don't forget to call me Renegade"—*because it's the coolest name ever*—"so the bad guys don't find out who we are."

We go in. I hold out my gun, with no intentions of firing. I don't see Kat anywhere. Light from the street filters in through the windows, leaving creepy, glowing streaks on the floor. I sneak down one of the aisles with Sarah a few feet behind me, my skin crawling. The projector around my waist makes a crackling noise, and when I glance down at my chest there's no *X*, just black. Crap. I smack the side of the projector device and my *X* flickers back to life. It must have only been out for a second, or Sarah would have noticed.

There's a noise to the left.

"Stop right there!" Sarah shouts.

I point my weapon at the sound. And then a whole shelf of superhero knickknacks topples down on us. We roll out of the way. "I'll get them," I say, and leap over the pile of crap before Sarah can argue with me. I skid around the corner and press the button to change clothes. I pause long enough to stuff my gun into the pouch. It doesn't quite fit, but I manage to close the flap over it anyway, with part of it sticking out one side.

I take off down the aisle, looking for Kat.

"*Psst*, Damien." She steps out from behind Dr. Doomsworth's recliner.

"I told you, call me Midnight," I whisper. "I don't want these superhero freaks knowing my name."

"Hey, did you see that guy?" Kat says, leading me toward the end of the aisle. "There's something familiar about him. I can't place it … I just feel like I know him."

"Come on, Shapeshifter. Since when do *we* know any superheroes?"

"Yeah, I guess you're right."

We creep through all the junk, keeping an eye out for

the "good guys" as we turn around the corner of the *L* shape. I'm wondering how I'm going to get away again when Sarah jumps out in front of us and shouts, "Don't move another muscle!"

I throw down some flash powder while Kat heaves the Masked Marauder's favorite beanbag chair on top of Sarah. We take off in opposite directions. I speed around the corner, pressing the hologram button. I loop around the entire store, leaping over the avalanche again, and catch up with my sidekick.

"They got away from me!" I pant, helping push the beanbag chair off of Sarah.

"X!" Sarah says, crawling out from underneath it. "Where's your firepower?"

"It's *Renegade*. Don't call me *X*." I pat my gun pouch. "It's right here."

Sarah narrows her eyes at me. "That's a stupid place for it. What if you need to shoot them?"

"Good point." I *might* want to horribly maim somebody for breaking and entering. Nothing wrong with that.

I speed up ahead of Sarah, trying to catch up with Kat. I make it around the *L* shape of the store, turning the corner to find the ring still in its display case. There's no one else here. Then there's a crash behind me. I turn around, and that's when Kat jumps.

She knocks me to the floor. I wriggle away from her and scramble to my feet, pulling out my weapon. I point it at her and we're both very still, not moving.

Kat fakes to the left. Maybe it's because my weapon looks homemade, or maybe she can tell by my body language that I'm not going to fire on her. She moves to the right, sidestepping the gun. I think she's going for the ring, even though the security's still on, but then I hear the projector make another *zap* noise and Kat gasps.

She stares at me, her eyes wide, and I don't have to look down to guess that she's seen through my disguise.

"Oh, my God," Kat whispers. "Dam—"

I panic. I do the first thing that comes to mind. I drop the gun and pull Kat against me, my mouth on hers. I meant for it to be quick, to stop her from saying my name, but then my tongue is in her mouth and everything feels warm and *right* and I forget where I am. And it doesn't hurt that she kisses back.

And then Sarah says, "Renegade?"

I reach out and slap my hand against the glass case. The alarms blare and I see Kat's face twisted in confusion. Then she's gone and the camera flashes and I'm seeing spots. The panel on the side of the ring display opens up and sprays out villain-deterring mist.

Sarah picks up the gun. Her nostrils flare in and out. "What was that?"

"I had to stop her." I yawn and turn away from her, waving my arm as I talk, trying too hard to look casual. "It worked, didn't it?"

Sarah crinkles her eyebrows. She shoves the gun at me, handle first. "Here. I guess you dropped this."

"I *had* to do something. I panicked." It's true.

"I suppose that's how you'd stop any old supervillain, right?" Sarah walks ahead of me, her footsteps heavy. Never has there been a sidekick so unhappy to have stopped the bad guys. Especially on Superhero Day.

I catch up to her right outside the store. The fresh air helps clear my head. "I, um … I might. You never know with me."

Sarah stomps her foot and glares. "You were the one who said no messing around with anybody else!"

"This doesn't count. It wasn't messing around—it was work." My voice is quiet. I feel like an idiot. I try to take Sarah's hand—I don't know why, to make myself feel better, I guess—and she jerks it away before I can touch it. "You're not jealous, are you?" I ask her.

"You made a rule. You have to honor that."

"Yeah, and what about you? You said this couldn't be more than a professional relationship, but that's not how you've been acting. Look, I panicked, okay? I had to distract her. It was nothing." I almost sound like I believe it.

"Nothing," Sarah repeats. "It didn't look like nothing." But she slips her hand into mine as she says it.

Guilt sinks into my chest until I feel like I'm on fire. I'm the worst not-boyfriend and supposed superhero on the face of the planet. And to top it off, I made a pretty lousy supervillain.

X·X·X

I make it all the way until the next morning before I take my phone out, start to call Kat, then flip the phone closed instead. I sigh. On the one hand, it hurts to be with her. On the other? Judging from how much I've been thinking about us since last night, it hurts a lot more to be *without* her.

I flop down on the couch. Alex is sitting on the floor, two inches from the TV, giggling at Saturday-morning cartoons. I try to pay attention to them. It doesn't work.

I take my phone out and stare at it. I should call Kat. She's probably up, right? I mean, I'm up. Alex is up, Amelia is up—it's perfectly normal to be awake at nine a.m. on a Saturday, even when you stayed up late the night before. Kat's probably sitting by her phone, waiting for me to call. Maybe she couldn't sleep because she was thinking about me. Like I was about her.

She probably hasn't called because she thinks *I'll* be asleep. I should call her.

Or she's pissed at me and never wants to talk to me again.

If she never wanted to talk to me again, she shouldn't have kissed back.

It doesn't matter, because I can't call Kat. Because Sarah and I have an agreement, and calling Kat means the kiss *wasn't* nothing.

I sigh, again, and put the phone away.

Amelia plops Jessica down in front of the TV and tells Alex not to sit so close. He doesn't listen to her, and Jessica immediately gets up and runs over to me. "Boy!" she says, poking me in the cheek, her whole face lighting up.

Aha. I gear up my phone so that it's on Kat's number. All Jessica has to do is press call. "Here, look at this!" I point to the call button. "Isn't it pretty?"

Yes! Jessica's outstretched finger moves slowly toward the phone. *Oh, oops, Kat, I didn't mean to call you. A two-year-old stole my phone and pushed some buttons! Crazy, huh? But since I've got you on the line, how about that kiss last night?* Jessica's almost there. I'm about to push the phone a little closer to help her out when Amelia yanks it from my hand.

"Why don't you call her and stop *moping*?"

"Give me that!" I make a grab for it, but Amelia anticipates my move and steps out of reach.

Amelia smirks at me and waves the phone around. "Is it your *girlfriend*?"

"I do not *mope*. And no, it's not. So give it back." I scramble to my feet.

Amelia sings, "Damien's in lo-*ove*," and makes a run for the kitchen.

I chase after her. This must be exciting stuff, because Alex actually tears himself away from the TV to watch.

I corner Amelia next to the fridge. She's wider than me, but I think I can take her. She pushes the call button on the phone. I lunge for it, but she elbows me in the collarbone. Which actually really hurts. A lot. "It's ringing," she says.

Oh, God. I rub my forehead with the palms of my hands. They're sweating. "Amelia, give me that. Right now." I tackle her and tickle her ribs.

It nearly works. Amelia's almost cackling too hard to answer the phone. "Hello," she says, in between bursts of laughter, "will you *puhlease* talk to my stupid brother, so he'll stop pining over you?"

"I'm not pining!" I reach for the phone. Amelia twists away again.

"He's so *in love.*"

"Agh!" I scream at her. I tear the phone out of her hands just as the front door opens. Gordon and Helen storm into the kitchen. Helen's in tears, and if Gordon didn't look so angry, I'd ask them who died.

"Everybody go to your rooms, *now!*" Gordon shouts. He shakes his head and points at me. He's so mad, he can hardly talk. "And *you …*" He can't even finish his sentence. He takes a deep breath and closes his eyes. "In the living room."

I flip my phone shut without saying good-bye.

X·X·X

I feel sick. I'd give anything for Mom and her laser eyes right now. At least she'd just shoot me and get it over with.

Helen can't look at me. She's crying her eyes out, and every time she glances over at me, she cries harder. She didn't give me any crap for being half supervillain or for being her husband's illegitimate kid. She let me live here and has been nothing but nice. What does she get in return? Me, breaking into her shop to steal an irreplaceable trophy of her glory days, her only reminder of why her sacrificing her superpower was for the greater good. It doesn't matter if that's not quite how it went down—I still hurt her. Guess that's what she gets for trusting a supervillain.

I sink deeper into the couch.

Gordon's holding a security picture of me with my hand on the display case in Helen's shop. "Is this you?!" He can't talk normally anymore, only shout.

I nod.

"So this is you. Dressed like a *supervillain*."

I can see why he would jump to that conclusion, even if you can't see the whole costume. I'm not about to point out that it was in fact my superhero outfit.

Gordon crumples up the picture and hurls it to the floor. "What were you thinking? Is this some weird kind of payback for me going out of my way to teach *you* to fly? Because you're not just hurting *me* with this."

He doesn't need to say Helen's suffering the worst and that she doesn't deserve it—it's already painfully obvious. I wish she'd leave the room.

"Were you trying to prove something?" Gordon goes on. "You hate it here this badly, is that it?"

I open my mouth. A little croak comes out, but no words.

"Damn it, Damien." Gordon seethes and paces in front of me. "I thought you learned something after the fire. I thought I could respect you, that on some level we could see eye to eye. It's a good thing a *superhero* came and stopped you." By saying "superhero" like that he means I'm not one and never will be. That's exactly what I wanted, but it still makes me feel like crap to hear him say it.

"Good thing," I mutter, avoiding eye contact.

"I don't even want to think about what would have

happened otherwise. I can't believe how far you'd go to spite us. I *trusted* you. No wonder your mother was so quick to agree to this arrangement."

"Gordon," Helen warns. She shakes her head, blotting her face with a wad of tissues.

Great. Now she's defending me. I know it's meant to help, but it only makes me feel worse.

He ignores her. "She'd probably had more of you than she could stand."

"Gordon, that's enough!" Helen snaps.

I swallow back a lump in my throat and stare very hard at my knees. It's hard to see their shape through my jeans, so I think about the wrinkles in the fabric instead.

"He's my son, I'm handling this! Damien, go to your—" Gordon realizes I don't have a room. When he can't think of where to put me, I expect him to tell me to pack my bags instead. Well, bag. In the singular. But he doesn't. He holds out his hand. "Phone."

I give it to him. I had to turn it off because Kat tried to call me back, after I hung up on her.

His forehead wrinkles as he tries to think of anything else that matters to me. "No dinner tonight. And no ... no friends over." He pauses, and I know he's wondering if I have any friends. "And I don't think I have to tell you that you're not leaving this house." He looks like he wants to say more, but he storms off into his bedroom and slams the door instead.

Helen comes and sits next to me on the couch. She puts a hand on my shoulder. "He didn't mean that," she says, her voice still thick from crying. "He'll calm down."

I don't deserve her sympathy. I turn away, curling up against the far edge of the couch, and bury my face into the cushions.

CHAPTER 15

I look like some sort of ragamuffin. I believe that's the technical term. I'm sitting on a park bench Sunday afternoon with Kat, devouring a peanut butter and jelly sandwich she brought me. It was easy to sneak out of the house while everyone was at church this morning. Gordon wanted to drag me along as punishment, but Helen convinced him to leave me alone. So I betrayed her trust yet again and ran off. But at least I know it's the last time, because I'm never going back. I've got everything I own, including Mr. Wiggles's remains, in my backpack. At least it's everything I had with me at the Tines house, except for my phone, which is still in Gordon's clutches. I'm shivering because I lost my coat. At least I've got my gloves. I'm wearing the same clothes I wore yesterday because I was too depressed to change them, and now I've got a big blob of grape jelly sliding down the front of my shirt.

I don't know where I'm going. I guess I can always make Mom let me come home early, though if she finds out I ran away, she might send me straight back to Gordon. I wish I could stay at Kat's house. Her mom likes me, and they have a guest room, and it's even on the first floor. Right now, it sounds like paradise.

"So your dad's the *Crimson Flash*?" Kat swings her leg back and forth against the park bench. *"Your mom* and ... and *him*?"

"I know. It's totally crazy." I've known for almost three weeks now, and I hardly believe it.

"So that makes you part superhero?"

"Yeah." I don't think Kat fully realizes what that means for me, that I have an *X* instead of a *V*. She hasn't said anything about it, and I haven't gotten to that part of the explanation yet. "And my stepmom owns the antique shop. And that ring really meant a lot to her."

"Oh, that stupid thing." Kat laughs and waves her hand. "Damien, don't worry about it."

She's taking all of this too well. I'm starting to suspect this is some kind of Kat robot I've been talking to the whole time, while the real Kat is locked up somewhere, wondering why no one notices she's missing.

"Kat, I just told you that my stepmom is the one who defeated your famous grandfather, and I said I'd help you steal his ring from her, then dressed up like a superhero and stopped you."

"If it meant that much to you, you should have said so." She stares off into space, all dreamy-like, and sighs.

I get the feeling she's not listening to a word I'm

saying. I raise my eyebrows at her, then wave my hand in front of her face. "You said you wanted that ring. You said you *needed* it, that it was yours and they were letting it collect dust; you—"

"So maybe I changed my mind." She shrugs. "Maybe I don't need it anymore."

A ring that protects from heartbreak, and Kat doesn't need it anymore. Because I kissed her when I was supposed to be with Sarah. "Listen, there's something else I have to tell you." I stuff the last of my sandwich into my mouth and tug a little on my right glove, cringing already.

"So," Kat says, "I hear you're in love with me."

I choke on the sandwich and cough, spitting out the rest of it. I cough some more until my throat is rough and I'm sure my face is red. "Be kind of hard to live out your dream of *marrying me* if I wasn't. You planning on wearing white, or just a dirty cream color?"

She punches me in the shoulder. "I'll be wearing black, at your funeral, if you don't shut up."

I tickle her—tickling is my new weapon of choice—and she screams and laughs and tries to fight back. And then somehow I have her pinned to the bench. I'm leaning over her, our faces really close. She stops laughing and slips her arms around me. I kiss her and wonder why there's never a bed and a locked door around when you need them.

"Damien," she says.

"Yeah?"

"You're getting jelly on me."

I sit up. We share the same jelly stain across our fronts, like one of those inkblot pictures.

I fidget with my gloves, tugging off the right one, then pulling it back on again. Tug, pull, don't look at Kat. My heart is pounding. I stare at the soggy bits of sandwich I spit on the ground. Finally I work up enough courage to speak. "Kat. I have to show you something."

"Ooh, Damien, not in public."

I look over at her, but I don't smile. The grin drains from her face.

"You know how I got my *V* last month?"

Her cheeks are pale. She nods.

"Well, I didn't."

She wrinkles her nose. "What do you mean? But you … I saw …" She bites her lip, probably realizing she never did see it. She just assumed.

"I told you. My dad's the Crimson Flash."

"So besides making you a lifetime member of the Safety Kids, that means …?"

I slip off my glove and show her my bare right thumb. Even without an ink pad, you can make out the clear shape of an *X*. "It's what happens to people like me, people who are half villain and half hero."

Kat pulls away from me, but I think it's more out of shock than revulsion. "Whoa. I didn't know that was possible."

"I have a chance to fix it. There have been cases, with other kids who got *X*s, and eventually they changed into an *H* or a *V*. It's just going to take me a little longer to get my *V*, that's all. As far as I'm concerned, I'm still one hundred percent supervillain."

She rubs her finger across my thumb. "Oh, my God,

Damien."

"It's okay. I'm getting used to it. Don't cry."

"I'm not." There are tears in her eyes, and she's shaking, but now I see it's because she's *laughing*.

My eyebrows come together in a scowl. "It's not funny."

"I know! It's horrible!" She can hardly breathe, she's laughing that hard. "But of all the people it could happen to … What's your superpower? Can you—" She interrupts herself with a burst of laughter. "Can you *fly*? Just like your dad?"

The blood drains from my face. I put my hands on my knees and stare straight ahead.

"Oh, my God, you *can*. I was totally kidding—I didn't think it was true." She falls against me, shuddering with guffaws and chuckles and whatnot. Then she finally gets ahold of herself, takes a deep breath, and wipes her eyes. "Damien," she says, "that's actually the worst news I've ever heard."

"I can tell."

But she sounds serious when she says, "So, does this mean you're going to have to wait to go to Vilmore? How long?"

I slide my thumb along the slats in the bench. "I don't know. I don't think it disqualifies me, and I'm going to talk to Taylor." Who mistakenly thinks I'm not Vilmore material, even without knowing about my less than sparkling parentage.

"We were supposed to go at the same time. Become real villains together." Kat rests her chin in her hands.

"Damien, we've got to do something big. We've got to be villains for real, so Taylor lets you in. We *both* have to go to Vilmore. It'll seem like we're so far away if we don't."

"Aren't you listening to me? I'm still going. The dean is marrying my mom—he'll let me in. I just have to talk to him."

"What if you *don't* get in? What if your *X* decides to become an *H*? I can't … with a hero … My dad would disown me, Damien!"

"It doesn't work like that—it's not just going to become an *H*. I can do stuff to influence it. It's based on my actions, not on who my parents are."

"What am I supposed to tell people next year when you visit me at school? This is my boyfriend Damien. He's a superhero. Don't beat him up, okay?"

"Kat, aren't you listening?! I'm still going to Vilmore. I said I'd be there, and you don't have to tell them anything, because I'm *not* a superhero! I don't care what anybody thinks!" I stand up, throwing my arms up and letting them fall back to my sides with a *thwack*. "I'm a supervillain! I was raised by a supervillain, I *think* like a supervillain, and I'm never signing any damn League Treaty! I do things my way."

"You certainly acted like a superhero the other night."

"Yeah, well, I had to, didn't I?"

"You have a *sidekick*."

"I don't! It—it doesn't matter, because I'm through with it! I tried living with my dad and his superhero family, and it didn't work out. I find out I'm half hero for my birthday, and suddenly everyone expects me to be some kind of saint. Maybe they should judge who I am based on my actions and not on some stupid genetic nonsense!"

"Damien, you can *fly*! Even if you get your *V*, you might as well wear a big sign that says I heart superheroes the rest of your life!"

"Who, me? I can barely get up the stairs! I'm never leaving the ground if I can help it!"

"What if you are a hero? I'm a villain—how are we supposed to be together?"

I kneel in front of her, my knees getting wet in the grass. I take her hands. "Kat, listen to me. Tell the kids at school to just try and mess with me. I'll show them what a real villain can do. It doesn't matter what anybody thinks, or if you've got your *V* and I've got my *X*, and it doesn't matter what my *X* turns into, as far as we're concerned. Because I've realized something. No matter how crazy things have been between us, no matter how much we've hurt each other, I still care about you—more than anything—and that's not going to change. I think you feel the same way, and it doesn't matter what our thumbs say, Kat, because I—"

Cold water splashes on my head. It trickles down my back and soaks through my shirt. Then a giant dog licks my face.

Sarah is standing behind me. With an empty water bottle. She says, "Come on, Heraldo. I thought I saw someone I knew, but I guess I was *wrong*." She tugs on his leash, turning and walking very quickly away from me.

I hurry after her, with one last glance at Kat on the park bench. "Sarah, wait. I can explain!"

She shoves me away with both hands. "It didn't mean anything? You're such a jerk! I can't believe I liked—I can't believe I ever wanted to be your sidekick! I guess it's a good thing I'm *not*, or else I'd resign!"

"Sarah, I didn't mean—"

"If you liked her more than me, you should have said so!"

My gaze falls guiltily to the ground.

"You don't want to be a superhero? Good, because you're not, Damien Locke! You're right, people should be judged on their actions, not their genes, because I can think of a ton of people more heroic than *you*. And they don't have a famous superhero for a father, and they can't even fly! And if all it takes to be a supervillain is lying and cheating to get what you want, no matter who it hurts, then I guess you're set! *For life.*"

"Sarah, it's not like that!" I move toward her, but Heraldo growls at me.

"Good boy," Sarah says, rubbing his ears. "And as for you, *Damien*"—she says my name like it's a swear word—"I don't ever want to talk to you again."

She storms off, and I actually stand there and watch her go. She's probably too mad to listen to me right now anyway. Not that she doesn't have a right to be mad, after how awful I've been. I'll call her later and sort things out. I mean about the whole romance thing. I don't know what I'm going to tell her about being my sidekick.

Kat comes up and dumps my backpack in my arms. "I've got to get back home," she says. "For dinner. I'd invite you, but my grandparents are coming over. Mom always freaks out when they're around, you know, so ..."

"No, it's okay. Don't worry about it."

"We'll talk later and figure out how to get you into Vilmore." She moves to hug me, then realizes I'm sopping wet. She hesitates and does it anyway. We embrace, holding on to each other too tightly, like it might never happen again. I whisper in her ear. "Let's dress like pirates for the wedding."

"Aw, but you were right—you'd look hot in a tux."

"Swords, Kat. I'm talking about getting to have *swords*. And a parrot who's also a sea captain to read us our vows."

"Let's tell everyone else it's a Renaissance theme and to dress accordingly."

"Better yet, we tell my side it's a fifties-diner theme, yours that it's World War One, *not* Two. Anyone who shows up without a costume gets the Renaissance garb we'll have on hand."

"Sounds like a plan," Kat says. We high-five each other.

I wave at her as she walks off to her warm house and warm food and cranky relatives. I don't look forward to deciding what to do with myself next.

And then I don't have to, because a dog licks my hand. I look down to see Heraldo dragging his leash, with Sarah nowhere in sight.

X·X·X

It's dark by the time Heraldo and I get to Mom's. My arms are sore from dragging a giant dog through the city. Every time he sees something interesting, he pulls me along after him. I don't know how Sarah does it. I also forgot my glove in the park—I think my right hand has leash burns.

"Mom!" I call as I get through the door. I set my stuff on the couch, take off my other glove, and let Heraldo loose. He takes off into the kitchen. I hear a deep bark and then Mom screams. She pokes her head into the room and seems relieved to see it's me. She's on the phone. She holds her hand over it and says, "Damien, what are you doing here? And more importantly, what is this *beast*?"

"I'm dogsitting."

She holds up a finger, signaling me to hold on. "You've got her this time? Oh, excellent. No, everything's ready on this side. Don't hold back—get results, honeybuns. Whatever it takes—keep me informed." She pauses, her eyes darting toward me. "He's here, actually. I'll make sure, don't worry." She hangs up. "Taylor says hello."

I'm sure he does. "Things didn't work out at Gordon's."

She flinches when I say his name. Heraldo jumps on her, knocking her back a step, and she pushes him away. "Damien, please keep that *thing* under control. I've got important work going on."

"For honeybuns?"

She fixes her hair. "As a matter of fact, yes. I have a surprise for you. You know Taylor and I have been doing some work together?"

"Is that what you call it?"

Mom clasps her hands together and beams at me. "Taylor's actually quite brilliant. He's worthy of more than being 'dean' of some school."

"Of *Vilmore*." I pet Heraldo, and his tail thumps really hard against my leg. "What's wrong with that?"

Mom tilts her head, her expression pitying. "You used to be so ambitious before you got that *X*." She puts her hands on my face, pinching my cheeks. Then she pats me on the head. "I shouldn't have let that *man* take you—"

"My *father*, you mean?"

She sighs. "People like me and Taylor, we've got untapped potential. And we're not getting any younger."

"He's the dean of *Vilmore*. Some people would kill to get there. It's ... Stop looking at me like that, Mom."

"You've got your whole life ahead of you. You can't understand. All right, Vilmore is a prestigious school, churning out many fine young supervillains who'll go on to do famous things. But that's just it. How many of those kids dream of sitting in an office at that same school? It doesn't make the history books."

"And what's so horrible about *your* life?" I slump down in the armchair and pick at a string hanging off it.

"Well," she says, very matter-of-factly, "I did have you at a rather young age."

"So? You were twenty-two, that's—"

"It's hard to build a name for yourself while having to put so much time into someone else. I think I did a pretty good job, considering, and I love you very much, you know. I wouldn't change a thing. But ... you're growing up now, and—"

"And it's so convenient that you have someone else to pawn me off on."

"—if I'm going to give my career an extra boost, now's

the time." Mom sits on the edge of the couch. She smells like chemicals from her lab. Sulfur and ammonia. It's good to be home, even if it feels really empty after being at the Tines house. Mom's whole face lights up, and I have to admit I haven't seen her this happy in years. "By this time tomorrow, we'll—Damien, where's your coat? It's cold out."

"Lost it. Guess I'm not as ready to take care of myself as you think." Heraldo suddenly leaps on me, his front paws punching me in the stomach. He slurps my face. "Get down! Boy ..." I add lamely, pointing at the floor. He doesn't listen.

"Anyway," Mom goes on, rubbing her hands together, "tonight, everything changes. Tomorrow, we'll be king and queen of this city—"

"Who? Us?" It's hard to listen with Heraldo's hot breath in my face. I fend him off with both hands as he licks my hair. I make the mistake of turning my head right as he barks, and then my ear is ringing.

"Taylor and I. And you'll be my little prince. Isn't that wonderful?"

"You're taking over the city? *Tonight?*" Did she call me little? I'm sixteen and taller than her.

"I've been bursting to tell you, but you've had so many changes in your life lately, I didn't have the heart to get your hopes up, in case it didn't happen." She slaps a hand to her chest and breathes out. "It's such a relief to share this with you! It's so exciting, I can hardly stand it. Think of it, Damien. We can do whatever we want, have whatever we want. You name it."

"Oh, so if this works out, you and Taylor won't get married? Because that's what I want."

Mom's selective hearing must be acting up again, because she acts like I didn't say anything. By "whatever I want," she must have meant the opposite. "That Sarah Kink girl's the key to making all our dreams come true. You were right, Damien—the hypno device wasn't Dr. Kink's invention after all. It turns out it was his daughter's. Now that we've got her in custody, our plans are going to go very smoothly."

Custody. Mom and Taylor nabbed Sarah and have her in "custody." Just like they had her dad. My insides go cold and it takes effort to keep from shaking. But if I have any hope of saving Sarah, it all depends on Mom and Taylor not finding out I care about her.

I force myself out of the chair and follow Mom as she dances into the kitchen, she's so happy about whatever's happening tonight. Something that involves kidnapping my sidekick. "Your plans?"

"You picked a good time to come back. I have to give you something. I tried to call you, but you had your phone off."

The counters are covered in chemistry beakers, and there are stacks of filthy pots and pans piled on the stove. Papers with what look like recipes and math are tacked to the cupboards. Intermingled between all the science-lab equipment are open boxes of Chinese food with dry noodles and chopsticks hanging out of them. There are stains on the floor, too, especially near the stove and the sink, where Mom must have spilled her concoctions and never cleaned them up. "Mom, did something happen to your lab?"

"What? Oh no, sweetie. With you gone, I got a little carried away."

"*Lazy* is the word I think you're looking for."

"Well, that, too. Ah, here it is." She grabs a small vial full of green liquid off the microwave. She holds it out to me. "I want you to take this as soon as possible. This will protect you."

I stare at it. "From what?"

"The hypno toxin I invented. Taylor and I are about to pump it through the sewer system. On its own, it doesn't do much, but when combined with Miss Kink's device, anyone who breathes it in will be susceptible to mind control. Oh, I shouldn't say *anyone*. Anyone who's not a supervillain. Once we've spread my toxin, all we have to do is speak into the device and set the trigger word. We're going to broadcast it across the city. Once the trigger word is set, anyone affected by the toxin who hears the word spoken through this device will be helpless, forced to obey my—our—command. But it's the superheroes I'm really interested in, not the nobodies. By morning, if all goes well, every superhero in Golden City will be like brainless robots, ready to do our bidding."

"I think the term is *zombie*."

"Don't be silly, sweetie. Zombies are undead and they eat brains. It's very different. We're not *monsters*." She laughs.

"And you think I might be affected by your … work."

She shrugs and tries to smile. "Well, you are half … you

know."

"Superhero."

"Anyone who's not a supervillain who breathes in the toxin I made will become susceptible when they hear my voice through the hypno device. I don't know how the toxin will affect you, but I don't want to take any chances. So you take this antidote, okay? *Promise me.*"

"Yeah, okay. Whatever." I put the vial to my mouth like I'm going to drink it, but when Mom turns her back to mess with something by the stove, I stick it in my pocket. *"Yuck.* You didn't tell me how bad it was going to taste."

Mom smiles. "We all have to make sacrifices, Damien. An unpleasant taste is a small price to pay for staying safe tonight. It's going to be worth it. With all the superheroes in the city under our command, rising to the top will be a cinch." She snaps her fingers. "The other supervillains will have to acknowledge our power. How's that for going down in the history books? First Golden City, and then who knows? With that much superpower under our command, we could expand. And someday you'll inherit everything. How's Kat going to like being an *empress*?" She winks at me.

Okay. That's a lot to offer a girl, I have to admit. "Kat likes me how I am. She doesn't need a whole city."

"So you are back with her?" Mom raises her eyebrows.

She's totally prying, but I don't care. "Yeah. I am." It feels good. After all the ups and downs over the past year, I finally know where I stand with her, and I can't say it's a bad place to be. More the opposite. "We're getting married. You should come. Wear a poodle skirt and roller skates."

"Oh, I'm glad," Mom says, and I don't know if she heard me, or if she thought I was joking about her wearing the roller skates. "And once we've taken over the city, you'll never have to see that man again. You can come home for good."

Come home? Never have to get yelled at by Gordon again? I'd have my own room—I could have my own *palace*. A one-story palace, of course, but it'd still be huge. Just let Gordon try and push me off a building again. No more trying to turn me into a superhero or letting villains burn in a fire just because they're going to grow up to have *V*s.

I picture Gordon and the rest of the fam as mindless zombie slaves, glassy-eyed, bowing to my every whim. Making me sandwiches and telling me how much they love supervillains. Especially me. Maybe I'll even let them live in my house, to keep them safe from Mom. She might get carried away and do something really awful to Gordon.

Something really awful like turn him into my slave? With no freewill at all?

Okay, that's pretty bad. My lungs feel heavy, and guilt prickles up and down my spine. Gordon rescued me from a fire. After I stupidly ran in there when he told me not to. He wasn't willing to go in for just anybody like I'd thought he'd be—he almost died specifically saving *me*. His intentions of turning me into a superhero, just like him, were totally misguided, but he was trying to help. It's not his fault he's an idiot.

And this new world of Mom's, with her and honeybuns at the top? Yeah, parts of it sound cool, like me and Kat having our own palace. But the rest of it sounds pretty awful. Who are we going to make fun if there are no heroes around? And, I don't know, before Gordon freaked out because he thought I robbed Helen's store, things were starting to go okay. I never had a problem being an only child before, but now that it turns out I'm not, it's not so bad. I kind of *like* my siblings. Even, dare I say it, Amelia, without whom Kat would not know that I might be in love with her and want to have her babies. Or something like that.

Another flaw with Mom's plan: you'd have to tell the zombies to feed and wash themselves, too. And breed. Otherwise this little empire isn't going to last. Or expand. There's an untapped industry: zombie-slave superhero porn.

I catch myself making a disgusted face, then quickly replace it with a grin. "Gee, Mom, it all sounds so wonderful. I can't wait."

She hugs me. "I know. I'm so excited."

"Are they going to torture that girl? Sarah something? To get her to fix the hypno device?" Not if I have anything to say about it, they're not.

"If they have to. I told Taylor not to hold back."

Crap. "Can I go help? *Pleeease?*" Hopefully I'll get there in time before they do something awful to my sidekick. I don't know how Sarah will hold up under torture, but I don't want to find out. I have to get to her before she's scarred for life and before she fixes that device.

"I don't know, Damien. I want you here where I can keep an eye on you. Things might get a little crazy tonight. I don't want you wandering around the city. *Without* a coat, I might add." She shakes her head in exasperation. "Besides, I haven't gotten to see you in a while. I missed you, you know."

"Mom, I hate to break it to you, but Taylor's not as great as you think. I know he's not sure if I'm Vilmore material, and I want a chance to prove him wrong. What could be a better chance than this? Let me go over there, and I'll make that Sarah girl talk. I have ways. And I'm *sixteen*. You don't have to worry about me going out by myself. I can handle it."

"Well, when you put it that way ... I suppose you can go over to Taylor's. You're right, it would be a good opportunity for you to show off your villain potential. Who knows? Maybe you two will bond tonight and you'll be a little more accepting of him joining our family. And you did take the antidote—that should keep you safe tonight." She looks around the kitchen and purses her lips, like she hadn't noticed how messy it was until now. "Pick up something on your way home, will you? Maybe Indian food."

I make a face. "No way."

She hands me twenty bucks. "Sushi."

"Mom."

"Fine. Get whatever you want, dear. And, Damien, change your shirt before you go. You look like a ragamuffin. You're going to be prince of Golden City soon —you need to think about the impression you're making."

CHAPTER 16

"I'm sorry, Damien." Taylor splays his hands in a "you're out of luck" gesture when I get to his house and ask to help them torture Sarah. "You're too late."

I try not to look like my heart just stopped beating. *Too late?*

Taylor shakes his head. "Besides, your mother shouldn't have let you come here. You don't need to get involved." He gives me a stern look, like he doesn't think I can cut it and should go back home.

He picks his way past piles of boxes in the living room and I follow him. Taylor inherited this house when his mother died last year. We helped him move here from his old apartment. It smells like an old lady—like mothballs and antiseptic spray and vanilla candles—and he still hasn't dealt with all her stuff, since he spends most of his time either at Vilmore or at my house.

"You mean I missed out on all the torture?" I say. "Did

you let her go, or could I still get in on it?"

Taylor whips around and accidentally elbows a pile of gardening magazines as tall as I am. The whole stack topples over, crashing into a three-legged table with a vase on it and knocking them both to the floor. He makes an exasperated scoffing sound, like it's all my fault for being here. "Damien, go home. You're not needed."

"But—"

A familiar face appears out of the hallway. A sinister grin slips across Pete's mouth as he takes his place next to Taylor. "Damien," Taylor says, "I think you'll find that I have all the assistance I need. Peter here will show you out. If you gentlemen will excuse me, I have a very important phone call to make." He disappears in the hallway and I hear his footsteps on the stairs.

I make like I'm heading for the door, even if I have no intentions of leaving here without Sarah. "Thanks anyway, Pete, but I can find my own way out."

Pete grabs my arm and twists it behind my back. "Not so fast, Damien. Who's winning now?"

"Oh, I see. Got a taste for me the other night, and now you want more?"

Pete lets me go. His fist comes at me so fast that I don't know what's going on until it's too late. His knuckles collide with my jaw in a burst of pain. The force knocks me back and I stumble into a glass cabinet full of china plates. It rattles and I feel some of the dishes inside it fall and break. Warm blood pours out of my bottom lip.

"Been waiting to do that," Pete says, cracking his knuckles, "for a long time."

"You're just mad because all those pockmarks uglied up your face." I touch my lip and wince. I pull my hand back and stare at my own blood staining my fingers. Nobody's ever hit me before. That's kind of surprising, now that I think about it. "I warned you not to scratch, Pete, just like I warned you not to mess with me."

Pete lunges at me. I step out of the way, but he grabs my shirt and punches me again, and this time it's my left eye and the bridge of my nose that erupt in white-hot pain.

"It was you on the cliff, wasn't it? You almost killed Sarah!"

"You catch on quick." Pete smiles and holds up his fist. "The first one was for the other night," he says. "That one was for being a lousy friend and stealing Kat from me."

I glare at him, even though my eye is throbbing. "You took *her* from *me*. We had a good thing going, and then you—"

"I saw her first!" Pete screams. He grabs me by the collar and shakes me, my head banging against the china cabinet. "You knew I liked her. You knew I was crazy about her, but you took her away from me anyway! I even introduced you." He laughs and shoves me to the floor. "I was an idiot."

"Maybe she just liked me better."

He kicks me in the ribs. Maybe I should learn to keep my mouth shut, but it's hard when Pete keeps spouting off nonsense.

"If she liked you so much," he says, "why did she agree to come to your room with me at your party? *Your* party,

Damien, at your house. Guess you weren't keeping her as satisfied as you thought, 'cause it was *her* idea to do it on your bed."

"Shut up!" I get to my feet, blood rushing to my head. I feel my ears get hot and my whole face feels like it's on fire. My wounds flare up, but I'm too busy thinking about how I'm going to kill Pete to notice. "That's not what happened."

"Not what she *told* you."

"I trust her more than you."

"You think she's going to tell you the truth? She wanted to go all the way, man. If you hadn't walked in on us ..." Pete smirks and shrugs. "Maybe if she hadn't been so into it, she wouldn't have been startled when you opened the door. She wouldn't have changed back to herself, and you wouldn't have ever known. Maybe it wasn't our first time, either—you ever think of that?"

I kick him really hard in the shins and pull my arm back, but Pete's too fast. He ducks before I can make contact. He grabs my arm and wrenches it behind me. I feel him pry my thumb out so he can see it. "So it's true," he says. "Damien Locke's only *half* a villain."

I struggle against him, but he twists my arm until I'm afraid it's going to break.

"Watch it, hypocrite," he says. "You didn't see me not being your friend when you took Kat from me. But the same thing happens to you, and suddenly we're enemies. It was her decision, too, not just mine. And now, get this, you're the son of a freaking *superhero*." He spits on the floor after saying it. He pushes me forward, into the hallway and not toward the front door. I get the feeling he's not "showing me out."

"Kat knows what I am," I say. "She loves me anyway. We're having a pirate wedding and you're not invited. And if you're lucky, I won't send you an invitation."

Pete slams his hand into my back, knocking my breath out of my lungs. "Yeah, she really loves you—that's why she was at my place the other night, begging all the guys to take her into the bedroom."

I kick at Pete, but I miss and he grabs my hair and jerks my head back. He pulls so hard that my eyes water.

"And next year," he says, "it'll be me and her at Vilmore. What do you think's going to happen without you there every day to remind her not to screw other guys?"

"You're dead, Pete. I hope you know that."

He laughs and opens a door. He shoves me into the room and slams the door behind me. I hear a key turn in the lock. "We'll see about that. If everything works out for me tonight, I'll be back. I still owe you, Damien—don't think we're squared up just yet."

$$X \cdot X \cdot X$$

I'm locked in what looks like an old guest room but has recently become a storage space for all the stuff that was in the gardening shed, which got knocked down in a bad storm last winter. All the furniture's been pushed against the walls, and there are various gardening tools leaning against the closet and getting dirt all over. God, Pete's an idiot; who leaves their victims in a room with a pickax? It doesn't take me long to find a screwdriver to take the doorknob apart.

I try all the other doors in the hallway until I find Sarah. I know it's her because I hear her sobbing, and because the door is locked. I run to the kitchen and check for spare keys and find a whole drawer full of them. Taylor's mom must have kept every spare key she ever owned. I take the drawer with me, which makes it hard to creep around quietly, and sit in front of Sarah's door, trying key after key.

"Let me out of here!" Sarah screams. She pounds her fists on the other side.

"What do you think I'm trying to do?"

She sniffs. "Damien?"

"Yeah, be quiet, will you? I'm not exactly supposed to be here." Key number seven is yet another dud. I throw it on the floor with the other failures.

Sarah goes silent. I don't know if it's because I told her to, or if it's because she said she never wanted to talk to me again. It takes me a while to work up the courage to ask, "What did they do to you?"

She starts sobbing again. "They made me fix it for them. I couldn't … They said …" She chokes and I only hear more crying until she gets ahold of herself. "They said Heraldo got hit by a car."

Key number fifteen is the last key. I close my eyes and pray that it works.

"They said he was lying in the street, dying, and … still twitching, and if I did what they wanted, maybe I'd get out of here in time to go save him. So I did, but they still didn't let me go!"

Fifteen is a dud. Damn. I look at the pile on the floor, then at the drawer, which is full of rubber bands and ten-year-old Post-it notes and expired film, but no more keys. "Who told you that? Was it a blond, middle-aged guy with a scraggly beard?"

"It was a boy. About our age. A little taller than you. Please, *hurry*." That last part comes out a squeak. "He's going to die!"

I can retry all the keys, I can go look for a different one, or … I dig through the drawer again, hoping to find something. "Sarah, Heraldo's fine. He's at my house." At the bad guys' headquarters. No problem.

"He's …" She draws in a sharp breath. "If you're lying to me—"

"I'm not." Cold metal scrapes across my fingertips as I grope at the bottom of the drawer. I grab another key and hold my breath as I fit it in the lock.

It turns. A click later, the door is open. I look Sarah over, still not sure that Pete wouldn't have hurt her. But she looks okay. The dog story must have been enough to make her give in. I could hug her, I'm so relieved, but I don't think she'd appreciate it.

"Wow," she says, poking the area around my eye with her finger. I wince. "You look terrible."

"Thanks for the update. Are you talking to me again? Because my mom and her fiancé are about to use *your* hypno device to take over the city, and we're the only ones who know about it."

CHAPTER 17

I didn't think I'd ever be back at the Tines house, but this is important. Amelia is sitting at the dining table, doing her homework. Helen is chasing a naked Jessica across the living room, trying to get her to take a bath.

Everybody looks when I come in, and I can practically hear them stop breathing. Amelia's eyes go wide and she mouths *Damien*, then quickly goes back to her homework, her eyes darting back and forth between her English book and her notes.

Helen grabs Jessica while she's conveniently too busy staring at me to run off.

"I thought Heraldo was here," Sarah whispers.

"My other house," I say. I take a step inside, not sure if I'm welcome here.

"Gordon!" Helen calls. "Someone's here to see you!" She lugs Jessica off to the bathroom.

Gordon comes out of Alex's room with Alex right

behind him. Alex starts to smile when he sees me, and then he notices how terrible I look and gasps.

Sarah tugs on my arm and points to Gordon. "I *told* you you looked like him."

Gordon's face gets really ugly when he sees me, all twisted up and angry. "Alex," he says, "go back to your room." Alex drags his feet, taking as much time as possible.

Amelia holds her book in front of her face, like she hopes Gordon won't notice her and make her leave.

"Amelia, you, too."

"I'm doing my homework—"

"You can do it upstairs!"

Amelia cringes and grabs her stuff, hightailing it out of here and up to her room.

Gordon marches over to me, studying the bruises on my face and my split lip. "I'm so angry with you right now, I could ..." He clenches his fist and doesn't finish. "You weren't supposed to leave this house, and then you wander off to God knows where—"

"I took my stuff," I say. "It's not like you couldn't guess I wasn't coming back. Listen—"

"Is that supposed to make it okay? What happened? Don't tell me it didn't work out and now you're back." He tilts his head toward Sarah. "Do you really want your friend to have to hear all this?"

That's my cue to kick her out, so Gordon doesn't have to embarrass me by chewing me out in front of her. "You don't understand. Something really bad is going down tonight and—"

"I don't want to hear it." Gordon folds his arms. "Do you know how worried we've been? I called your mother about a million times, but the line was always busy. Finally I got through and she said you'd come home."

"Mom and Taylor Lewis are spreading some toxic formula through the sewers. It's going to turn everyone except villains into their personal slaves. They're taking over the city!"

"Damien, shut up!" Gordon's face is red and mean. "I've had it with you! You leave for good without even *telling* us, you make us worry all night, and then you show up looking like *that*. Like you just—"

"Got beat up? I told you, something bad is happening."

"I don't know what I'm supposed to do with you." He rubs his forehead and turns away. "If you want to live with your mother, fine. I've failed. We clearly don't need another three weeks to figure that out. You win. If your mother can handle you, then—"

"Dad!" That gets his attention. It's the first time I've called him that. *"Listen* to me! You have to stop them. You're a superhero—you have to stop Mom and Taylor, or the whole city's going to be theirs by tomorrow morning!"

He looks at me like he's considering it. Then he just looks exhausted. "I can't trust you anymore," he says. "Bringing you here was a ... Just do what you want. I don't care."

"He's telling the truth," Sarah says.

Gordon glares at her. He squeezes my shoulder. "I'm sorry it worked out like this." He gives me my phone. I guess he doesn't need to punish me, now that I don't live here. Then he turns his back on me and wanders off into the kitchen and that's it.

My chest feels heavy, and not just because the Crimson Flash refused to save Golden City. Sarah and I leave, with me dragging my feet.

"I can't believe I met the Crimson Flash!" Sarah says once we're outside. "It must be so cool that he's your dad."

"Yeah, real cool." I lean against the front of the house. The cold air feels good on my bruises. My mom's about to take over the city and enslave everyone, and all I can think about is I just got kicked out of a house I thought I didn't want to live in.

The front door opens and Amelia clomps over to us. "I believe you," she says, looking really proud of herself.

"Great."

"If you were lying, you'd do a better job." Amelia twists her thumbs together, fidgeting and scuffing her foot against the ground. "Alex is going to be really sad if you go," she says. "He's gotten used to you living in his room."

"Tell him I'll never sleep on another floor without thinking of him."

"The attic's kind of big," Amelia goes on. "Dad could probably put a wall in it. It could be two rooms. Alex could live up there, and then—"

"You guys would have a guest room that smelled faintly like cheese. Sorry, Amelia, but I know when I'm not wanted."

X·X·X

Amelia was right about one thing. If I was lying, I'd do a better job. Just because I'm telling the truth doesn't mean there's any reason I shouldn't get results.

I crowd inside the phone booth as Sarah calls up the Crimson Flash on his emergency hotline. She talks a little deeper than normal, disguising her voice in case he remembers it from five minutes ago, and tells him there's a fire at Taylor's address, and people are trapped on the top floor of an apartment complex.

She hangs up and says, "I hope you're happy. Now you've got *me* lying."

"It's for a good cause. Now to get Heraldo." I dust my hands off as we leave the phone booth and make our way toward Mom's house. I remember the twenty bucks Mom gave me and ask Sarah if she's hungry.

She gives me a funny look. "How can you think of food at a time like this?"

"Like what? The Crimson Flash is on the job—problem solved, right? He's a *real* superhero. He's got experience with this sort of thing. He'll get there, realize there's no fire, and figure out what's really going on."

"And see that you were right," Sarah adds.

I shrug. "Listen, Sarah, about what happened earlier, in the park ..."

"When you were with that girl?"

"I thought I was over her." Only kind of a lie. I wanted to *believe* I was—that's close enough.

"Clearly you're not." Sarah holds on to the edge of her glasses and looks down her nose at me.

"But I should have told you first, as soon as I realized it

wasn't going to work out. Between you and me."

Sarah's quiet for a minute. Then she clears her throat. "I … I liked you, Damien. I *do*, I mean. I should have told you that from the beginning. Guys aren't usually into me, and I thought it would be easier if you were my science experiment instead of my boyfriend."

"I'm sorry we won't be going to any dances. It could have been fun." I want to tell her she'll find somebody. Somebody awesome—not awesomer than me, of course, but still cool—but I think it would just make things worse.

"Not as fun as with her, though." Sarah hooks her thumbs in her pockets and scuffs her shoe against the pavement. "It's probably better we keep things one hundred percent professional anyway. To avoid awkward situations."

Like this one? I don't have the heart to tell her we don't have a professional relationship, either, and that she's still not my sidekick because the superhero thing isn't going to stick. I let it go for now, thankful that she accepted my apology and things are going to be okay between us.

We get to my house about half an hour later, opting to go straight there instead of getting dinner. I tell Sarah to wait outside while I get Heraldo. He leaps up on me as soon as I open the door, giving me a face full of dog, licking my cheek and pounding me to the ground. When he's done, I pick myself up and notice a note on the table from Mom. She says not to worry about dinner because she and Taylor are already busy with their plans and won't be back until morning. P.S., she can't wait until I'm her little prince of the city, yada, yada, yada.

Great. At least the Crimson Flash is on the job and we don't have to worry. Plus, with Mom and Taylor gone all night, I don't have to leave Sarah standing in the cold.

I tell her she can come in. She shoves past me and throws her arms around her dog. "Heraldo!"

I crumple up the note on the table before Sarah sees it. She doesn't need to know that Mom is one of the bad guys and has big plans for me. Plus, being called her "little prince of the city" is kind of embarrassing.

I'm home. Finally. I flop down on the couch while Sarah glomps Heraldo and he licks her hair. No wonder it's so poofy all the time. But at least she's safe, and the Crimson Flash is going to put a stop to Mom's plans. And I'm out of the Tines house, back at Mom's where I belong. Where it's quiet and I have my own room and nobody freaks every time I move a muscle.

I breathe deeply and stretch out, taking it all in. Nothing to worry about.

Then my phone rings.

Sarah freezes, like she thinks it's going to be bad news.

It's probably Kat. That would be great. I could walk Sarah home, then go over to Kat's house, and—But the number on the screen isn't Kat's. It's Pete's.

I flip open my phone. "Screw you."

"That how you answer the phone now?" he says. "You have so many enemies, you don't even bother with hello?"

I'm on my feet, pacing. "What do you want, Pete? You going to cry some more about how Kat likes me better than you? I told you, I always—"

"Lose? Funny you should say that about Kat."

My insides go cold and watery. I stop pacing.

"'Cause she's here," Pete says. "You want to say 'screw you' to her?"

"She's not—"

"Damien!" Kat's voice comes on the phone, scared and desperate. "Don't listen to him. It's a—"

"I got your girl," Pete says. "And I got a whole lot of superheroes under my control."

"What about my mom?!"

"Nothing. Taylor bought that I was the eager, helpful assistant. While he and your mom went to spread their stuff around the city, they stupidly left me with their magic machine. I broadcast my voice all over town before they could, and now I'm the one in charge of all the zombies. I was on every radio and TV in Golden City, on all the stations."

I wince, remembering that Pete's superpower makes him the human radio signal. He could spread the hypno powers of Sarah's device all over town faster than anyone. "The Crimson Flash was supposed to stop you."

"Yeah, I got him here, too. He's real useful, and he can't wait to see you. Listen, Damien, I know how jealous you get when Kat fools around. So I'm going to be nice and give you a heads-up. We're on top of the tallest tower in Golden City, the—"

"Banking and Finances building."

"Enjoying the view. It's real nice at the top, Damien. Too bad you're always stuck on the ground. Anyway, if you want to walk in on us again, you know where to find us. And Damien? I'd hurry if I were you." He hangs up.

I hurl my phone at the couch. It bounces off the cushions. I shout a couple expletives that make Sarah and Heraldo both gape at me.

I dig through my backpack and pull out the gun Sarah made. I still don't know how it works, but it's the best I've got.

"What's going on? Damien? What did he say?"

"It's happening. It's …" I swallow and run my hands through my hair. "Mom and Taylor didn't take over. Pete —that guy who told you Heraldo was hurt—did. And he's got Kat and the Crimson Flash." I pull the antidote Mom gave me out of my pocket and hold it out to her. "Take this. It'll protect you against the toxin." Probably.

She stares at it. "But Damien, you're a *superhero*. You need that."

I shake my head. "I'm only half superhero. I don't know if it'll even affect me. I don't want you turning into one of those pie zombies we met in Ruthersford."

"That's uncharacteristically sweet, but—"

I force the vial into her hands. "But nothing. Drink it. Now."

Sarah tries to protest, but I don't take no for an answer. Grudgingly, she downs the whole thing, making a disgusted face the entire time. She looks like she's going to puke it back up when she's done. *Bleuh! That was awful.*"

"I'll bet. Now go home."

"What?! But I took the antidote. You are *not* going alone."

"Take Heraldo home, and … be safe." I shoo her and Heraldo to the door, shoving them outside and locking up behind me. "I know you think I'm a lying jerk, but I really don't want anything to happen to you."

Sarah folds her arms. "You're not just a lying jerk, you're really, *really* stupid."

I salute her. "If I don't see you again, it was nice knowing you, Cosine."

CHAPTER 18

The Banking and Finances building is dark when I arrive, but I don't doubt Pete's up there. Way … up … there. I tilt my head back, the wind blowing through my hair. I feel dizzy already. Better not to think about it.

I hurry inside the building. It's unlocked. It smells funny in here, and the air looks a little hazy from the toxin Mom and Taylor spread all over. I tear through the lobby, but I skid to a stop when the computer screen on somebody's desk flickers to life and Pete's face appears.

"Hey, hey, hey!" he shouts, clapping his hands together. "It's time for the 'What Will Pete Do Next?' show! Damien, if you're watching, this one's for you, man." He points at the camera, then makes a fist and places it over his heart. There are a couple of his superhero minions marching back and forth behind him.

The camera zooms out, then in on Kat. She's tied to the stairwell house on the roof, the same one I was clinging to before the Crimson Flash threw me off the building. Kat has a golden choker clasped around her neck. She doesn't wear that type of stuff, but I'm guessing it's not meant to be jewelry. I think of Bart the Blacksmith, Kat's grandfather, and wonder if it's his handiwork. After all, without something to suppress Kat's powers, there's no way Pete could tie her down and not have her change shape and slip out of her bonds.

Her arms and legs are tied so that she's spread-eagled against the wall and can't move. Pete kisses her. She struggles to pull back, but there's nowhere to go. Pete breaks from her and looks at the camera. "Is this about where we were at your birthday party?" He taps his chin. "No, I think we were farther than that."

"Damien!" Kat screams.

I move away from the monitor and run for the elevator. I hear Pete's voice on another screen say, "You know you like it."

I push the elevator button about ten times. It's so slow, and my heart is beating so fast. The elevator's never going to get here. One long, agonizingly slow ride to the top separates me from saving her.

A little voice in the back of my head says, *You should fly, you idiot.*

It's not going to happen. I feel sick thinking about it, and my knees wobble. My muscles get weak, and I almost drop my gun. A wave of hot guilt pours through my chest. Kat's in trouble, and I don't know how I'm going to handle being on the roof—I can't even fathom flying up there.

My fingers tighten around the gun in self-loathing. I

hear screams coming from the monitors, and I think if the elevator doesn't get here in the next five seconds, maybe ... maybe I'll go outside and just *try*—But then it dings and the doors open.

The Crimson Flash steps out. His face is twisted in a sinister grin, his mouth lopsided. He tilts his head one way, then the other, looking me over.

He reaches out and grabs my arm and *pulls*. I think it's going to come out of the socket. I jerk forward and stumble into him. His hand moves for my neck, but I'm getting more experienced at ducking. I move out of the way in time to not get strangled. I stomp on his foot. It should have hurt, but he doesn't even flinch. I twist and turn, trying to get my arm out of his grasp. I hold up my gun, thinking maybe I can risk firing a warning shot, but the Crimson Flash knocks it out of my hand. It skitters across the floor. It's enough of a distraction that his grip on me loosens a little. I get free and run under a desk.

He picks up the gun off the floor. So much for the "only superheroes can use it" safety. He walks down the rows of desks. Above me, Pete's voice on the computer claims it's halftime, then, "Come on, Damien—it's time to blow out your birthday candles. You'd better hurry." He wishes me a happy birthday, then starts singing, as if we were kids having a party. He stops and yells at Kat to join in. "Don't be shy!" he screams at her. "You know the words!"

The Crimson Flash kicks a rolling desk chair across the floor. I wonder how much Sarah's hypno device affects him and if he recognizes me at all. I wonder if any of him's still in there.

The Crimson Flash kicks another chair. He's getting closer to my hiding place. I hug my knees to my chest. I can't sit here and let him find me. I make a run for it.

He chases after me. I weave between the desks, trying to slow him down, but it only slows *me* down instead. I push chairs behind me to create obstacles. The Crimson Flash flies over me, cutting me off at the other end of the aisle. Great. I've got him on one end, and a whole lot of chairs on the other.

I leap onto the nearest desk and dive into the next aisle as he pulls the trigger on the gun. A laser shoots out of it, cutting the monitor on the desk in half, just as Pete says, "She's not *singing*! I'll have to *make* her if you don't hurry up, Damien."

The Crimson Flash fires off another laser and I scramble out of the way. He flies over so that he's standing right in front of me. He doesn't rush or anything, just points the gun and walks toward me, steady and relentless, as I get to my feet and run like hell.

He fires again. *Zap!* The laser misses me. That hypno device must be pretty powerful, because the real Crimson Flash wouldn't be caught dead trying to murder his own son. Even if I might be somewhat of a disappointment.

Another *zap!* This one splits open the heel of my shoe. I pick up the pace.

I hit the wall and run alongside it, hoping I can double back and get to the elevator before Gordon. He shoots the next laser in front of me, stopping me in my tracks. I duck down and make for the elevator as fast as I can. I push the button, but the doors don't open. Who else is using the elevator in this place?! I push the button about twenty more times, each time expecting to feel a laser in the back, right through the heart.

Gordon closes in on me.

I can't move, paralyzed with fear. I have to get through these doors, no matter what, and I have to not get killed by my own superhero dad in the process.

"Some part of you has to be in there," I say, my voice shaking. Maybe I can distract him until the elevator gets here. Maybe I can actually appeal to his good nature, the one locked up deep down inside, and bring him out of his zombie state. At least enough so he doesn't shoot me. "Come on. You don't want to do this. You'll be really sorry when you wake up tomorrow and realize you killed me!" *If* he wakes up tomorrow. *If* I manage to stop Pete and get everything back to normal.

The Crimson Flash smiles and points the gun right at my heart.

"Dad!" I scream, a last, desperate attempt to snap him out of it. "I know you're in there! The real you wouldn't do this, you—"

"You made Helen cry," he says, and everything turns to slow motion as I watch his finger move on the trigger.

But he doesn't fire. He unexpectedly drops to the ground, the gun slipping out of his hand. A little dart sticks out of his neck.

I look over and see Sarah, a dart gun in her hand. She blows over the end of it, like in the movies, and grins at me. "My own special blend. You still want me to go home and be safe?"

"If it isn't the Cosine Kid. My hero." I lean against the doors just as they open, and tumble backward into the elevator.

X·X·X

"I bet he didn't mean to do that," Sarah says on our way up. She can't get over her hero firing lasers at me, even if he was a zombie at the time.

"Listen, Sarah, about what I said earlier today ..." I tap my fingers against the metal railing in the elevator, holding my gun in one hand. I stare at the trigger and think about Gordon almost firing on me and what could have happened if Sarah hadn't shown up when she did. "I didn't mean for things to turn out this way."

"He's the Crimson Flash. He wouldn't normally have done that."

"I shouldn't have said you weren't my sidekick. I just ... Being a superhero wasn't exactly in my life plan."

"I mean, he *is* your dad, right?"

"Sarah," I say, cutting her off, "you need to go back home."

"Are you nuts? I just got here. *And* you needed me. I think that's pretty obvious."

"You can't go up there with me. He's already got Kat." And is going to do something awful to her if I don't get there in time to stop him. Can this elevator go any slower, or would that break some kind of world record? "What am I supposed to do if he gets you, too? Give me the dart gun and get out of here."

"Ohhhh, no. I'm not going anywhere. You just said I was your sidekick."

"No, I said I shouldn't have said you *weren't*. It's a little different."

"You called me Cosine." She shakes her head at me, like she thinks I'm insane. "I've already saved your life once tonight. I'm not going to get caught, and even if I do, so what?"

"So what? He's got Kat tied to a wall. He's going to hurt her to get to me, and if he finds out I care about you, too? He'll be all over that. You'll be taking a huge risk, going out there to face him with me."

"How am I supposed to be your sidekick if you worry about me all the time? We're both going to get hurt in this business—we have to accept that. You have to trust me."

"Do you trust *me*?"

She conveniently finds a speck of dirt on her dart gun and shines it clean with the edge of her shirt, pretending she didn't hear me. "I'm not going home, Renegade."

"Fine. Stay and help me if you want; see if I care."

The elevator dings and the doors finally open to the top floor. The elevator doesn't go all the way to the roof—we'll have to take the stairs from here.

"You know you're walking into a trap, right?"

"Yep." I hold my gun out in front of me as we leave the elevator, but the coast is clear.

"Just checking," Sarah says.

CHAPTER 19

We burst onto the roof, and I don't look too far to the edge, afraid of getting dizzy and blowing this. Two superheroes stand guard at either end, and a third mans the camera, aimed at Pete. I point my gun at him, ready to fire, but I can't. Pete's standing right in front of Kat. There's no way I can get him without getting her, too.

Sarah shoots her dart gun at Pete, but one of the guards zips in front of him at super speed, taking the blow. The superhero crumples to the floor.

"Grab her," Pete says.

The other guard and the cameraman seize hold of Sarah as she takes aim again. They wrench the dart gun out of her hands and one of them breaks it in half. I'm guessing he has super strength, or that he works out a lot.

"Let them go, Pete." I aim for his chest.

He jerks his thumb over his shoulder at Kat. "Go ahead," he says, "kill us both. If that thing even works."

"Of course it works!" Sarah shouts. She kicks the shins of one of her superhero captors, but he doesn't notice.

I flash Pete a smile. "I'll make you a onetime offer. Let them go and do whatever you want to me."

"Is that right?" Pete pulls Sarah's hypno device out of his pocket. It looks how I remember it—kind of like a tape recorder, papered in red and blue cellophane, with colored wires spliced into the side—only now with more duct tape. "Damien," he says, speaking into the device. His voice gets tinny, echoing across the roof. And then I'm not sure if I really heard him or not, or if he said it directly into my brain. As I look around to see if anybody else heard him, a smile creeps over Pete's face. He says four words, "I am your *master*," and something snaps inside my head. I remember what Mom said about a trigger word.

"Give me the gun," Pete says.

Sarah struggles against her captors, but it's no use. "Damien, don't do it!"

I march over to Pete against my will and put the gun in his hands. I can still think, and maybe talk, but I can't stop myself from doing what Pete says. Mom wasn't sure how her toxin would affect me. I must not be as susceptible to it as a normal person or a full-blooded superhero. Not a lot of good that does me. It means I'm aware that Pete's in control of me, but I can't do anything about it.

Pete turns the gun over, inspecting it. He raises his eyebrows at all the wires and buttons. "What'd you do, make this yourself?"

I can almost hear Sarah gritting her teeth.

Pete points it at me. He lowers it so it's aimed at my

foot—I guess he isn't ready to kill me yet—and fires. Nothing happens.

Kat exhales in relief.

Pete tosses the gun down, calling it a piece of junk. Then he rubs his hands together. "It's great, isn't it? The city is falling into my hands, I've got the girl, and now my old buddy Damien has to do everything I say. What should we do to celebrate?"

"I should steal her away from you."

Pete punches me in the mouth, knocking me to the floor. I taste blood and move to get up, but he says, "On your knees, boy," and I have to listen.

The other superheroes on the roof don't seem to have any freewill. They stand around until Pete tells them to do something, their eyes glassy.

Pete holds out a foot to me. "Kiss it, and bow to your master."

I lean forward and put my mouth on his dirty shoe.

"With your tongue," he adds.

I do what he says. It tastes like rubber and mud and it's Pete's *shoe*. I guess I should be grateful that's all it is. And that he hasn't stepped in anything gross lately.

"Get up."

I stand. I catch a glimpse of how high up we are, how the whole city splays out below us, the ground so far down. I feel dizzy, like I'm going to fall, even though I'm not near the edge. I wince and shut my eyes. I wish I had something to hold on to.

Pete laughs. "That's right, my boy's afraid of heights."

"It's okay, Damien," Kat says.

Pete turns and glares at her. He raises his hand like he's going to hit her, then holds off. "You need to learn not to dirty your pretty mouth with his name. You'll figure that out soon enough."

"I wish I'd never met you," she says.

"Be careful what you wish for. Remember I introduced you to *him*." Pete snaps his fingers. He points to one of his superhero minions. "You. Back on the camera. It's time for another show. Damien, go stand next to Kat." He makes *L* shapes with his fingers and peers at us, like he's going to take a picture.

I do what he says and move closer to her. "It's going to be okay," I whisper.

Kat nods, but she doesn't look all that convinced. It might have something to do with her being tied up, and me being under mind control.

"Don't talk to her," Pete says. "I was going to do her and make you watch. But then I thought the only thing worse than making you watch me rough her up is if I make *you* do it." He grabs a pocketknife out of his jeans and flips it open, locking it into place. He puts it in my hands. "A little foreplay. You can only use it on her."

Pete's so retarded sometimes, always giving me weapons. But he's got me—I will my hands to turn the knife on him, and it's like the signal doesn't get through.

"Smile for the camera," Pete says. "The whole town's going to be watching."

Me, a knife, and Kat. With Pete directing. Not a recipe for fun. My mind races. This whole situation seems hopeless. Pete's holding all the cards, and what can I do?

I can talk, that's what. As long as my mouth works, I've still got a weapon. My most dangerous one.

"You know, Pete," I say, before he can tell me what to do with the knife, "this plan isn't going to work."

"Nice try, Damien."

I shrug. "It's flawed. You want to know why?"

I wait for Pete to take the bait. I'm patient. I don't offer him the answer until he mulls it over, curiosity getting the better of him, and finally says, "Why's that?"

A slow, wicked grin twists up my mouth. "Because, Pete, I hear you like torture. So I'm guessing you want me to torture Kat while you watch. But you know what, Pete?" I laugh. Pure and sweet maniacal laughter that I pull seemingly out of nowhere. It's a strain to make it sound real, but it's this or let Pete finish ordering me around. That's not going to happen, not while I'm still breathing. "I like torture, too. Too bad we couldn't have stayed friends."

"Yeah," Pete says, a scowl pulling on his face, "too bad."

"Boy, are you dumb. You could have had me live out my worst fear, and instead you're giving me kinky S and M." I hold the knife toward Kat, pointing it at her stomach.

Pete gets all ruffled about it and glares at me. "Did I tell you to do that?"

"This is going to be great. And here I thought you were going to make me jump."

"If I tell you to jump, boy, you ask me how high."

"Off the building, I mean. That would have been ..." I

shudder just thinking about it. I don't have to fake that part. I lower my voice a little and shoot Kat a wary look, like I don't want her to hear, before turning to Pete and going, "I might have *cried*. On TV."

"And you'd be dead," Pete adds.

"I would," I agree. "But you're not going to do that to me. It's one thing for you to torture people you don't know because Taylor tells you to. Notice you're not touching Kat—your first instinct is to make me do it. So, you know what you're *not* going to do, Pete? You're not going to kill me—you don't have the guts."

One side of Pete's face twitches at the insult. "You just made the biggest mistake of your life."

Oh no, Pete. That's what *you're* about to do.

"Drop the knife," he says.

It clatters on the ground.

"Get away from her."

I take a step back.

He points to the ledge. "Get over there. Now."

I do what he says. I want to close my eyes and block this out, but I can't or I might fall. Last time I was here, I did. And if all goes well tonight, I will again.

When I can't make myself walk any closer on two legs, I get down on my knees and crawl to the ledge. *This is for Kat. And Sarah.* "Please don't do this!" I shout. "Don't make me! We used to be friends, Pete, I—"

"Jump."

"How high?"

"As high as you can."

I get to my feet. The drop below is sickening, and I feel

my stomach wanting to heave. I look over my shoulder. Sarah closes her eyes, tears on her cheeks. She's mumbling something to herself. She looks like she's praying, but knowing her, she's probably reciting the periodic table of elements.

Kat's eyes are on me, willing this all to stop. "Don't do it," she whispers.

"Aye, aye, mateys," I say. "I guess it's time to walk the plank."

My knees are weak. Some part of me would give anything to not have to do this, even if it means not saving the day, anything so that I'm somewhere else, safe on the ground. But the compulsion to do what Pete says is stronger than my fear. Good—it's what I'm counting on.

I tell myself everything's going to be okay, as long as my heart doesn't stop beating before I can carry out Pete's order. Which it might do, it's beating so fast.

I jump as high as I can and leap off the edge of the tallest building in Golden City. Kat screams what might be my name, or what might just be a cry of agony. It's garbled and I'm too busy hurtling through the air to figure it out.

My mind races, swearing inwardly and panicking. *Fly! Fly, damn it!*

Nothing happens. I'm plummeting, like I did the other day, like in my nightmares. Gordon said I had control, but I don't. I will myself to use my power, to save myself, but it's no good. I think through what Pete said, my blood pounding in my ears. He never said don't save yourself, he never said don't use your power, don't fly. This is all *me* and my hang-ups and my fears.

Cold air whizzes by me, stinging my skin and making my eyes water.

I imagine what it'll be like to hit the pavement—*splat!*—and then not breathe or think or feel anything anymore. And I *don't want to die.*

I will myself to fly. Because making Pete tell me to jump off a building and then *not* flying and *not* saving Kat and Sarah and *not* stopping that bastard is really, really lame. If I can't do this now, just this once, I don't deserve a name like Renegade X.

The wind slows. The ground stops rushing toward me. I freeze in midair. I'm too afraid to move, in case I fall again. I half wish I'd let Gordon teach me this stuff, because maybe then I'd know what to do.

I get ahold of myself. My mouth tastes like metal, like blood, and I realize I bit the inside of my cheek. The wind carries the sharp scents of garbage and motor oil. I don't look down. I think about floating up, and that's what happens. My ascent feels slower than the elevator ride. I'm inching my way up, wishing I could go faster but not knowing how and too afraid of falling. I keep myself as calm as I can, telling myself moving is better than not moving. Saving Kat is better than not saving her.

But it'd be way better if I could get there sooner than later. I think about going faster, and this time I speed up.

I stay below the edge of the building when I get to the top. Everything now depends on Pete not knowing I'm back from the dead. I peer over the ledge. Kat's crying silently and trying to look brave about my death. Pete's standing in front of her, ranting to the camera about how he beat me, how he finally won.

Sarah's glaring at Pete, her face streaked with tears. She keeps looking over the edge, like she knows my plan and is wondering what the hell happened to me. Or she's looking for my body on the pavement.

I slip over to the side near Pete, keeping my hands on the ledge for support, even though I don't need it. Physically, I mean. Mentally, every time I breathe I think I feel the air give way and I'm plummeting again to my doom.

My gun is still on the floor. I reach for it, very carefully, silently. Pete's too busy to notice my arm creeping across the ground behind him, but his two superhero minions might. My fingers close around the handle. I fly up over the edge and set myself on solid ground.

Pete's still too close to Kat, but I come at him from the side. I pull the trigger.

"Damien, watch out!" Sarah shouts.

I roll out of the way in mid-fire, heeding her warning just as the hero with super strength who was holding her tackles me. I don't see where the laser hits, but I hear Pete cry out. The super-strength guy kicks my gun away and stomps on my wrist. It crunches in a way it's not supposed to, and I feel like I'm going to be sick.

"Stop her, you idiot!" Pete screams. He's near the ledge, trying to get to his feet, babying one foot like someone just shot a laser at it. Sarah runs toward him. She takes advantage of his weakened, one-footed state and gives him a good shove before Mr. Super Strength grabs her and drags her away.

Pete falls. *Off the building.* Even though I hate him, my heart still stops, watching someone else live out my worst fear. But then he catches himself, his fingers clutching the ledge.

"Damien! Save me!" He sounds desperate. I don't know why he picks me and not one of his cronies. Maybe it's to torture me—maybe he'd risk his life to make me a little more uncomfortable—or maybe in his panic mine is the only name he thinks to call out. We did used to be friends. Once upon a time.

I walk toward him. I can't help it—the power of the hypno device drags me against my will. If I save him, this is all over, with me on the losing side. I don't have a weapon, Pete knows about my ability, and I won't get a second chance. All I can do is creep slowly, dragging my feet as much as I can without disobeying him, and hoping he slips before I get there. If he dies, the hypno spell is broken, and we all get to go home.

"Damien! Faster!" he cries.

Oh, tell me they got that one on tape. "I'm not going to let you hurt my friends, Pete. I'm not going to help you."

"You don't have a choice!"

Step. Step. My shoes scrape against the roof as I struggle to slow myself down, but Pete's order to hurry up takes effect and I can't help but pick up the pace.

I pass Kat on the wall. I hate to think what Pete's going to do to her if he gets up from that ledge. I touch her hand, squeezing her fingers. I cling to her as long as I can, but my legs move on without my consent. Just our fingertips are touching, and then they're not anymore.

"You're going to die, Pete," I tell him. "Nobody's going to save you."

"Shut up and get over here!"

My heart sinks, heavy and dead. I don't look back at my friends. I don't think about how badly this all turned out. I cross the last stretch of roof and kneel down.

Pete loses his grip with one hand but catches himself again.

I'm shaking, trying to fight it so hard, but I can't. I'm going to save this bastard, and he's going to kill me, torture Kat, and do who knows what with Sarah. And then he's going to rule over Golden City like a king.

"I order you to save me!" Pete screams. I've never heard him so desperate, so freaked out.

He's losing his grip. If I could hold out a little longer— but my hands move on their own, reaching for his, even with my injured wrist. It's all over.

Then, out of nowhere, a pair of lasers *joop* by, nearly missing my hand. They cut across Pete's fingers, and it isn't pretty, and he falls. A. Long. Way. Down. His screams echo in my ears. His order to save him still stands, and I'm going to jump again without wanting to, but then Mom grabs my arm and doesn't let go. Now I know where the lasers came from.

"Damien! What happened to you?!" She hugs me so tightly to her that I couldn't get away even if Pete told me to. And then the urge to jump after him and save him disappears, and I know he's dead.

There are tears in my eyes, I'm so relieved to see Mom

and for this whole thing to be *over*. I don't cry, though. Standing here, getting hugged by my mommy, still on TV, and crying like a baby would be too much.

The superheroes on the roof blink and stop what they're doing, which includes holding Sarah hostage.

I break free from Mom and grab Pete's knife off the ground and cut through Kat's bonds. I have to use my right hand to do it, and my wrist is swollen and hurts like hell, so much that I can barely use it, but I don't care.

Kat drops to the ground. She sinks into me and I wrap my arms around her, and we both slump to the floor as one person, in one big heap.

"God, Damien, when you jumped, I thought ..." Tears spring up in Kat's eyes. She swallows them back and clings to me, her words trailing off unfinished.

"It's okay. It's over now." I unclasp the choker from around her neck. It feels like it takes forever, and my fingers keep fumbling. It doesn't help that it's so cold out here.

Mom bends down and picks something up off the ground and puts it in her pocket. "We should get you kids out of here," she says.

"You're an idiot," Kat tells me, wiping the tears from her eyes. "What was I supposed to do if he killed you?"

"Die of heartbreak before he could hurt you, of course." I wink at her. "It was all part of the plan."

And then I remember Sarah, having to stand around watching me, her former potential boyfriend, comforting the girl I chose instead of her. Sure, Kat was the one tied up, but I didn't even ask if Sarah was okay.

I get to my feet and turn to face her. Sarah's standing there with her arms folded, watching me. At least she's not writing this down in her notebook.

"Sarah," I say, feeling more awkward than ever, "I'm sorry, I ..." I walk up to her, holding my wrist close to my chest to minimize the jostling. "Are you okay, Cosine?"

She nods, then grins. "I told you to trust me."

"I'm sorry it didn't work out," I tell her, though I keep my voice a little low, not really wanting Kat to hear. "You know. Between us." We already talked about this, but I can't help still feeling guilty about it.

Sarah rolls her eyes at me. "Please, Damien. I'd *much* rather be shoving people off of buildings with you than dating you. This was way more fun, and I'm better off being your sidekick. I *am* your sidekick, right?"

"Yeah," I say, smiling at her. "I wouldn't have it any other way."

CHAPTER 20

Kat and I are sitting on a cement planter outside the Banking and Finances building. A building I wouldn't mind never seeing again—if they ever decide to tear this thing down, I'm going to get front-row seats. I have my arm around Kat, and she has her head against my shoulder. Sarah's dad came and picked her up, but she told me to call her tomorrow, to make sure I'm okay.

One of the superheroes called an ambulance, and the paramedics bandaged up my wrist. They said it was just sprained, but they still want me to go to the hospital and get checked out. They wanted to take my gun away at first, but I told them it wasn't real. They believed me when they saw all the wires hanging off of it.

As a rule, villains don't go to the hospital. Medical villainy is actually a pretty lucrative career, because villains who get hurt in situations not on the up and up are willing to pay top dollar to get healed without any of the authorities asking questions.

"Damien," Kat says, curled up against me. "I love you." She swallows. "I ... I just wanted you to know."

I kiss the top of her head. "Aw, you're just saying that because I saved your life."

"No, I mean it." She sits up and gives me a stern look. "I know Pete said some crap to you about me and him—he was bragging about it. It wasn't true."

"You only want me because you like the idea of a cool pirate wedding and I'm the only one who can pull it off and *you know it*. But," I add, my eyes darting toward her, "I love you, too. Just so you know."

I hold her closer, and she settles back into me, one arm across my stomach like she's never going to let me go. "Kat," I whisper, "I have another confession to make."

"You want to start your own circus with dancing robots instead of clowns, and ferocious penguins instead of lions?"

"Yes! But no, that's not it. I'm afraid I have bad news."

"Bad news? After tonight?" She sounds skeptical.

I nod. "Mr. Wiggles is dead. I've tried to reanimate him, but ... you know how that goes. He still dances to music, but now he wants to eat brains all the time."

Kat laughs. "I think I can forgive you."

"Because you love me or because I saved your life?"

"Both." She grins. "My dad should be here soon. I called him over twenty minutes ago. He freaked when he heard what happened and said he'd take the new computerized car he's got, the one with the ultra-efficient GPS." Kat rolls her eyes. "He made a point of telling me that, so I'll know he cares. Like I wouldn't anyway. I'm sure he'll give you and your mom a ride."

"Thanks, Kat." I'm not looking forward to explaining to her dad how his daughter got kidnapped because of me or how I'm only half villain. Something he might not approve of, especially now that I'm dating his daughter. "I should go find Mom and let her know."

"Where is your mom?"

Good question. I realize I haven't seen her in a while. I nearly got killed, I'm injured, and Kat and I are obviously back together. Mom should totally be hovering over me. The only thing that would stop her is if she had something big going on.

Something really big. And I know now what she picked up off the roof. And I know I have to stop her.

X·X·X

Mom's on her cell phone in the lobby, the scene of my fight with the Crimson Flash. She says, "Fine! I'll do it myself!" and slams her phone shut. Sure enough, in her other hand is the hypno device.

She gasps when she sees me. "What are you doing here? What did the paramedics say about your wrist?"

"Who was that? On the phone?" I circle around her, keeping my distance.

"Taylor." She rolls her eyes. "He's being ridiculous. He doesn't realize this is our chance, that this Pete thing was only a little glitch."

"Maybe he's upset that one of his favorite students is

dead. Just a guess. Can I see that?" I hold my hand out for the hypno thingy.

Mom smooths out her hair, flustered because I'm right. "No, dear, it's very delicate and you already broke it once."

"This thing with Pete wasn't just a little 'glitch.' Kat could have gotten seriously hurt, and I almost died. Don't you care?"

"Of course I do! But it's not like I planned for that to happen. And if you'd taken the antidote like I told you to, instead of *giving it away*, there wouldn't have been a problem." She gives me a look. "Once I take control, everything will be fine."

"Mom, you can't! You put everyone I care about in danger tonight!"

"And you handled it very well, considering the circumstances. I'm very proud of you."

She holds up the hypno device, ready to speak into it.

Before I know what I'm doing, I draw my gun on her. "Mom. I can't let you do that." I have to hold it with both hands, partly because of my injured wrist and partly because I'm shaking so badly.

"Damien Locke!" She scolds me, then laughs, not taking me seriously. "What do you think you're going to do? I'm your *mother*. Put that away."

"Didn't you hear me?! I said I can't let you do this!"

She lowers the machine, her face set in a scowl. Her lip curls in disgust. "You sound like a superhero."

"I *am* a superhero!"

I'm as shocked as she is that those words came out of

my mouth. My arms shake so much that the gun rattles.

"Clearly sending you to your father's was a mistake." She didn't even flinch on the *f*-word this time. "I don't want you seeing him anymore. You're going to stay home, and we're going to—"

"We're not going to do anything unless you give me that." I gesture to the device with my weapon.

Mom's eyes flash. "Damien, put the gun down."

I shake my head.

Mom's silent, and when she speaks, her voice is soothing, like she's talking to a scared animal. "It's over now. Everything's going to be okay."

I aim the gun at her chest and feel like I'm aiming at myself.

"You're not going to use that on your mother. Now, cover your ears—"

I shoot. A laser flies past her head. It got a little closer than I meant it to. "That was a warning. Put it down *now*."

"Damien, you don't want to do this." Mom isn't scared —she's pissed off. "You're crossing the line."

"What does that mean?"

"It means you'd better hope Gordon keeps his word, because I won't have a superhero living in my house!"

"He will," I say, mostly to bother her. But I know he will, even if he hates me. I move in closer and, keeping the gun in my left hand, hold out my right, not caring how much it hurts. "Give it to me."

Mom's face is impassive. "If you do this, you're not going to get into Vilmore." She puts the device in my hand. "You're making an enemy of your own mother.

That's the choice you're making here."

"No, that's your choice, Mom." I feel like all my insides are dying. I want more than anything to give it back to her and tell her I'm a supervillain and beg her to take me back. But I can't. I don't feel like a villain anymore—not one hundred percent, not after tonight. I could have gone along with Mom's plan and become prince of the city, but I had to save Kat and stop Pete. And I couldn't let her hurt Sarah or Gordon or anybody close to me, even if that meant sacrificing everything and not getting into Vilmore. Even if it meant I'm that much closer to getting an *H* instead of a *V*. I may not be all hero, but I can't pretend I'm all villain, either.

Mom's lasers flash. Everything happens in slow motion. The lasers hit my gun, exploding it in my hand. She lunges, reaching for the hypno device. I turn away. I hurl it as hard as I can at the wall.

"Nooo!" Mom screams. I can practically hear all her hopes and dreams breaking as the hypno device smashes against the wall.

"Don't even think about bothering Sarah again. If you do, I'm sure the police and every superhero in town would be interested in finding out where you live and how to get into your secret lab. And I'll be wanting the recipe for the antidote. When I come to get my stuff."

I turn my back on her and walk out on the life I've known for sixteen years.

I stay the night at Kat's house. Her parents don't invite me, but I "accidentally" fall asleep on their couch, because I don't want to deal with the fact that my mom disowned me and I'm dreading having to call Gordon.

Kat's mom cried for an hour after we got back to their house, even though Kat assured her she was fine, and her dad shuffled around and said he would buy her anything she wanted, because he doesn't know any other way to handle things. Nobody asked me how my wrist was. It hurt a lot, and maybe I should have gone to the hospital, but I wasn't going to bring it up.

Kat's mom wakes me up about noon, her hand on my shoulder. I blink, still tired. I want to go back to sleep, because sleeping means avoiding reality, but it also means nightmares and falling to my doom over and over. It means confronting my mom, who may or may not still care about me, and in my dreams it's me who pushes Pete off the ledge. Sometimes I fall with him. Sometimes it's just me who tumbles down to the pavement, while Pete does whatever he wants with Kat.

"There's a man here who says he's your father," Kat's mom says. "He's waiting for you outside." She looks a little guilty, and I'm guessing they didn't want to let him in the house, since he's a superhero. "Your phone rang about a hundred times, and I answered it and told him where you were."

I sit up. I stare bleary-eyed at my knees. My stomach growls. I can smell myself—I don't remember the last time I needed a shower this badly. And my wrist is throbbing and my face hurts all over.

"You don't have to go with him," Kat's mom says. "I can call your mother."

My eyes water when she mentions Mom. Mrs. Wilson's so nice, and she doesn't know Mom doesn't want to see me again. I press the back of my arm against my eyes and breathe in slowly. I shake my head.

She hugs me and tells me it's going to be okay. I kind of wish she wouldn't. It makes it harder not to break down.

I get ahold of myself and tell her it's fine, I'll go with him.

Gordon's waiting for me on the front porch. Relief washes over him when he sees me. Then he looks awkward and like he doesn't know what to say.

"I guess you won. I'm a superhero now, right? I saved everyone and Mom doesn't want me." I stomp down the steps. "Lucky you, now you're stuck with me."

"I thought Helen was going to slug me this morning when I told her I didn't know where you were." Gordon squeezes my shoulder. I shrug him off. I don't want anybody touching me. "You did a good thing last night," he mutters, scratching the side of his head.

"Everything's messed up."

"It could have turned out a lot worse."

"Like Mom not disowning me? Like Kat not getting kidnapped? And my ex–best friend not falling off a building and dying?!"

Gordon sighs. "Sometimes it's not easy, doing the right thing. It's not as black and white as you think."

"Fine, so I'm a superhero. I guess that means you have to keep your promise and take me in."

"That's still an *X* on your thumb, Damien. I wouldn't say the events of one night are going to decide your whole future. You've got time yet to decide which way you want to go."

"You only have to put up with me for two years. Then I'll be eighteen and on my own. It'll fly right by. I'll try and stay out of your way."

"What are you talking about? If this is about what happened last night, well, I was under mind control. I wasn't myself."

"Not that." He wouldn't normally chase me down and shoot lasers at me—I know that much; I'm not stupid. "Last night, at the house, you said you didn't care. You said taking me in was a mistake."

"I didn't say that."

"You wanted to." I sit down on the porch steps. I consider going back inside and telling Kat's mom I can't go home with him.

"I was wrong. It wasn't a mistake." He squats down so we're at the same eye level. "Everybody wants you to come back."

I rest my head on my arms, propped against my knees. "It's okay if you're only doing this because you feel like you have to, but don't tell me everyone wants me when they don't."

Gordon pales. He looks like he's going to be sick. Then he smiles and shakes his head. "I don't think they'd let me in the house if I showed up without you. And I know I'd never forgive myself." He holds his hand out to me. When I don't take it, he grabs me and pulls me to my feet.

"You're a good kid, and I'm proud to have you." He puts his arm around me and hugs me so hard, my ribs feel like they're going to break. He kisses my forehead. "Come on, son. Let's go home."

CHAPTER 21

"That," Kat says, looking up at the shark swimming by behind the glass, "is a triangle, mister."

"Square. You lose again."

Amelia rolls her eyes at us. "It's a *shark*."

It's been a week since the whole Pete fiasco. We're at the Golden City Aquarium with my family. At first Gordon wasn't going to let me bring Kat, on account of her being a supervillain. He *claimed* it was because the aquarium trip was only for our family, but then I played up how much my wrist hurt and said I didn't know if I could leave the house without Kat there for moral support. He scowled at me and said she still couldn't come, and then I told him about the robotic scorpions I put in his closet that only I know how to disable. That changed his mind pretty fast.

The front of my T-shirt has a picture of a shark with a word bubble that reads, SHARKS BITE PEOPLE! RARR! There's an octopus on the back holding a sign that says I'M

A GOOD SOURCE OF INK.

Kat's wearing a silver evening gown. Heads turn as she walks by, and then people stare and mutter to themselves when they see me. She looks like she's going to prom, and I look like I don't respect sea life. It's great.

I trace another shape on Kat's palm with my finger.

"Circle," she says. "Don't patronize me, Damien. I can take the hard stuff."

"Apparently not, or you wouldn't keep getting them wrong."

Amelia looks at the stingray gliding past the window, then looks at us like we're crazy.

Alex runs by, chasing after the shark. He's practically glued to the glass. Gordon tells him "No running," and Alex slows to a jog.

Kat shuts her eyes as I draw another shape. She shakes her head. "What was that?"

"Dodecahedron."

"It was not."

"Was, too. Now you owe me ten dollars. I accept cash or credit. No checks or money orders."

"How about I forget that you were late yesterday and call it even?"

"Ten-dollar late fee. I must be awful important." I take her hands and pull her to me, pressing her against the shark tank. I move in to kiss her, but she kisses me first.

I hear an "Oh, gross!" from Amelia and some giggles from Alex.

I wonder how long we can go at it before aquarium security tells us we're not supposed to touch the glass.

There are angry voices behind us, and I catch snippets from Helen like "came in the mail yesterday" and "that girl's a bad influence." Then Gordon marches over to us. He clears his throat. "Damien. Can I have a word with you?"

"Kind of busy."

He ignores me and holds up a little card that says, *Your subscription is on its way!* "Helen tells me this came yesterday. Addressed to *me*."

I break away from Kat and take a better look at the card he's holding. It's from *Hottest Villains*. I raise my eyebrows at him. "Wow, Dad, you didn't even give them a fake name? That's pretty bold."

"I didn't order it. But I think you know that." He folds his arms, his jaw set, waiting for me to confess.

"I thought the thing with my mom was a one-time fling. I didn't know you had a supervillain fetish."

Gordon scowls. His face gets red, and he looks like he's about to chew me out in front of everyone at the aquarium. But Kat interrupts him.

"Gee, Mr. Tines," she says, "this is a real let-down. You're always so clean and on the up and up on your show." She sighs. "I guess it's true what they say about not meeting your heroes in real life."

Gordon's scowl fades into a look of confusion. Then he beams at her, clearly entranced. "You watch my show?"

"All the time." She claps me on the back and stage whispers, "So does Damien, but he doesn't like to admit it." She conveniently leaves out the part about how we make fun of it nonstop.

"I might have seen a few episodes," I tell Gordon, "but I'm not a diehard fan like Kat here."

She forces a smile while reaching over and pinching my arm.

Gordon's so shocked by this news, he stands there, smiling and gaping at us for a minute, as if he we just told him the world was made of sunshine and rainbows and he believed us. "Listen, Damien," he finally says, waving the subscription card, "we'll talk about this later. And you're going to give me the deactivation code to those scorpions the second we get home."

"Of course." I salute him, which seems to throw him off. He mumbles something about us enjoying the aquarium and makes his getaway.

I'll tell him whatever codes he wants, but the joke's on him because the scorpions don't use a code. The only way to deactivate them is to wait until their batteries run out.

"We make good partners in crime," Kat says.

"Yeah, sure. Today we do. Six months from now, when you're going to Vilmore and I'm not ..."

"We'll figure something out."

"Even if I had my *V*, there's no way Taylor would ever let me in. Not since I ..." Since I chose Gordon over my mom. "Not since Mom disowned me. Vilmore and me—it's never going to happen."

Kat bites her lip. "A change of plans doesn't change who we are. Or how we feel."

"But—"

"Damien." Kat grabs my shoulders. "I love you. That's what matters."

She smiles at me, and I know that she means it.

Kat and I have barely started kissing again when Helen stomps over to us, Jessica squirming in her arms. "Damien," she says, addressing me and not Kat and not sounding particularly friendly, "we're getting lunch. Are you coming?"

I give her a thumbs-up without breaking from Kat.

"Is that a yes or a no?"

"Kat!" Jessica shouts, and then laughs like it's the funniest thing in the world.

"Maybe you two should give it a breather," Helen says, in a tone that says by "maybe" she means "definitely."

"Come on, Helen," Gordon says, coming up behind her and taking Jessica. "Let the boy have his fun. You're only young once."

Helen shoots Gordon a look, like she plans on murdering him later but doesn't want to say so in public. I can tell the last thing she wants is to let me "have my fun." Maybe she's the type who thinks teenagers shouldn't be allowed to date until they're thirty, but considering how she reacted when I told her about my supposedly kissing "Joe," I think her getting so pissed off has more to do with who my partner is. Maybe bringing Bart the Blacksmith's granddaughter to our family outing wasn't the best idea in the world, but I love Kat, and Helen's going to have to get used to it.

"You wouldn't say that if you'd seen them yesterday," Helen says. "I caught them *timing* it. With a stopwatch."

I pause long enough to explain. "We were going for the world record."

"But we were nowhere near it," Kat adds, disappointed.

Helen sighs. "We'll be at the food court if you decide you're hungry. Otherwise, meet us in half an hour in front of the eel exhibit." She calls for Amelia and Alex to hurry up.

Gordon ruffles my hair. He sounds extra friendly when he says, "Have fun, kid," possibly to make up for how sour Helen's being.

"Hey, Dad?"

He looks over his shoulder.

"Are people staring at us?"

He glances around. "No more than usual. You're going to have to try harder."

"Aw, nuts." I snap my fingers.

Gordon's laughter fades as he hurries to join the others. I go back to kissing Kat.

Things pick up and we get some good mutters from people walking by. An old lady calls us "obscene." I'm beginning to think we should have brought the stopwatch when my phone rings.

"Don't answer it," Kat mumbles. She puts her hands on my face, holding me to her.

"Sorry, Katfish. Duty calls." I answer it. It's Sarah. "I thought I told you never to call me here."

"Renegade, did you see the paper this morning?" she screams.

"You know I don't read anything before noon."

"There's been a series of robberies all across town. The police can't figure out the connection, but it's *so* obvious they're going after items owned by the Mad Baroness. It's so infuriating! I know where they're going to strike tonight. Not only are they going after Mad Baroness collectibles, but they're doing it in this spiral pattern. We have to be there."

"Got it."

Silence. Then, "So get down here!"

"I'm a very busy man, Sarah. I can't drop everything every time somebody needs me."

"Psh. I know what *you're* busy doing, and this is more important. Besides, I've got a new weapon for you to try out."

"As a matter of fact, I'm on a family outing. It's very important. Do not disturb and all that."

"How is your family outing 'do not disturb'? Fine. I guess I'll go walk Heraldo."

"I'll be there in two hours." I hang up.

Kate takes my phone and turns it off. "So you're mine for two hours, huh?" She locks her arms around my waist.

"I'm partial to telling all the sharks they're not as cool as they think they are, and that it's people like them who bankrupt the tooth fairy and don't leave any tooth money for the rest of us. Or we can make out some more. I'm planning on moaning, 'Oh, Salty! You bad sea demon!' next time. Just so you're prepared."

Kat grins. "Who says we can't do both?"

"I knew I loved you." I lean in and kiss her. And then a shark swims by and I shake my fist at it and ask it where all my quarters are.

ACKNOWLEDGMENTS

I'd like to thank my awesome agent, Holly Root, for using the L-word and swooping in to save the day at exactly the right moment. I'd also like to thank Greg, Elizabeth, and all the other wonderful people at Egmont (the book's original publisher) for believing in this story and making the magic happen. Without them, this book wouldn't be the physical entity you hold in your hands, and would still be intangible words on my computer screen—and if that's not magic, I don't know what is.

As for everyone else, putting up with a struggling writer is no easy task, but supporting and encouraging them for years on end? I'm pretty sure that puts you in the running for sainthood, which is why all these people get my most heartfelt thanks: Chloe and my family, for supporting the hell out of me, even when things looked their darkest; the writing group, for making Friday nights at the Black Drop my favorite part of the week; Dianissima and the rest of the Latin crew, for listening to more about writing than they ever wanted to know; and everyone down at The Pat's, for taking me in when I needed it, teaching me Dianglish, and bestowing upon me the wisdom of Misty the Sphynk, a great oracle who definitely knows all.

The adventure continues in …

THE TRIALS OF RENEGADE X

CHAPTER 1

K at pulls back a little as I kiss her. We're sitting on my bed in my room at Gordon's house. That's right. *My room.* It used to be my little brother Alex's room until Gordon remodeled the attic. Now Alex lives up there, and I live down here, on the ground, like any sane person. Any sane person making out with his really hot supervillain girlfriend, that is.

Kat's eyes dart toward the door, as if she expects it to spring open any second, even though no one's home. "Damien … what about your mom?"

She means Helen, Gordon's wife, the mother of my three half siblings. I kiss Kat's neck, making her shiver— one of my favorite perks of being her boyfriend. "She's *not* my mom."

"She *really* hates me." Kat keeps her voice low, like she's afraid to say the words out loud. This should probably be the part where I deny it and reassure her that deep down my stepmom really does like her, but we'd both know it was a lie. Kat's deceased grandfather was Helen's nemesis and the reason Helen lost her superspeed and why she walks with a limp. So how she feels about Kat isn't exactly a secret—one she doesn't mind telling me every chance she gets, as if I didn't hear her the first million times. She's also banned Kat from the house, and especially from my room—and, if she could, I'm pretty sure she'd ban her from my pants—but what she doesn't know won't hurt her.

Kat shakes her head. "What if they come home? You know I'm not supposed to be here."

"I also know what tomorrow is." Tomorrow's the day Kat moves into her dorm at Vilmore, the local villain university. Villains and heroes start college at sixteen, and not just because neither of them wants the enemy to get ahead, but because it turns out high school is boring and pretty much useless. And now Kat's starting up at Vilmore. *Without me.*

We were supposed to go together. We were supposed to sleep in each other's dorm rooms and partner up to ace all our classes and totally rule that place. Now she's going to do all that stuff—excluding the sleeping in other people's dorm rooms thing, I hope—on her own. Or, God forbid, with *other people*, even if they're not nearly as awesome as me.

I've had all summer to prepare for this, ever since Kat got her acceptance packet and I got my official rejection letter, but I honestly thought she'd tell me she'd changed her mind by now. I mean, if she has to go without me, what's the point? Just because her dad would kill her if she didn't go, and just because he'd *especially* kill her if she wasn't going on my account. Her parents aren't crazy about her making life choices based on "a boy," even if that boy is me, and even if I am not just "a boy," but "*the boy*" in her life. Plus, they've known me for about two years now, so they should understand why Kat would want her life to revolve around mine.

But anyway, tomorrow my girlfriend moves to Vilmore, *our school*, without me, and even though it's only a forty-minute train ride away, it feels like it might as well be the moon. I want to make the most of the time I have left with her, and that doesn't involve worrying about what Helen and Gordon will think of what we're about to do to each other. In my bed. Pants not required.

Plus, we've spent the summer doing it all over Golden City—we have a checklist of all the places we've graced with our love—and my room hasn't been covered. We even managed to do it in Kat's room last month, even though her mattress squeaks and her mom watches us like a hawk, but only because her parents were gone all day moving her grandparents—the ones who are still living, *not* Helen's nemesis—into a retirement home for supervillains. The home is really nice and has special walls, so when the residents lose control of their powers, they can keep it isolated and don't accidentally shoot anyone with laser beams or start any fires.

I wanted to put the retirement home on our checklist and volunteer to help them move, like the wonderful, upstanding citizens that we are, but Kat said it was probably our only chance to rip each other's clothes off under her parents' roof, so I gave in.

"You know, I saw your mom the other day." Something

gets weird about Kat's voice, and she doesn't quite look at me, so I know that when she says she saw my mom, she means my *real* mom. "Damien, there's something you should—"

"I don't want to talk about her."

Kat hesitates, taking a deep breath. "Yeah, okay. But ..." She shakes her head, letting it go.

Good. Because my mom is the last person I want to think about right now, and not just because it's a total mood killer. It's been five months since she disowned me. Five months since we've spoken, and she probably hasn't thought about me once, so why should I think about her?

"I don't want to go tomorrow," Kat says.

I grin at her. "Liar." I wish she meant it, but I know she's excited about going. How can she not be? At least for now. A week or two in, when she's missing me like crazy, she might change her mind.

She smiles, but she still looks sad. "I wish you were coming with me, that's all. We were supposed to ..." She swallows and lets the rest of her sentence hang in the air.

We were supposed to go together. It was going to be the two of us, partners in crime. But that was before my sixteenth birthday. Before my thumbprint changed to form an *X* instead of a *V* like it was supposed to. Now she gets to go to Vilmore, and I'm starting at Heroesworth Academy on Monday.

Heroesworth. Ugh. Not exactly my dream school—the exact opposite, in fact, since it's a university for heroes, not villains—and not where I'd ever pictured myself. And yet I volunteered to go. It wasn't even Gordon's idea, though his whole face lit up like it was Christmas morning and he'd just opened a new pair of tights when I told him I wanted to enroll.

Want might be a strong word here. But I made my choice. I'm not a villain. I chose Gordon and his family—*my* family—over my mom. Over taking over Golden City and turning all the superheroes into zombie slaves. And I can fly. That's a superhero power if there ever was one, like even my genetics are trying to tell me this is who I am. A hero.

I've still got an *X*—thanks to my mixed parentage and the virus some scientists released years ago that marks heroes and villains with letters on their thumbs—and depending on my actions, it could still turn into an *H* or a *V*. But I live with heroes now. I have a sidekick. If I picked up a Magic 8 Ball and asked it if I'm going to get an *H*, it would say, *Signs point to yes!* Because they do. So I figure I might as well embrace it. I might as well try for an *H*, because then maybe it'll get here that much faster. Then I won't feel that hot rush of shame every time one of Gordon's or Helen's relatives comes over and asks if "that boy" is still staying here. Even though I *live* here and they know that. Or in the case of Helen's sister, glares at me like I'm some kind of demon spawn.

Which normally I'd take as a compliment. But not fitting in *anywhere* is getting old. And if I had my *H*, Gordon could tell people I'm his son without flinching. Without worrying about having to explain how he had a one-night stand with a supervillain. He wouldn't have to stand there, stammering, his whole face going red enough to match his cape.

"Let's not think about tomorrow," I tell Kat. "Or Monday."

"Or how we'll be going to rival schools and never see each other?" she asks.

"Exactly." I kiss a slow trail down her neck, making her melt against me and forget about what's going to happen after tonight.

She kisses me back, her tongue hot on my ear, and she might not be the only one who's melting. "I could change," she whispers. "Just in case someone comes home."

Kat's a shapeshifter. So even though normally she has shoulder-length black hair, blue eyes, and a thin nose, she could look like anybody in the world. But I don't want anybody else—only her. "Never," I tell her. "I'll risk it."

She sighs and relaxes into me, and I know that she liked my answer, despite her worries about getting caught. Her hands slide under my shirt, her fingers running up and down my spine. Resting just inside the band of my jeans.

There's a zap when I kiss her, a jolt of static electricity that sparks between us. She winces, but just for a split second, and then she's kissing me again. Ignoring anything else.

I forget about everything except the feeling of Kat pressed against me. Right now we're just two people making out, about to do way more and cross a significant location off our checklist, and it doesn't matter what letters are on our thumbs or what schools we're going to.

Her phone buzzes from inside her purse on the floor. That'll be her mom, checking up on her. Making sure she's not alone with me long enough to get into any "compromising" situations.

You know, like the one we're in now.

Kat ignores the phone. The buzzing stops for a few moments, then starts up again as her mom calls back.

"You know," Kat says, "it's not too late to, like, go out for ice cream or something."

Something our parents would approve of, she means. Though in Helen's case she's made it clear she doesn't approve of me spending *any* time with Kat, compromising or otherwise. Not that she gets a say in it.

"Oh, isn't it?" I ask, playfully pushing her down to the bed. It is *way* too late to go out for ice cream. In my humble, still unfortunately fully clothed opinion.

She grins. "We could go to that one place where they name the ice creams after zoo animals, the one where you kept pointing to the Bald Eagle flavor and saying you were going to report them to the endangered species people."

I smile at the memory. "The one we got banned from, you mean?"

"The one *you* got banned from." She pokes me in the chest. "I got a coupon for a free ice cream cone because they screwed up my order."

"You're going to be gone tomorrow. Do you really want to spend the rest of our time together messing with people? Because, I mean, if that's what you want, we can go—"

"Don't even think about it." She pulls me down to her. I kiss her, my hand sliding under her shirt. My fingertips brush against her stomach, then up against the edge of her bra. "You're sure you want to do this?" she asks.

"Uh, when have I ever not been sure?" For the record, I am *extremely sure* I want to do this. Like, right now.

"Never, but that was before you decided you wanted to get your *H*. I'm the bad-girl villain. You're the hero now."

I swallow, not liking what that implies. As if choosing to go for my *H* means having Kat in my bed is off-limits. That makes it sound like what we're doing is wrong, and I so disagree. I love her, and so what if that means I want to take her clothes off?

Besides, I said I wanted to be a hero, not a saint.

"Are you telling me you want to be a bad influence?" I ask her.

"Definitely," Kat murmurs, kissing me again, her mouth hot against mine. She grips the edges of my T-shirt and starts to pull it over my head. So I don't see so much as hear when my bedroom door flings open and Helen, my stepmother, says, "Damien, are you—"

She cuts off there. Kat freezes. My heart pounds in my chest.

I pull my shirt back down—it's blue and says, SUPERHEROES DO IT WITH CAPES!—and run my hands through my hair. They weren't supposed to be back for at least another hour. Never mind the fact that no one was supposed to just *barge in*, like they, you know, own this place or something.

Helen's standing in the doorway, her eyes narrowed at Kat, who sits up and stares at the wall, not looking at anyone. She was already a bit flushed from our compromising activities—okay, more than a bit—but now her cheeks turn a bright, shameful red.

"You could have knocked," I say, shattering the tense silence that's filled the room. And even though I'm the one breaking the rules by having Kat here, I can't keep the annoyance out of my voice. There is such a thing as respecting other people's privacy, after all.

Amelia, my fifteen-year-old half sister, rushes up behind Helen, putting a hand over her mouth. She manages to both smirk and look genuinely horrified at the same time when she sees me and Kat in the bed together, even though we're both still fully clothed. "Oh. My. *God*," she says, drawing each word out extra long. She makes the situation sound ten times more dramatic than it is, as if we'd been caught running a prostitution ring out of my room, which isn't exactly zoned for business. "You are *so* dead."

"Amelia," Helen growls.

But Amelia's already running off, shouting something about having a million phone calls to make.

"Tell them I charge one hundred dollars an hour," I call after her. "Kat's my reference if they have any questions about quality of service!"

Kat punches me in the shoulder. "*Damien*," she says out the side of her mouth, her teeth clenched. She jerks her head ever-so-slightly toward Helen.

Helen, who is staring at us in shock, as if how I feel about Kat—or that I can't keep my hands off of her—is in any way news to her. "This isn't a free show," I snap. "You can stop staring at us like we're animals in the zoo." *And to your left, everyone, you'll observe the mating ritual of the teenagers of the species. Notice how the male specimen becomes agitated when said ritual is so rudely, and prematurely, interrupted.*

"What's going on?" Gordon calls, his footsteps in the hallway.

"Your son and that—" She swallows back whatever she was about to say, but I can't help glaring anyway. Because I'm pretty sure "that wonderful supervillain girlfriend of his" isn't how she was going to end that sentence. I'm *pretty sure* Helen thinks Kat is a slut for giving it up to me, even though I'm the only guy she's been all the way with and we are in love and have plans for a pirate-themed wedding.

We don't find out what Helen was going to say, though, because apparently she can't even finish. She can't even look at me for one more second and instead holds up her hands in an "I'm done" gesture and turns away, leaving Gordon to deal with me.

He glances after her, then at me. He takes in the situation. Me. Kat. The slightly rumpled bed. Then he suddenly gets real interested in his shoes. This from the guy who did it with my mom in a dirty subway bathroom and made her lose her hairpin. He wasn't so shy *then*.

Kat's phone starts buzzing again. She reaches down and snatches it out of her purse, hitting a button to silence it.

"Damien," Gordon says, clearing his throat, "I think Kat had better—"

"I have to go," she says, not letting Gordon finish. "I'll see you, um ..." She pauses, realizing that for the first time in months she doesn't know when we'll see each other again.

I lean in to kiss her good-bye, but her eyes dart toward Gordon, and she pulls away, too embarrassed.

She gets up from the bed, slinging her purse over her shoulder and stuffing her phone into it.

"Kat, wait—I'll walk you home."

I get up to follow, but she shakes her head, already hurrying for the door and pushing past Gordon. "I just … My mom's going to be freaked." That's all the explanation I get before she makes her escape, though not without one last glance over her shoulder at me. Our eyes meet. She bites her lip. Then she rushes off, leaving me on my own to explain to Gordon where babies come from.

X·X·X

It's not that I dislike Helen. In fact, for a stepmom, she's pretty awesome. I mean, I'm her husband's illegitimate love child with a supervillain, and even if the little incident that spawned me happened before she and Gordon met, it's cutting it pretty close. She could have freaked when Gordon first brought me home six months ago, just out of the blue, no warning. She could have refused to let me stay here or had crazy ideas that I was evil or something. But no. She welcomed me into the family. And even if she misguidedly felt sorry for me for my supervillain upbringing, she never made me feel weird about it.

And considering that my real mom disowned me for disagreeing with her and showing even the teensiest signs of maybe leaning toward my hero side, Helen gets major points from me for treating me like one of her own kids. Even though we're not technically related. And even though we might disagree on who I should be allowed to associate with.

I sigh as I glance at the clock—it's almost six—and dial Sarah's number on my cell phone. Sarah's my sidekick. She's an ordinary citizen, not a hero or a villain, though she *is* pretty heroic. She's all for me getting my *H*, for obvious reasons. And, also for obvious reasons, she's on Helen's list of people that are actually allowed at the house.

Sarah answers after only two rings. "What's the emergency?" She must know it's me.

"No emergency. Can't a hero call his sidekick just to chat?"

I can practically hear her rolling her eyes. "What is it, Renegade?"

"It's a nice night for crime fighting."

"I thought you said you were busy?"

"I was." That was when I thought I was spending the evening with Kat, before Helen chased her off. "I had a change of plans."

My door opens. I half expect it to be Helen again, or Gordon, coming to tell me off for earlier. He was too flustered at the time to do much more than stammer. And then I told him that when a bird and a bee love each other very much, or when they meet randomly in a dirty subway bathroom—which is *not* on our list, by the way—they want to rip each other's clothes off and do things to each other that birds and bees would never do in real life. And that sometimes when people meet randomly in a dirty subway bathroom, they don't use protection and end up with an illegitimate love child who then has to explain the facts of life to them sixteen years later. Because if they already knew, they wouldn't be gaping at him with their mouths hanging open like that.

Then he stormed out.

Which is why I expect him to be back for round two, but instead of Gordon, Amelia pokes her head in, her eyes darting right to the bed, as if she expected to catch a second showing. Which, considering that no boys will ever touch her—what with her sparkling personality and all—is probably the closest she'll ever get to the real thing.

Amelia's got dyed black hair, blond eyebrows, and is slightly pudgy. She also wears way too much mauve eye shadow, something that was popular for some reason with all her friends at our old school.

I glare at her. "You could have knocked." Just because she has no life of her own and has to live vicariously through mine doesn't mean she can barge in whenever she wants.

"Then you would have told me to go away."

"*Exactly.*"

"You had a change of plans?" Sarah repeats through the phone. "So I'm your second choice."

She makes that sound like it's a bad thing. As if it's not an honor to be chosen at all. "We could just hang out. You know, if you think all the evil-doers of the world are taking the night off or whatever."

"Your girlfriend bailed on you and you're lonely, you mean."

Okay, maybe there's some truth to that, but the way she talks, you'd think it was a crime to want to spend time with her. "We can watch a movie. Your pick."

She makes kind of a snorting sound. "You said you were busy, so I made plans. With *Riley*."

I make a shooing motion at Amelia, directing her toward the door. I mouth the words *Get out.*

Amelia acts like she didn't notice and plops down on the bed. I don't know if she's just misguidedly making herself at home, or if she's hoping to get a better look at the scene of the crime. The *almost* crime, anyway.

I ignore her and tell Sarah, "Cancel them. Wouldn't you rather spend time with me?"

"Spend time with you instead of my boyfriend? Yeah, right, Damien."

"I'll let you pick the movie. Something sci-fi, if you want. With a really technical plot I won't be able to follow." Sarah convinced me to go see some futuristic, super-convoluted sci-fi movie with her this summer while Riley was out of town, visiting his grandparents. My brain just about melted out of my skull, and I spent the whole time asking Sarah what was going on while she kept saying she'd explain it to me later, after it was over. I *considered* faking an illness and pretending I needed to go home, but the fact that I didn't and sat through the whole thing, melting brain and everything, just goes to show what a good friend I really am and how lucky Sarah is to have me.

"Riley and I are watching a rom-com. In my room. And I'm turning off my phone."

Erg. "Riley's a total douche. You know that, right?" He's also got an *H* on his thumb, marking him as an official hero—just Sarah's type.

"Uh-huh. Sounds like someone else I know. Funny how you only started wanting to hang out with me so badly after he entered the picture."

"Not true." Okay, totally true. I don't know why, but the guy just irks me. And I know I shouldn't care, but the fact that Sarah likes him better than me, and might actually believe he's a better *hero* than me, really pisses me off. I'm supposed to be the hero in her life. The only one. I don't need a do-gooder type like Riley showing me up. Especially since he's the type who will watch *The Crimson Flash and the Safety Kids*—my dad's kids show— with her while keeping a straight face. Something I could never do, though, thankfully, neither can Kat. It's one of our favorite shows, as long as we get to make fun of it the whole time. Sarah watches it intensely, like the Crimson Flash's words of wisdom about how to safely cross the street is the most important advice she'll ever hear. I'm surprised she doesn't take notes.

"And," I tell Sarah, "just to prove how not jealous I am, I'll come over and watch the movie with you guys. I'll even sit between you, to equally share my presence."

"The last time I let you hang out with us—"

"Let me? Don't you mean, 'was honored by me wanting to spend time with you'?"

"The *last time* I let you watch a movie with us, you

pretended Riley had gone invisible and that you couldn't see him."

Riley's superpower is turning himself invisible. *Lame.*

"I'm entertaining," I tell her. Which is true and she knows it.

"No, you're a jerk. You *sat* on him, Damien, and pushed him off the bed."

"I didn't push anyone. He fell in his frantic attempt to get away from me."

"He broke his finger! He had to go to the doctor."

How is this my problem? "It's not my fault he doesn't get enough calcium. I didn't *intend* for him to get injured." It was just an added bonus. "Plus, it healed, didn't it? I don't see why I can't hang out with you guys."

"Because you're not my boyfriend. And you're not the only guy in my life anymore."

I was her boyfriend, sort of, once upon a time. During a very brief period where I was mistakenly denying my love for Kat and thought fooling around with Sarah would be easier than dealing with my real feelings. Which it turned out wasn't true, and Sarah and I were better off keeping our relationship romance-free. Not that there was a lot of romance going on, just some making out, but whatever.

And yeah, maybe I enjoyed being the only guy in Sarah's life, before she met Riley at some sci-fi convention back in June. And it's not like I want to date Sarah now or anything. I just don't want Riley putting his mouth all over her. Or making her think that having an *H* makes him a better hero than me. "That doesn't mean you're not still my friend."

"But it does mean you don't have a right to be jealous."

I clench my fist. "I am *not*—"

"You only want to spend time with me because you can't have me. That's kind of the definition of jealous."

"You're my sidekick. How am I supposed to get my *H* if you're spending all your time making out with some guy?"

"You say that, but every time I have a mission for us, you're too busy with Kat. Slipping certain parts of your anatomy into certain parts of hers.'"

"*Language*, Sarah." The mouth on her. Seriously.

"Those were *your* own words, Damien. And besides, who says we're making out?"

"Great, then you won't mind if I—"

"We could be doing *much* more than that, but you know what? It's none of your business."

"Come on, Sarah, don't be like that."

"I have to go—Riley's here with the movie. Good-bye, Damien." She hesitates, then adds, "Don't call back," before hanging up.

"I'll watch a movie with you," Amelia says. She's sitting on the edge of my bed, idly kicking one leg against the mattress.

This is what it's come down to. Spending Friday nights watching movies with my half sister, who will always be free because she has no life. This is what I have to look forward to now that Kat's moving to Vilmore without me and Sarah's preoccupied with the Invisible Douche.

"Or I can go make sure Sarah's not doing anything I wouldn't do."

Amelia snorts. "Is there anything you wouldn't do?"

I pause, thinking it over. "Homework."

She rolls her eyes, then brightens. "Have you started it? I bet you haven't. You're going to be *so* behind."

"On what? School hasn't even started yet."

"Um, hello? Didn't you get Miss Monk's email? We already have a project assigned in Intro to Heroism, and it's due *Wednesday*." She says *Wednesday* like it's the day the world's going to end.

Did I mention that it's not just me who's starting at Heroesworth next week, but also Amelia? Even though she's eight months younger than me and was a grade below me at our high school, she applied for early admission to Heroesworth this year, since she'll be sixteen in October. They let her in—a decision that probably had more to do with her dad being the Crimson Flash than it did the ten-page essay she wrote them—which she bragged about all summer. At least until I got accepted, too, and then she said they'd let *anybody* in.

"I don't even know what classes I'm in yet." What with us not being allowed to choose any of our classes our first semester, plus I was kind of a last minute addition, thanks to Gordon pulling some strings with a friend on the admissions board. But I'm going to take a shot in the dark and guess that my classes are all, how you say, really stupid?

Amelia gapes at me. "Didn't you read your intro packet? New students have to take Intro to Heroism. That means both of us." She narrows her eyes a little, as if waiting for me to argue. Then she clears her throat. "If you want, I could help you start the assignment."

Work on an assignment before I've even started school? For a class I may or may not even be in? "Yeah, that's exactly how I want to spend my Friday night. Don't you have flying lessons to get to? Oh, wait, that's right. You *don't.*" Amelia spent months telling me how much better at flying she was going to be than me when she got her power. Then a few weeks ago she discovered she could teleport items to her, but only if she'd touched them before. It was apparently her great grandmother's power on Helen's side, meaning she didn't inherit "the family power" like I did. And after enduring months of her being a snobby bitch about it, I'm taking every chance I can get to gloat. "It's too bad, really. I wanted to see him push you off a building." Like he did to me, no thanks to her.

She flicks a piece of fuzz off her shirt. "You're such a jerk."

"Yeah, I am. But you, Amelia, you're *delightful.* A real pleasure to be around." Just thinking about falling from the tallest building in Golden City still makes me sick, especially as I remember the pavement rushing toward me, which I *still* have nightmares about. My fear of heights was bad enough, and then Gordon had to go and make it worse. This from the guy who supposedly teaches safety lessons to kids. Good thing my flying power kicked in at the last second, or else he'd have had a lot of explaining to do.

"I've changed my mind," Amelia pouts. "I'm *not* going to help you with your assignment. And you'll be sorry on Wednesday."

Sure I will. And pigs will sprout wings and Gordon will

sleep with a supervillain. Oh, wait, that last one already happened.

"You'll be the only one without a poster to present."

A poster. Yeah, I think I can make a poster in two days, *if* I'm even in that class. "I'll manage."

"Okaaaay," she says, drawing it out to convey just how skeptical she is. "But don't say I didn't warn you."

ABOUT THE AUTHOR

CHELSEA M. CAMPBELL grew up in the Pacific Northwest, where it rains a lot. And then rains some more. She finished her first novel when she was twelve, sent it out, and promptly got rejected. Since then, she's earned a degree in Latin and Ancient Greek, become an obsessive knitter and fiber artist, and started a collection of glass grapes.

Besides writing, studying ancient languages, and collecting useless objects, Chelsea is a pop-culture fangirl at heart and can often be found rewatching episodes of *Buffy the Vampire Slayer*, *Parks and Recreation*, or spending way too much time on Twitter and Facebook. You can visit her online at www.chelseamcampbell.com.

CPSIA information can be obtained at www.ICGtesting.com
Printed in the USA
LVOW11s1216270315

432300LV00001B/155/P